Beyond the Surf

hwneild

For Isabella
11.03.2016

THE MARTINEZ ISLANDS

'Two little full stops and a big comma 500 miles off the Coast of Africa'.

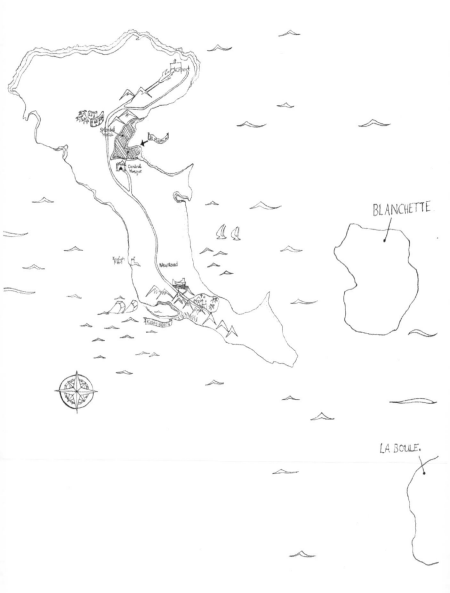

BLANCHETTE.

LA BOULE.

Contents

Chapter One

Latitude

Kayte, shaken from her daydream by a sudden bump, instantly turned towards the plane's window. She realised the Boeing 737 had merely bucked on an air pocket, and the subsequent pitch revealed a sapphire blue ocean with a multitude of glorious islands scattered directly below. Her birds-eye view of the atolls palm fringed golden beaches and sparkling white reefs formed the picture postcard vision of a paradise Kayte had been crying out for. It was only now, strapped in and glued to the porthole, that she finally realised her desire to flee home had become a reality. Not only that but, for the first time in her life, she appreciated the power of her imagination. If she really wanted something in life, she now knew she could get it.

She pinched herself, remembering that she'd been at her lowest ebb only three weeks ago; when she'd sat shivering in her dressing gown, slumped in her cramped little kitchen staring out through the salt smeared window at the bleak Solent sprawled out before her. It'd been either raining or overcast; day in, day out, windless and dreary for weeks. She hadn't kitesurfed for nearly a month. There had been no wind for weeks. That lack of wind had become a vital issue for Kayte. It had made kiting impossible and she lived to kitesurf. Think intelligently about wind, she'd reasoned. If we've had no wind for weeks then surely it must be due soon, mustn't it?

The Solent, Kayte's homebody of water, seemed to permanently resemble a mass of rusty iron sheets shifting aimlessly around. Above the corrugated surface, bruised clouds had persistently hung low in thick shrouds. The sea and sky forever stitched together by a drizzle that zipped up the canopy of murk seamlessly.

On top of inertia, she'd been broke too. Pot-less. As a result, her sinking spirit had found it harder and harder to pierce the embedded gloom engulfing her. Her whole entity felt grizzled, inside and out. If she hadn't been so lucky, she'd have allowed herself to carve a well of sorrow so deep, she'd never have been able to clamber out. She'd felt like the clouds would never lift and could hardly remember a day when they hadn't been swirling around her.

As the aircraft commenced its descent and headed towards a larger group of very green islands that had appeared out of the azure Indian Ocean like droplets of shimmering emeralds cast in a silver setting, Kayte stole an uncomfortable glance at her boyfriend, squeezed up beside her with his eyes closed. She could see each exquisite island, individually encased in a ring of frothing white. The waves breaking on to the offshore reefs created what looked like water haloes that surrounded each island.

'Steve, Steve, look at this,' she said, tugging her boyfriend's arm. 'It's like paradise down there.'

'Alright, Kayte, alright. I believe you.' He brushed her arm away.

Stunned, she turned very slowly back to the window. Her excitement hadn't just dimmed, it had been extinguished. As she stared at the beauty below her mind was elsewhere. Perhaps it was just the mere presence of Steve himself, or his negativity, which took her back to the depressing memory of that ragged day three weeks ago when she'd stared, locked in, at the dullness outside.

A red and white emblazoned Isle of Wight car ferry had appeared, just at the right time, ploughing its lonely way through the grey-green messy swell of that bleak February morning. It was literally the only spec of vibrant colour visible. She desperately needed colour, something bright and uplifting, and there it was. That bright ship, a flashing orb in a churning pool had offered Kayte a slight glimmer of hope, which she'd tried to grasp with all her might. As she focused as hard as she could on the ship's bright visual properties willing it to hoist her spirits out of the doldrums the familiar, tinny rattle of post being shoved roughly through the letterbox visibly shook her. To Kayte, the paper letters felt as if they were actual bombs falling on to the doormat. Her heart sank further into the abyss. More unpayable bills! It was like a final straw moment, one that broke the camel's back.

'Oh God, no,' she'd said out loud, putting her head in her hands. She couldn't take any more bad news.

She clutched her mug of coffee reverently, desperately trying to console and calm her quivering self, and puffed the steam, inhaling it through her nostrils as her panicked heart beat ferociously. It was a desperate act, a final escape. She conjured a vision where the feeble waves she could just make out through the gloom below were in fact perfect arcing rip curls softly cascading on to golden sand on a bright tropical beach.

'Stop it!' she snapped out loud. She forced herself to get going and, slurping down the creamy mass at the bottom of her mug, went to dress. She hauled herself up, wrapped her towelling dressing gown tightly round her shoulders and stepped out into the corridor.

As she shuffled past the front door she glimpsed an envelope lying on the mat, sunny side up and embossed with two exotic stamps. One was a bird of paradise and the other, a mesmerising psychedelic shell. Hullo, what's this? she thought. She looked at it cautiously for a long moment, as if the strange letter was an explosive that would detonate with any sudden movement. She leant down very slowly then snatched it up, ripped it open and tore in to her cluttered bedroom.

Flopping down on the unmade bed she read the letter and, shaking her head, laughed out loud. This had to be some sort of joke, she reasoned, it couldn't be real. It had to be an elaborate prank from one of her friends. It just has to be.

The letter, typed on official-headed paper, read:

Dear Ms King,   12th February 2003

On behalf of our esteemed and honoured Life President, Prince Jaffa, I am writing to you, as the current female kite surfing speed record holder, to invite you to improve your record on The Martinez Islands, our nation State on 14th March 2003.

We are delighted that Mr Chuck Schneider, the men's record holder from America, will also be attending.

As soon as you accept Prince Jaffa's invitation in writing, I will send you two airline tickets and a cheque for $5,000.00 to attend. If you break your record whilst here on The Martinez Islands the Prince will be delighted to present you with another cheque for $15,000.00.

This will be an all expenses paid one week trip. The Prince will pay for all yours and a kite caddy's travel costs, including taxis to the airport, excess baggage and all accommodation and expenses for both of you during your stay.

I very much look forward to hearing from you, at your earliest convenience, to confirm your attendance. My office will be in touch immediately afterwards regarding all the travel arrangements.

If there is anything else you would like to know please do not hesitate to contact me.

Yours sincerely,

Signed Jon Mabenge Director of Tourism.

And here she was, exactly three weeks after receiving the letter, coming into land on The Martinez Islands, two tiny full stops and a comma in the middle of nowhere - five hundred miles off the east coast of Africa. She hadn't really believed the invitation was 100% genuine until the moment she'd seen the islands clearly come to focus.

She'd never seen anything as unspoilt as what was unfurling beneath her. As the aircraft banked and lowered Kayte clearly saw palm trees fringing empty beaches and small black fishing canoes peppering the coastline. Massive red granite boulders stood out in the coves, like sculptured mythical creatures. She glimpsed a ramshackle city flickering between high peaks and, as the plane pitched again, St Martin shone, silhouetted with glinting minarets and bulbous rooftops.

Kayte soaked up the wonderful apparitions, flashing from one view to another, and began to shiver; something had electrified her, as if she'd been bitten. All memories of that ghastly day vanished in an instant and Steve had gone somewhere far, far away. She stared, googly eyed through the plane's oval window, stunned, writhing to a new beat. She questioned herself: this can't be the same planet, it's another world I'm flying into, surely? Then, in suspended disbelief, Kayte clicked it was only the spirit of adventure screaming in her bloodstream.

Kayte had never been out of Europe. Lanzarote was the furthest afield she'd ever been from England. These sorts of views were reserved for books or her imagination only. Wow, what a wonderful world we live in, she realised. The oblivious Steve squirmed uncomfortably beside her.

The airfield they approached was precariously positioned. Squeezed onto a flat piece of land at the base of a steep escarpment, the runway reached out as far as the actual coastline, which forced the plane to shoot down dramatically, land abruptly and then screech to a halt as rapidly as possible. A few relieved passengers actually clapped at the Captain's skill as the aircraft taxied past a large construction site.

Kayte could see a new tinted glass terminal was being built to replace the small old military affair they were marshalled in to across blasting hot tarmac minutes later. The decrepit, if charming looking building, had clearly been neglected. It looked completely empty from a distance, through the heat haze, but was in fact half filled with heavily armed guards. Squat, flat-nosed, dark-skinned, hard looking individuals greeted the passengers officiously as they were led into the tiny arrivals area. Kayte noticed a stern, blond German looking soldier with a short, cropped, flat top haircut scrutinising everyone from the control tower as they all stumbled across the sweltering runway. It was so hot, Kayte's sneakers had felt tacky on the melting asphalt.

The terminal actually had an old fashioned rustic pleasantness about it, Kayte thought as she entered. And with the paint flaking off the walls and the old baggage carousel looking as if it hadn't worked for years, it felt like they were going back in time, to a slower pace. All the steel-framed seating had rotted so badly that the upholstered seat pads had completely lost their mould and sunk into awkward posterior shapes.

The thirty passengers were jammed into the baggage claim area, all sweating profusely and gasping for air in the close, musty atmosphere. Steve was leaden, completely deflated and hunched over like an anaemic orangutan, arms drooping by his sides.

Between the passengers and the exit was a passport check

point, more like an old ticket booth at a fun fair - a silly phone box with a rickety old table next to it for bag checks.

'Ze kitesurfing party will come forward now,' the German GI shouted out. 'Slowly, one at ze time.'

As they shuffled forward like convicts, queuing for their passports to be stamped, the heat became increasingly uncomfortable and the atmosphere, although still, was intense with frustration. At moments it was so quiet, just like in Nairobi, where they'd all met in transit. The only sound Kayte could hear was the hum of four old ceiling fans slicing, with great difficulty, through the dense air above them. And then the bang of a passport being franked echoed out, boof-boof, with long gaps in between.

Steve had found a random chair and flopped down with his head in his hands, trying to hold his hangover in.

'You, get up, now,' roared the German.

Steve got up lazily, stood vaguely to attention and, under his breath, muttered, 'F-k you, what the hell is this place?'

'Hey, hey, Steve, take it easy, man. It's no worse than going to America believe me. Just keep calm, do what the prick says,' whispered Jim, the British journalist they'd only met three hours earlier.

After having a rather elaborate visa, accompanied by a bright stamp, embossed in their passports and without an item of baggage missing, the group finally emerged outside in to the open - a full two hours after touchdown, squinting like prisoners released from a dungeon.

'F-king hell, that was intense,' Steve exclaimed.

'Yeah, quite unnecessary,' Jim agreed.

'It felt like a welcome to a police state paradise,' Kayte chipped in. She couldn't believe how bright it was. A glinting, hazy brilliance that her soft, British wintered eyes were having difficulty adjusting to.

They were welcomed by Jon Mabenge, the Tourism official who had written to Kayte the previous month. He was a small, chubby man with thinning jet black hair that was oiled back, big bright bulbous brown eyes and a small round, apple cheeked face. Loudly, in high pitched pidgin English, he said:

'Welcome, welcome everyone, on behalf of our esteemed President, Prince Jaffa, I welcome you all. My name is Jon Mabenge.' He clapped his hands. 'But everyone calls me Papa Jon. I will be looking after all your needs while you are here on our wonderful island. Please just ask if you need anything, anything at all. I will be most happy to oblige you. Please be seated, we will go to your hotel just now.'

'That's the first happy face I've seen since we got here,' commented Kayte.

Chapter Two
Bump!

It was three o'clock by the time they'd loaded up and boarded their two mini-buses. One had a roof rack and a trailer.

'Steve, get in with us,' said Kayte.

'No, I'll get in this one, keep an eye on the kit.'

They left the airport on a perfectly surfaced road lined with street lamps, but after five minutes it all came to an abrupt end. The road transformed from tarmac to a dust track in an instant. From a big, wide and smooth carriageway to a dirt road, bordered by occasional 1950s, two-storey villas painted in faded aubergine or avocado, the small convoy bounced along, jostling around potholes, with the trailered minibus in front.

'I'm sorry about what happened back there in Nairobi, Chuck,' Kayte said, above the racket.

'What happened Kat?'

'You know, with Steve.'

'Ah, heck, don't worry about it. It was nothing.'

'Well, it was bloody rude. I don't know why he did it. I shouldn't have really brought him. He's been getting worse and worse since that accident. I was going to bring my friend but my mum wouldn't let me.'

'Oh?'

'Yes, she said that, because of all the dodgy political upheaval here, she thought I needed a bloke with me. She insisted I did.'

'And what am I?' he said smiling.

'Ha, ha, anyway, Steve can't do much now.'

'Aw, heck. I know, it's tough,' Chuck said, all too aware you can be a cockerel one day and a feather duster the next in the kitesurfing game.

'Yes, it is. He was one of the first people to kitesurf in UK, he kicked off the scene seven or eight years ago.'

'Yeah, I know. What's happened to him now though? He looks like…'

'…a bum?' finished Kayte. Chuck nodded. 'I know he does. He takes God knows how many painkillers, can't do any sport, and he drinks way too much.' She had to shout and hold tight now. The bouncing intensified and then calmed.

'That must be tough on you babe. What's he doing now?'

'He's a chef in our local pub.'

'Oh, wow man. Booze and pills, and a hot kitchen. Bad combo, babe, bad combo.'

She'd felt obliged to apologise. Earlier that morning, in Nairobi airport, Steve and Jim had gone off for a beer. She'd been sitting, annoyed and alone in the domestic departure lounge when, coming through the lounge entrance like a shimmering apparition, Chuck had arrived. In the middle of his small entourage, like a modern day Jesus with his disciples, Chuck's blonde, healthy brightness positively burst into the tired old waiting room. She'd smiled, feeling instantly pedestrian by comparison, and put her hand up and waved sheepishly. When this rather forlorn-looking, solitary girl was pointed out to Chuck, he waved back and led his acolytes over.

'Hey, babe. How's it going?' he'd called out, as he approached. 'On ya own? Real cool to see ya. You're looking great.' He exuded Californian warmth and friendliness.

'You too, Chuck. You too. No, my caddy, well actually, you

remember my boyfriend, Steve, is over there having a… um… a coffee with… um, Jim Singer, a sport journalist we've just met, do you know him?' she mumbled, as they gave each other a brief hug.

'Na, babe. Jim Singer you say? Na.'

'Me neither, strange.'

They'd been chatting for fifteen minutes when Steve tottered up, alone and tipsy, much to Kayte's obvious embarrassment.

'Hey man, how's it going?' Chuck had said, straight away holding out his hand. 'Good to see ya.'

'Yeah, yeah, awright man. Not too shabby,' Steve replied, completely ignoring the gesture of friendship. Kayte was gobsmacked. She couldn't believe how he'd just turned his back on Chuck purposefully to start rummaging for nothing in particular in one of their bags. My God, she'd yelled to herself. She was so embarrassed. Aghast, she'd looked at Chuck and could read his thoughts: the guy's a friggin' bum, it read. It was obvious; one man in the bloom of his life, the other going to seed. It was immediately clear that she should have brought someone else. It was all just too much for Steve, he couldn't cope with the fact that it wasn't him kiting on the big stage. After all, he'd been a player too, once upon a time.

Back in the bounding minibus, Kayte stared forward as the two vehicles rumbled onwards into St Martin, the island's capital she'd glimpsed as the plane hiccuped. Through the dust she could see the trailer ahead, loaded with her precious boards, bumping wildly. She spotted a small scruffy dog appear out of the scrub between houses to their left, a few cars ahead of their convoy. She gripped the seat in front as she followed its blind dash across the road. It hesitated. Then bolted. No, it's not, is it? It can't be.

'Stop!' she yelled. Everyone but the driver spun around. The minibus ahead carried on. The dog hadn't reached the other side when it should have. Her mini-bus swerved. She spun around to look out of the rear window. Kayte could see the dust kicked up by the minibus settle to reveal the dog laid out near the opposite side of the road behind, twitching in its last throes of life.

'Oh, my God, oh my God!' she shrieked. And then leant forward and began to retch. She heaved, but nothing came out.

'Jesus Christ, babe, are you OK? Babe?' said Chuck, sliding across and rubbing her back.

'Didn't you see it, didn't you see?' she spluttered.

'See what, babe?'

'The dog, the dog, the trailer in front hit it.'

'No, I didn't.' Chuck turned and called out, 'Did anyone else see it?' Only negative responses came back from the other passengers as they sped on.

'Stop, stop, we've got to stop. It's someone's pet we've just run over,' Kayte called out.

'Miss Kayte, it is only a dog, please don't concern yourself,' said Papa Jon above the din, turning back from the front passenger seat.

'But, but it's illegal. We have to stop,' she pleaded as the small convoy rumbled forward regardless.

'Don't worry about it, Kat, just let it go,' Chuck urged.

'Let it go!' she repeated. 'I don't believe you Chuck.'

Shocked in to silence, Kayte, with tears in her eyes, withdrew. She sat, hunched up for the rest of the journey. She couldn't help but realise that this sort of tragedy was obviously a complete non event here; no one took a blind bit of notice.

How can you dismiss your values so easily? a voice inside her said. Just by getting on a plane and landing a few hours away, she said to the voice. As easy as that? It seems like it, she said nastily to the voice, and went catatonic.

Even exotic sights of people sitting lazily around, shaded from the afternoon heat in brightly coloured robes, or curious

Moorish buildings, or green-shirted children playing football on the white tropical beaches, couldn't lift her out of her reverie. She sat numb until they pulled up outside their hotel.

The Splendid Hotel was a shabby 1970s soviet style edifice, with a whitewash exterior that had gone sooty and mouldy from the moist tropical atmosphere. The crescent shaped five storey building was, however, undergoing some sort of cosmetic refurbishment. Kayte could see one solitary man at work as they arrived. He was leaning out precariously, with his roller on a stick. He'd only managed to paint fifty patches. So, one third of the building was made up of flashing white irregular squares, like an unfinished jigsaw puzzle, the rest, well … grubby.

The vast foyer they entered must have looked luxurious when the establishment first opened decades ago, but now it had a rather spartan, depressing, post communist feel to it. There was a pathetic little gift shop in one corner selling postcards, a few kitsch gifts, cigarettes and a vast selection of half bottles of spirits, which no doubt oiled the nefarious activities that went on behind the closed doors upstairs. Papa Jon gathered them all around and, in his jovial manner, informed them:

'The rest of the day and evening are free for you to do as you please. I am sure you are very tired from your journey, so please make yourself comfortable and use all the facilities at your leisure.' He then clapped his hands, his signature call, which echoed around the empty space. 'I will be back at nine thirty tomorrow morning sharp, and we will go to Kidd's beach for the day. I pray for great winds, inshallah, God willing.' And he clapped his hands again. 'My friends, please do not leave the hotel compound as there are still some bad elements around.' They all looked at each other. 'Now, if you require anything, anything at all, my telephone number is here with the receptionist or ask for the manager, Mr Toyful, who will only be too happy to assist. Please be aware that we have no mobile telephone coverage here on the islands yet. You can book calls through the reception if you wish. On that note, the Prince will not be paying for these calls or any extras, like alcoholic consumption. Am I clear my friends?' Unanimous nodding. 'Then I bid you all a very good evening, and again welcome, welcome.'

He bowed and walked backwards a few steps before turning and skipping out of the hotel. The moment he was outside, he began shouting ferociously at the minibus drivers who were busy unloading. Some of the group looked at each other, impressed with the performance from this lively character whilst the rest seemed more stunned at the prospect of no mobile reception. They stared glumly at their screens, occasionally shaking them, wondering how on earth they'd survive without the devices. Kayte could even see one or two look as though they were having withdrawal symptoms already.

'What's up Kayte, are you alright?' said Steve, having lugged their kit in.

'I thought your van ran over a dog back there. Did you see it?' she snapped.

'No, we didn't. Are you sure?'

'I'm pretty sure, yes.'

'Well, come on, let's go up to our room and take it easy.'

Kayte and Steve were allocated two adjoining rooms but entered the first one they came to. The room was large and airy with two single beds pushed together. It was decorated in a retro 70s style, with one dark stained, wood-panelled feature wall. A pair of large cubist-style prints dominated two other walls and the fourth wall was all glass with a sliding door that led out onto a balcony. Shattered from the long journey, they dropped their bags down and flopped on to the beds, falling asleep instantly.

Chapter Three
Longitude

As Kayte and Steve collapsed onto their beds, across town, Roger MacGill stepped out of his sleek, black Mercedes and entered the peaceful courtyard adjoining St. Martin's central mosque. It was half an hour before evening prayers.

He took off his soft Gucci loafers and approached the imam barefoot. He sat down with his legs outstretched. His crossed feet, exposed to the sunshine, absorbed the late afternoon rays. The perfectly starched creases in his cream slacks contrasted rudely with the flowing white robe of Imam Bakri, who was sitting cross legged on a little rug opposite him in the shade.

'Mr MacGill, I mean Omar, so sorry. I must thank you for your kind presents during my illness,' the seventy year old elder statesman said, opening the conversation in perfectly polished English.

'You are most welcome, sir. You look very well, refreshed, a new man,' Roger said.

The imam's slip of the tongue reminded Roger that he was now known as Omar on these islands. He was now an official citizen and brother of The Martinez Islands. One month ago, he'd copied the deliberate act of his hero, Napoleon Bonaparte. When stranded in Egypt in 1797, Bonaparte had converted to Islam as a tool for consolidating his authority and popularity with the indigenous population. Roger had done the same here and adopted a Muslim name, Omar. He chose that name as it sounded like Omai, the first Pacific islander who'd come to England at roughly the same time as Napoleon was marooned in Middle East. He'd recently bid for a painting of him by Joshua Reynolds but had been pipped at the gavel.

Roger really didn't give two hoots for religion. He thought the lot of it was mostly mumbo-jumbo. To him it was just a form of keeping order and controlling people. All over Africa, he'd seen do-gooders, Christian God squads, the tens of thousands of charity workers and busy bodies; they all presumed they were working towards some greater benefit but were, in actual fact, generally creating black markets and supporting criminals. He wasn't going to be part of anything connected to that, or this lot for that matter. Roger knew very well that nothing is written in stone, or straight forward in life, it's all fluid. He just wanted peace.

'You're very kind to say so. I am feeling much better,' the imam replied. 'Ever since you arrived on the island I have been unwell. It is a shame I haven't seen more of you.'

'Yes, it is, sir. You have been sorely missed.'

They looked at one another. Imam Bakri broke the silence. 'How can I help you Omar? What is it you wish to see me about?'

'Well, sir, I'm concerned that … how can I put it … the atmosphere on the islands seems to have deteriorated in recent weeks. I can't quite put my finger on it, but my men have noticed and felt a steady escalation in tension over the past few days too, and we fear it may spill over to violence. Can you shed any light on this matter?'

'No, no. Of course not. No,' the Imam said, emphatically. 'I am not aware of anything that you need concern yourself with.' Then, after a moment's silence he reconsidered. 'However, I admit there are certain domestic issues, unresolved family squabbles which may be resurfacing. Yes there are,' he shrugged. 'But this is of no concern to you. This is island life after all,' he said, smiling.

'Okay,' Roger replied slowly. He was serious now. 'That is all very well, I understand. However what would you like us to do, sir? Me and my men, how can we be of help?' he sighed. 'We cannot simply sit back and allow unrest. You must understand that. I'd very much like to work through this matter with you in the absence of Prince Jaffa.'

'Do nothing Omar. Just relax, my friend,' Bakri said immediately. Leaning back, he began to laugh. 'Tell your men to do the same.' He held his hands out wide. 'Enjoy the beauty of our islands and do not concern yourselves with business that is not yours.' He leant forward, whispering for maximum impact, 'Do not get involved. Do you hear me?'

Silence. One of Roger's eyebrows twanged in surprise. I am involved though, I police this godforsaken place, he thought. I don't give a monkey's gland what you do to each other but I've got my interests to look after. He cleared his throat.

'Yes, I do, sir. I do understand. However I must maintain peace on the islands.' He was deadly serious now. 'You do appreciate that don't you?'

Imam Bakri's response was a conversational swerve, going off-piste, he caught Roger off guard. 'Are you happy on our islands, Omar?' he asked.

Two small birds began to squabble furiously on top of a water fountain in the centre of the enclosed courtyard. The two distracted men craned their necks to see a ball of fizzing spray created by their flapping wings, effervescing rainbows in the golden light of sunset.

'Indeed, sir. I am very happy here,' Roger lied nonchalantly, still mesmerised by the feathery hullaballoo.

'That is good, very good. You are welcome, most welcome. Now please tell me, Omar, we still have a few minutes left. Remind me how you met Prince Jaffa, if you would be so kind?' the imam asked. 'I know nothing about that.'

Taken aback slightly further, and to buy a little time, Roger asked if it would be OK to smoke. He was annoyed now. He pulled a packet of Dunhill Internationals from the top pocket of his salmon-pink shirt, lit one and began pulling on his cigarette.

Both men were well aware that, when chit chatting, it's just as important to read between the lines as it is to listen to the answers. You learnt more about people through seemingly innocuous conversations than you would by engaging them in philosophical discussions. It was the imam's business to know who the murky stranger in his midst was, and what made him tick. After all, this renowned mercenary was currently funding all The Martinez Islands' public services and, as a result, was currently the major power broker on his islands.

'Well, sir, I met Prince Jaffa, on a mutual friend's yacht in the South of France two years ago. It was perfect timing as I'd finished a big job and was waking up to the fact that I'd actually had enough of fighting other people's wars for them. I wanted to retire from that. Prince Jaffa asked me to help him. I was exhausted and wanted to take a step back. I know I'm still a young man …'

'… and how old are you, Omar?'

'43, sir.'

'My apologies, pray continue.'

'Where was I? Yes, this work I do … did, I'll call it privateering. You may call it something else, but it's now fast becoming unacceptable to modern sensibilities, however you look at it. You have my word of honour, I am not involved here with any nation; I am here on my own freewill.' He took another drag. 'Well, it was over those few days on the yacht that Prince Jaffa explained the problems you were having here on the islands back then. He asked if I could help and I agreed; that is it. And here I am two years later.'

'We all enormously appreciate what you did. You are a saviour to us. But why, Omar, did you agree to do it?'

'Basically the reason I am here, sir, and I'll be frank, is to legitimise myself.'

'To make a decent human being of yourself?' the anglicised imam interrupted, still smiling.

'If you like, sir. Yes I am,' Roger said with a grin. 'I have fully funded Prince Jaffa's Presidency here, and am paying for all the reconstruction costs out of my own pocket, as you are aware. There is no one funding me, all I am doing is out of my own pocket. Everything I've earned, literally everything, I am pouring in to your islands. I want to live my life here in peace, inshallah, God willing.'

'Inshallah, God willing,' the imam echoed.

Just then the muezzin rang out across the capital, heralding the day's last call to prayer. Within minutes the courtyard was full of barefooted men, quietly making their way across the marbled passageways.

Imam Bakri slowly got to his feet. 'I must go now, Omar, but I thank you for being so open with me,' he said. 'I look forward to continuing our conversation soon.'

'But sir, although I thank you for your time, I still haven't received any clear direction from you,' Roger said, standing up too.

'My brother,' Imam Bakri said jovially, with arms outstretched again, 'enjoy yourself, tell your men to do the same. I will contact you if need be.'

'Umm, sir, I will come and see you the day after tomorrow at the same time.' Roger held out a hand to his new religious leader, which the old man took. The Englishman squeezed. It was limp and slithered out the moment he exerted pressure.

'Inshallah Omar, inshallah. Come if you like,' Imam Bakri said smiling broadly and warmly. He leant forward again and spoke slowly. 'And take this as a compliment, my friend,

please, I mean it ... consider yourself ... welcome to die here.'
He laughed. 'I mean that. I wish you well. Go in peace. Come
again soon.' And with that he turned.

What the hell did he mean by that? Roger was taken
aback. He took a sharp intake of air. He was lost for words and
missed the moment to reiterate that peace on the streets was
of paramount importance to him. Roger bowed his head as
the imam wafted silently away. He told himself there was no
way he was going to f-ing die here.

Roger sighed deeply. He turned and returned to his
Italian shoes, which he'd left by the entrance, against the grain
of ghost-like men flowing around him. He wasn't going to
prayers - kneeling down and kissing a carpet - no bloody way.

He did feel slightly, and only slightly, more secure on
these isolated islands - these ravishingly peculiar islands,
which he now called home - than he did when he'd woken up
that morning in a feverish state. But not by very much.

As Roger's car purred out of town through the small third
world city, he stared out of the window thinking, not about the
conversation he'd just had, but about something else. 'Are you
OK, sir?' his driver enquired.

'Yes, yes, fine Frank. Thanks,' said Roger, coming to. 'Just
thinking about home actually.'

'And what a beautiful home it is too, sir. I'd think about it
a lot if it were mine.'

'Nah, nah, nah, not this place. Home home ... Blighty.'

'Oh, England!'

'Yes, of course, man, home. Don't you think about it too?'

'Yes, of course I do, sir. I miss the old place like mad.
What I'd do right now for a few pints in a local pub and good
ol' banter.'

'Yup, second that, old boy.'

Chapter Four
Bearings

Kayte and Steve woke in darkness two hours later. They had quick showers and headed straight down for bottled water and something to eat. The lobby shop was shut but, in the opposite corner of the empty foyer, there were signs of life.

'Come on, let's try there,' said Steve, and he was off like a homing pigeon, flying across the vast marble hall.

'Hey, hey, wait for me.'

The bar room they entered was decorated with dark wood panelling in the hotel's signature retro 70s theme. The actual bar itself was a single slab of thick mahogany, highly polished with a wavy cut edge. Alongside were six zebra-skin upholstered high stools and small clusters of low tables and soft cushioned comfy seats sprinkled around the spacious interior.

Before ordering a drink, Kayte urged Steve outside through big glass windows on to a decked terrace, which had smart bamboo style furniture and glass-topped tables with small nightlights burning in red bowls. Kayte couldn't quite make it out in the shadows as her eyes were adjusting, but there was obviously a lush garden beyond as she could smell a dense, fragrant sweetness permeate the dark. The air was scented with the white flowers of the night. Faint hubbub of nearby city traffic wafted in on the evening breeze, along with pulsing waves of crickets and tinny pop music cutting in occasionally. An intoxicating mix of exotic natural beauty with raw human energy that made Kayte's soul leap, hardly able to bear the confines of her body.

As they stood on the terrace taking in their new environment, Steve turned to Kayte. 'Well, I hope there's a bit more wind than this for you tomorrow, or the kiting's gonna be crap.' Steve could see she was miles away, so turned and re-entered the bar.

'Yes, right,' Kayte mumbled dreamily, as her head went back and her eyes drifted upwards. She wobbled significantly, taken by surprise. She was hit by the twinkling millions and billions of the African sky at night. There is nothing quite like it.

'My God!' she said out loud before gulping. 'I never imagined in my wildest dreams that our universe to be so heavily occupied,' she exclaimed to herself. 'It's not just our world, even the heavens seem over-populated!' All she could add was a stupefying, 'Wow!' And feebly pointed up at the awesome spectacle for no one in particular to appreciate but herself.

'Oi, Kayte, whatcha havin' to drink?' rang out Steve's voice from the bar, bringing her right back down to earth.

Oh, sh-t, here we go, she thought. She didn't want to encourage a drinking session on night one. 'Just a juice of some sort,' she called back.

But Steve had other ideas. When Kayte walked back, she saw he'd joined Jim, who she'd wanted to avoid when they'd first walked in. He was rapidly sinking a cold beer.

'I left your drink at the bar,' Steve mimed, and pointed.

Kayte found her sad looking drink on the bar and settled on an empty table near the group, yet apart, and placed herself where she could survey the whole room. Aside from her small group, there were only two other customers in the room, both on high stools at either end of the bar. She sat back and looked at each of them in turn. Firstly a grand, Spanish-looking, middle aged dame was perched precariously like a human flower sipping a pina colada through a straw. It amused Kayte that, in order to prevent smudging her purple lipstick, she had to pucker her fulsome lips right out. It looked like she was going to kiss the straw before sucking, like she was whistling up her cocktail. The other customer was a much younger tanned European. He was kitted out in white linen trousers, brown loafers without socks, and a crumpled, light weight matching jacket worn loosely over his T-shirt. He was crunched over his brandy and ginger, thoughtfully pushing the ice around and occasionally glanced lazily in front of him at the dark- mirrored wall to survey the scene behind. Kayte caught a glimpse of his medallion, a flash of gold in the mirror. His pendant, his badge of honour, rested below the profile of a dark, very good looking, clean-shaven Italian type. With his fine hooked nose and jet black hair, oiled, perfectly parted and brushed back, he looked more suited to Portofino or St Tropez than the windswept Martinez Islands.

A few more of the kitesurfing group came in. Apparently Chuck was staying in his room and calling in room service. Smart chap, Kayte thought. The gap Kayte had wanted to create between Steve and Jim narrowed. Going for a meal was fast becoming a distant memory. Just then a singer, a crooner, arrived.

He quickly setup his keyboard and banged straight in to 'Quando quando, quando', followed by a barrage of similar easy listening cheese. The floral lady at the bar soon withered, drooped and left. But the good looking, dark- haired guy swung himself around and to face the singer, who was now fully in to the croon. A new group of loud, swarthy men had come in briefly, emitting an aura that they could do exactly what they wanted. The sort of people who think everywhere is a manners free, arrogant zone. With them were two local ladies, dressed to kill, who seemed to be giggling constantly at everything and anything. They resembled puppies that liked licking their master's faces and performing little tricks on command. The loud group had a quick drink and trotted on, upstairs no doubt. Kayte just wished she was with her best friend, Lisa, who was pregnant and back in England. They would have had a real laugh together. Or even Sam, who was going to come. People spotting, then tearing them apart, was their favourite pastime in the seaside resort where they lived. She looked at Steve, who was on his third pint and leering across at one of Chuck's caddies.

With a slight stumble, the smooth Italian got off his stool and sauntered over towards Kayte, lighting a cigarette as he approached. Exhaling, he coolly asked, 'So, waddaya doin' 'ear in St Martin?'

'We're here for the kitesurfing challenge.'

'Oh yesss, kitesurfing. I 'ear you were comin'. Cool, cool, ya, very cool. Iz OK to join you?'

She snuck a look across at Steve. He looked piqued.

'Yes, please do,' she said. He was already down and grinning at her. 'And you, what are up to?' she enquired.

'Oh me. Ze flowers, 'ass what I'm 'ear for. I worka for a company, iz called Fragonard in Cannes in France. You know it? I buys flowers for ze perfume.'

'Oh wow, that's interesting,' said Kayte. 'Why here?'

'Iz a flower called Ylang-ylang, it only grow 'ere. We use it a lot. It iz in most perfumes … Coco Chanel, Hermes and most aromatherapy.'

There was no stopping him. Aflame with brandy, he launched into talking to the group rather than with them. At one point, with a backward tilt of his head, he pointed back at where the wild bunch of 'harrowgant people jus' zere,' were sat. Leaning forward, and quite unnecessarily, he lowered his voice for faux drama to inform everyone, 'Zat lot, who were zere, are some of di mercenaries who run zis place jus' now. Be careful of zem, be real careful, zeya outta control, even cuttaoffa your 'ead and not looze sleep, belieb me.'

He leaned back again, and laughed. The group were left thinking, 'ha, ha, yeah right!' sheepishly, not really knowing whether to belieb him or not. They looked at each other. Was it just the brandy talking?

This Italian smoothie was the sort of person who wouldn't naturally gravitate towards the easy going surf crew, but in this hotel's environment it was perfectly acceptable to mix and be pleasant.

Jim joined in and immediately began to ask the Italiano questions about the island's politics.

'I'ma gonna tell you, my frien'. Two 'ears ago, when I came to buy ze 'arvest it was crazy 'ere, man. I mean real crazy. Ze leader then, 'e take away all politz. No politz 'ere at all and 'e take away all elder men and festivals, all the 'istory, everything gone and 'e let all ze teenagers rule ze place.'

'What was the leader's name?' It was Jim again, cutting in.

"E was called Zafir. But can you belieb it, man! I mean it was crazy, man. All 'zese gangs of kids running around like kings, zey ze bosses. Juss' likea da mob. This leader, Zafir, 'e legalize smoking marijuana too, you know?' he went on, laughing and acting out someone puffing away like a buffoon. 'Canna you belieb it? So all ze kids 'is stoned in charge, it was dangerous man 'ere, I mean it was anna … anna … whazza ze word? 'elp me please.'

'Anarchy,' Jim supplied.

'Exactamento, ya, anarchy. Real crazy. Oh ya anutter zing, 'zey calt it Ze Young Revolution or somezing 'cause only they, ze kidz, are people that like ze new. 'Is funny, no? Anyways, zis man, Zafir, 'e say all old ways are bad, old people bad. And they stop dealing with the West, Hamerica or Great Britain or France, nuttin', nada, all finish, all out, but now these guys …' He gestured his head back again, 'zese guys commma 'an change it all back ze way it was, so ze peeple zey like them, it fantastico when I come 'ere last year. But zis 'ear the peeple donna like zem nomore. Zey sez zey don't wanna go home, zeez mercenaries. No, no zey very happy being top doggies, but zey are bastardos, you know. I 'ear they done some really bad things and the people now want zem to go, and go fast, they all 'ave 'ad enough.'

Mister Italiano slurped his drink and slunk off to the bar for a refill.

'Wow, man, that sounds like one hell of a cool experiment. High teenagers in charge,' said one of Chuck's assistants.

'More like Lord of the Flies,' Kayte said.

'Reminds me of our politicians back in England, if you ask me,' chimed Steve.

'Yeah, right. Half the countries in the world seem as though they're run by kids, they're called naïve Lefties!' said Jim. No one else got the joke. He then got serious. 'In fact, from what I read, the Young Revolution, as it was called, was actually a fundamentalist group who wanted to revert to a more agrarian, self sustaining, simple life. Pretty commendable ideals, but really all pie in the sky stuff. Local resentment just got too strong.' Everyone turned to listen. 'Like, for example, no public servants had been paid for years and rubbish wasn't cleared. There were no police, only rampaging, stoned brutal teenagers in charge. I believe there were no historic festivals and the elders had no role. It was bonkers. Therefore Prince Jaffa's coup, supported by this bunch of mercenaries who are still here,' he too nodded over to where the hard bunch at the other end of the bar had been, 'went completely unopposed and they took control easily, assassinating the old leader, this Zafir … I'd forgotten his name … in the process.'

'Hey man, you're mighty well informed. When did all this shit happen?'

'Just doing my research. Just doing my research. I'm a journalist, remember. Time spent in reconnaissance is seldom wasted, my friend, seldom wasted. The coup happened eighteen months ago. But these islands have this sort of stuff going on all the time. I think they've had something like 15 different leaders in the past 25 years, five of them were military dictators. The locals are as fickle as they come.'

'Yes, we heard that,' said Steve. 'It's bonkers. The locals must be so bored here, in paradise, that having this sort of shit going on all the time is their idea of entertainment, nut cases!'

Mister Italiano reappeared, sat down and continued his diatribe with gusto:

'Zis Rodger Mc-something, ze mercenary leader, 'e call

'imself Omar now. 'E very powerful 'ere, very powerful. 'E really damman in charge. 'E do good zings but ze people zey no like him no more. Zey scared of 'im. And 'e white and 'e foreign. Iz ze old people and young people and estudents they all come toogedder now to kick him out. Foreshore. I tell you iz gonna be soon man, belieb me. I feel it inna ma bones,' the Italian said gushing.

'What's your name, man? Where you from?' Jim asked quickly, changing the subject.

'Oh, oh me, I'm Marco. I'za from a town called Bordighera in Eataly, very near ze French border, 'iz beauty full. But 'ere, when all this sheet calma down, I gonna open me a restauranto 'ere. Zis izzy most beauty full place in ze world. Eh look, I tell you iz more beauty full 'ere than Mauritius, sheet 'ole, or Sayshellts. Zis place, it beat 'em panz down. Hey you guys, do a good job anna bring in ze touristos for me, ya?' He was slurring. 'Hey, I zorry, I godda go to beddy now, I a beet peased.' He'd finally admitted defeat.

'Oh Marco, one last thing. What's this we hear about the Americans, and the air base?' Jim enquired. 'Do you know anything about that?'

'Okay, you win,' Marco giggled. 'I go a'ead 'n talk. I getta one more drink. I tell you, iz importante.'

The air was cool and still now, the music had stopped. The sour impression the load of mercenaries dumped had finally dispersed. All that could be heard was a wall of cicadas chirping ferociously in the foliage outside and the clinking of glasses being washed behind the bar. While Marco left the table, Kayte urged Steve up and they slipped off to bed with a few others. It was only Jim and another four of the diehards finishing their drinks or waiting to hear the next instalment of the islands intriguing political history who hung around.

Marco swiftly appeared. 'Well, to answer your question ma frien',' he said sitting down. 'I 'av been 'ere tree weeks now and I go tomorrow. But when I flew across to Blanchette, you know, one of de udder little islands, I spoke to my friends on de farms zey say zey seen a war ship. Yes zey did. Zey say it may be to stop pirates from Somalia, but zey not sure. No, no. And people 'ere not happy about any talk about an Hamerican base. You know ze yanks zey kick allah ze people off islands when zey zoo zeese zings, local people jus' 'avva to piss off, so of course, zey worried, man. Like zey did in Diego … Diego,'

'Garcia,' said Jim.

'Ya, Diego Garcia. Ze people 'ere very worried. Hey look guys, I real zorry, I juzza gotta go to bed, jus' 'ave a great time 'ere, be 'appy. Zat Kidd's beach you are going to iz fantastico. Bon soir tout le monde, nitie nite, a demain, see you tomorrow.'

And off he went, chuckling and weaving away, shaking hands with the solitary barman en route.

'Wow dudes, this is quite a place,' one of the team said. 'Mercenaries, military takeovers, loads of bud, it's wild here man, wild.'

The conversation they'd just heard left a couple of laid back surf types stunned in to silence. It was all quite a revelation to fully appreciate quite where they were. Yet Jim, he twitched with excitement. The dying candle lit up his sharp angular features like a frightening mask. His eyes disappeared, his mouth became a black hole and his shadow on the wall behind pulsed with menace as the candle finally spluttered and snuffed itself.

A definite chilly sea breeze suddenly picked up and swirled into the bar room, spooking the group off their seats, urging them up to their rooms. And as the unnerved remnants of the group moved across the ghost-like emptiness of the darkened foyer, they felt as though someone was watching them. They positively ran for the lift, their footsteps echoing around the voluminous space.

Chapter Five
Vamos A La Playa

At nine o'clock the following morning, Kayte, the kitesurfing party and their baggage were assembled in the foyer. They were being snapped and flashed at by two local photographers. Kayte loathed the attention and just wanted to get out to Kidd's beach, but Chuck was in no rush. He was in his element, switching on a series of megawatt smiles. Especially when interviewed at length by an attractive raven haired local journalist who, flirtingly, seemed to be asking him every possible question under the sun.

'For sure, if the wind's right and the conditions are cool, then hell yeah, that's what I'm here for, to break some records. I'm right up for it,' he gushed. 'I can't wait to get out there and bust some bad moves for you guys and smash my record here on the Martinez Islands, yes sirree, I'm comin' 'agetcha.'

Kayte's interview was over in an instant and delivered in a typically prim English style - polite and self depreciating, with words like, 'Yes thank you, thank you. I'm delighted to be here, it's such a lovely island. I really am looking forward to it. It's my first time kiting on the Indian Ocean. And, 'Yes I am very excited about that. I'm certainly going to try my hardest ...'

Eventually, cajoled and corralled by the ever-smiling Papa Jon, they all bundled onto the minibuses.

Kayte sat in front of Chuck waiting, for the last bits of kit to be loaded.

'So, Kat, what gear have you brought over? I didn't get a chance to ask you yesterday,' he asked.

'Oh, I just brought my favourite twin-tipped board and my speed board and another one I've been working on with a shaper over the winter, and three kites; seven, twelve and fourteen metres. And you?'

Chuck proceeded to launch into a long-winded list at least twice as long as Kayte's, leaving her feeling totally ill-equipped with second-hand old junk.

It was well past 10am when they rumbled off through the dusty streets, which were now packed with folk in brightly coloured skirts, sarongs, shirts, shorts and elaborately turbaned headdresses bustling on either side of the pavement less roads. Kayte, getting her first flavour of downtown life in the tropics, sat glued to the action outside her window. Men and women sat on either side of the road with a myriad of goods for sale, laid out on coloured cloths, such as garlic, mangoes, fish, peppercorns, spices, chickens, batteries, cigarettes and bottled water. Kayte didn't know where to look, into ancient courtyards, up Moorish narrow lanes, into cars or at the rooftops. Strange scents wafted into the cramped bus, along with dust, car horns and human chittering constantly dominating the background. A true feast for the senses, which all leapt onto high alert. The smell was more intense than in England; colours seemed sharper here and the sounds harsher. The taste of the truly exotic was all around. She'd definitely arrived on the other side of her world and, although she had never experienced anything quite like this before, Kayte felt oddly comfortable and strangely at home.

'Hey, Pappie, what's that building over there? A night club?' Chuck asked, pointing at a churchlike, red bricked, turreted building, replete with stained glass windows and a garish flashing neon sign outside.

'No, no Mr Chuck, that is our National bank,' Papa Jon replied proudly.

Chuck cracked up. 'No, way man. That's cool. Funky money eh!'

'No Chuck, that's weird,' said Kayte giggling. She sat back, feeling the blues of the British winter evaporating with every happy convulsion.

Sharp braking snapped Kayte forward. The convoy had been halted by an immaculately dressed policeman directing traffic from a podium. He was fully kitted in bright white military fatigues with sparkling gold epaulettes and matching white gloves that flashed brilliantly in the sunlight.

'Hey everyone, look at him, the guy looks like he's popping to a Michael Jackson video,' quipped Chuck, still on form.

'He is, look at him, he's actually making the traffic boogie to his tune!' added Jim.

As they waited for their turn to move, a group of scruffy teenagers walked past. Seeing Europeans inside the minibuses they started swearing and cursing at them, even spitting on the ground and shaking their fists violently at the vehicles, as if to say 'foreigners go home'.

'F-k you too,' hissed Chuck through pursed lips.

'Do they want to be isolationists or what?' Jim added, prissily.

'Yeah right, Jimbo, frikkin' losers,' said Chuck out loud when they'd pulled off.

'Just ignore them, please. Please. They are our lost boys,' said Papa Jon.

'We're here to make this a better place for them!'

'Here, here,' said Jim.

And they were off again, speeding out of town. Kayte glimpsed inviting beaches flickering past through trees, and small fishing shacks perched on the shoreline between low- rise tenement buildings. She could make out small dugout canoes plying their craft out in the little coves they rumbled past.

On leaving the busy, potholed outskirts of St Martin town, they abruptly encountered another new half-built single carriage road. Some sort of ring road. All was suddenly smooth and quiet. Again, street lamps were erected and evenly spaced. Fifteen minutes later though, they turned off the freshly tarmacked carriageway and took a precarious route that veered up and away from the newly built road. From this higher angle, Kayte looked down to see the road was brutally carving its way through a beautiful fertile valley.

Climbing for another ten minutes, the small convoy levelled out onto a crest. Kayte looked across at the rugged expanse of jungled mountains rippling into the distance; deep green in colour with a purple luminescence. On the adjacent hillsides were tiny villages and habitations where pristine hills should have been. On the lower slopes sprawled wastelands, which had been cleared of vegetation. It made them look scraggy, as if the jungle had been thrown back by a battalion of strimmers. All human activity stopped at certain flush points, finally allowing lushness to soar free. The upper reaches were still hidden in deep pockets of mist, waiting for the midday sun to burn them off and reveal their peaks. Below lay Kidd's Beach.

'This is where our wind's made, Kat,' said Chuck. 'At this time of year these mountains mimic a sort of capillary action. They draw winds in from the sea below and then hurl 'em back down around the beach in one big constant motion. That's the idea, anyway. Looking good.' Kayte nodded and furrowed her brow in agreement. She was trying her best to put on a look that could be construed to say, 'I know'.

The road then slipped gently over the hogs back hill and dropped over the other side. The narrow lane zigzagged its way through thriving terraces of vegetable plots and luxuriant fruit tree groves, weaving its way down to sea level. On certain turns, Kayte saw the spectacular Indian Ocean dead ahead, unencumbered in all its choppy, greeny- blue glory. She let the warm tropical air blow through her hair. She inhaled deeply and sighed, intoxicated by the smell of the tropical sea spray effervescing from the coastline below. I've finally arrived, she said to herself, smiling.

With a jolt at the bottom of the hill, they joined a heavily pitted sand track that skirted a large tranquil lagoon. The dust swarmed vehicles veered left, squeezed between the lagoon and an extensive castellated wall of sand dunes to their right that hid the beach and sea behind. They bumped and swerved along this dirt road for about a mile.

'Wow, man, this looks like the goddam daddy of a beach for us Kat, look how long it is!' Chuck exclaimed. Ahead of them were sand dunes, seemingly unfolding to infinity.

'Yes, it sure is, it looks ruddy perfect,' replied Kayte excitedly. She looked over at Steve who was grimacing in pain, his skin tone had paled a shade. 'Are you alright, Steve?'

'Yeah, I'm fine, don't worry about me,' he said through gritted teeth.

Then the convoy stopped. 'Wait one moment, please,' said Papa John. The dust ball created by the vehicles caught up with them and passed over. 'Open now.'

The group all tumbled out. Kayte could see they were in the middle of an arcing spit, about two miles long, that housed just the track, dunes and beach. The crescent shaped strip of land was only about 50m wide from the seashore to the lagoon's edge. The lagoon itself was twice as wide, maybe a little more, and looked so serene compared to its neighbour, the throbbing ocean. It felt so protected and safe. The lagoon was not quite green in colour but a beautiful Bombay Sapphire, a gin-clear turquoise shade, with no sign of stagnation or disease.

On the other side of the lake was a rounded, gently sloping hillock. Kayte could see a derelict old colonial style guesthouse directly opposite. It had obviously been empty for a long time as the garden was overgrown; wild roses and creepers rioted over the walls, rambling bougainvillea spilled up and through many of its crevices, and red effervescing flowers stood out perfectly against the dense green backdrop. The vehicles had disturbed and thrown up a flock of white, screeching, long legged marsh birds who, ruffled, began to settle themselves back down in the reeds surrounding the water's edge.

Kayte squinted. She could make out a large low rise, hi-tech, glass fronted eco building, appearing through the vegetation. The structure, in its final stages of completion, and placed perfectly in its environment, looked like a modern Frank Lloyd Wright designed construction. It emerged from the natural landscape harmoniously. The vast lengths of tinted glass, framed in dark wood, had a continuous subtle balcony running the whole length of the upper floor, which created one enormous shaded canopy for the floor below. The shadow hid the ground floor and tucked it back into the foliage. Exposed, newly landscaped terraces ran down to the lagoon shoreline. Kayte could see small, thatched lodges within the gardens which would soon be hidden once the planting took.

As her eyes moved further across the ridge, she could see there were a number of private homes hidden within lush compounds all along the hillock. Each property enjoyed the same sensational view through their green gardens - across the blue lagoon to the golden dunes below and then out across the uninterrupted chopping azure Indian Ocean.

'Oh, my God!' Kayte spluttered, as her gaze was arrested by a vast mansion complex, a stuccoed English Regency palace, on top of a high bluff at the apex of the ridge. All the other buildings harmonised with their environment, but this edifice shone out rudely and glared a blinding white in the unforgiving late morning sun. A small army of people teemed in and out like ants, working on the final stages of the build. It had the most perfect reflection in the still water below, like a wedding cake, which was briefly interrupted by a small boat coming across to meet the new arrivals.

All along the far shoreline were a series of jetties coming out from below each property, with small pleasure boats moored up. Though, of course, below the white monster that dwarfed the others, was an elaborate boat house, again all white with a cedar tiled roof.

'What the heck is that Pappie?' Chuck pointed at the edifice opposite. He'd noticed it too. 'It looks like the friggin' White House, man!'

'That, Mr Chuck, is the new home of Omar, our island's saviour,' Papa Jon replied, gushing with pride, false or real Kayte wasn't absolutely sure. 'It is very nearly completing, as you can see, and I am correct that furniture will be arriving any day now. I am in charge of organising the house warming party.' His face lit up like a brass chalice. 'Many foreign dignitaries will be coming for a long weekend of festivities. And, Mr Chuck, entertainment will be by Brenda Fassi, Lou Bega and Gypsy Kings, have you heard of them?'

'No man, sounds like a blast though, I'll have to hang around for that bash,' the young American chuckled.

'Sadly it will be in one month Mr Chuck, but I am sure you will be most welcome. There will be a most spectacular firework display, many delicacies will come in from South Africa, much wine from France and, Mr Chuck, the party tents are coming from Nairobi,' Papa said blithering excitedly. 'No expenses spared, no sir. No corner is being cut, believe me. Come now please.'

The American contingent weren't fazed by it one bit. Kayte, however, not quite able to articulate it, felt slightly nauseous as she listened to Papa Jon while staring at the creation opposite. They had just driven through extreme poverty and fifteen minutes later here they were, viewing eye-watering wealth and hearing of gross opulence.

Simultaneously, the group turned toward the welcoming beach, lured by the distant waves drumming the offshore reef.

They picked up their bags and boards and followed Papa Jon through a gap in the dunes to reveal the Indian Ocean up close, bursting onto the cream speckled sand ahead of them. They could smell a pure, raw equatorial windswept saltiness, spicy and ozone dense. Here they were, at last, ready to kitesurf this beach, this coast, this island for the very first time. The newcomers fanned out onto the beach, staring around agog, like lost astronauts or reincarnations of Captain Kidd's pirate crew who'd made this very beach their base two hundred and fifty years ago.

As they stumbled onto the sand, Kayte turned and discovered, tucked up on one of the dunes, a fantastic large beach bar. Heavy polished wooden trunks supported a neat palm-fronded thatched roof. Housed within, stood a beautifully crafted horseshoe shaped bar. Its vast selection of bottles and spirits, displayed in tiers, glistened invitingly. A generator gently thumped away behind the bar, masked by the sound of breaking waves, as it cooled the fridges and powered a sound system that emitted welcoming low level samba beats. From where she stood, it seemed to Kayte that the music was whispering to her, but really she knew it was nothing louder than fitful wind carrying the sound away from her, and then back again in wisps.

Laid out on a flat area in front were a few fixed umbrellas, again with palm thatching and an assortment of chic ethnic furniture. Low slung rattan chairs, Arabic poufs and sleek designer leather loungers completed the scene.

'I'm in heaven.' Kayte heard Jim exclaim and, to her dismay, Steve echo, 'Me too, that is the dog's bollocks of a bar.'

To the left of the gap, high up on another dune opposite the bar, was a slightly smaller, empty shack. It had flat wooden window panels at the sides that acted as shutters but could be opened up on their hinges and propped up with rods to create sun shades. This was where the group would base themselves for the days they would be here on the beach. The official time recorders could setup their equipment, view the course and be able to monitor the kiting action from a higher point.

'Hey, Pappie, this is cool man,' said Chuck, looking around, 'this is one helluva setup.'

'We aim to please, Mr Chuck. We aim to please. Do you like it too Miss Kayte?'

'Oh, yes, I agree. You really couldn't design a better beach for speed kiting, it's absolutely perfect.'

'It sure is. It's long an' exposed, and I can see the winds'll come whistling down from them hills we've just come down from and run cross off, parallel to the beach,' Chuck enthused, staring around and pointing at the peaks behind.

'Do you know if the winds here are constant, Papa Jon?' Kayte enquired.

'Oh yes, Miss Kayte, they are. I believe afternoon is generally best. Only at this time of the year though.' Kayte hadn't clicked that Papa Jon was the sort of person who tried to say exactly what you wanted to hear. It was cultural.

'Yeah, Kat, that's what I said up there, babe, the sea air is sucked up into the mountains overnight where it cools. When the day warms up, them hills'll chuck it back down again.'

'Chuck it back down, very funny, very funny,' said Papa Jon, laughing and slapping his thigh.

'Whose idea was it to kitesurf here in the first place Papa?' Kayte asked.

'Miss Sonia and Mister Kirk I believe, Miss Kayte,' he said when he'd recovered. 'They run the bar here. You will meet them just now. They are setting up the water sport shop for the hotel over there.' He pointed through the dune to the modernist building. 'They told Omar, he looked into it and then he told me to make this trip happen. It is a very happy day for me.' He rocked his head from side to side. 'Indeed. Oh, happy day.'

'It is for me too. It's an ideal beach for what we do, just perfect.'

'My God, Miss Kayte,' Papa Jon puffed, as he helped her carry equipment up the slippery dune. 'What is all this for?'

'Well, in these rucksacks are our actual kites, pappa, and the bars and lines for steering the kites.

'And this?' he asked, pointing to the pump attached to the outside.

Steve had remained by the vehicles, doing rheumatic exercises on the side of the minibus. He was drenched, like he'd just stepped out of the shower. His back had taken a pounding on the journey.

'I'm going to go for a little walk, get my toes in the water and get a feel of the place,' Kayte told Chuck a few moments later as he supervised the laying out of his kit down the whole of one side of the shack. 'There's nowhere near enough wind to kite yet. And we want to make a splash, don't we?'

'Damn right, babe, for sure.'

The ocean beckoned.

A small group of locals had appeared from nowhere and were gathered in a cluster to witness the new spectacle that was soon to unfold on their beach. The bush telegraph, local radio and television stations had been broadcasting alerts about the event. The same news crew that had been at the hotel earlier soon arrived and began setting up their dated camera equipment on the beach.

Chapter Six
Kidd's Beach

A couple of local barefooted, skipping children followed Kayte down to the surf, excitedly jumping up and rabbiting questions in a quick fire, high pitched patois, which she couldn't make head nor tail of. She instinctively knew that simply smiling, joining in and laughing was the best solution, as it was for most things in life. She held her hands out and led her two new chittering buddies down to the shore.

Kayte, wearing long flowery shorts and a tight brown T-shirt with no footwear, went straight into the sea the moment she reached the water's edge. Going up to her knees, she felt tropical warmth surging around, massaging her limbs. An occasional invigorating swell of coolness would burst through the warm water having risen up from the deep. She waded further out. Waist high on water, she raised her head reverentially to the sun and closed her eyes, stretching her arms out wide. To the casual observer watching from behind, she may have been keeping her balance, not conducting an incantation.

She turned and waded back to shore, the kids had run off. She turned up the beach alone. It's not quite there yet, she thought, as occasional forceful gusts were beginning to develop into sustained, steady breezes. As she paced the shore away from the base, leaving footsteps that faded in the wet sand behind her, she could see tiny waves breaking five meters from the shore. Getting up on the board was going to be sweet. The surface beyond the surf was flat but not completely though, more corduroy in texture.

After about ten minutes of walking, when the two huts were faint blots of activity behind her, she came to a spot where huge red boulders jutted out into the sea like a roughly made pier. The granite rocks arced around, creating a wonderful still pool of aqua blue water protected from the choppy sea beyond.

She pulled off her top and stepped out of her wet shorts, leaving them where they fell. She froze for a moment in her green bikini and looked around furtively, embarrassed by her white skin. There wasn't a soul around. Confident the coast was clear, she waded out into the crystal clear body of water, with only calm water ahead and smooth sand between her toes. The sea bed had obviously built up here over time as her progress to deeper water was gradual; rare for the Indian Ocean as invariably there is a steep shelf not far off the beach. She stood, holding her breath as the sea caressed her midriff, relishing that hesitant moment of goosebumps before she gave herself up to the unknown. Rising on tiptoes, she leapt up slightly and dived forward immersing herself fully in this great ocean for the first time. She opened her eyes as she swam under water, thrilled by the field of mosaic pentagrams of sunlight flickering on the sandy bed in front of her. She soon came up for air and rolled over onto her back and lay still, floating on the calm water, looking up at the shimmering sun and hearing the waves flapping gently on the sea wall beyond her pocket of peace.

Rolling over she swam smoothly ashore and sat a little way up the beach near the dunes, staring out to sea, loving the serenity and privacy of the moment. She lay back in the sand, closed her eyes and felt the chill in her marrow thaw and soften as she dried in the baking sun.

She sat up and subconsciously pinched herself again. Here she was, virtually naked and completely alone on a huge beach, on a tiny sundrenched island in the middle of a massive ocean.

48 hours ago she was huddled in her freezing kitchen. Phew, she sighed to herself, what a relief, it was real! She almost felt like praying. Thank you ... Lord.

A flicker, a movement on the horizon caught her eye. It was heading straight towards her. The speck grew into form and, out of the fuzzy off-shore reef, a sublime 1950's motor launch appeared, carving its way effortlessly through the slight swell. Its pure white bow, which resembled polished ivory, glinted and sparkled royally in the sunshine. When the craft was about 100m from where she sat, Kayte could see a pair of binoculars clearly aimed directly at her. They were held by a blond haired man standing next to a seated driver, who was dressed in an immaculate white uniform. As the boat neared the beach it swung away and ran past her, broadside for the first time. She could see, seated in the stern, the torso of a good looking, dark-haired, bronzed man. He wore an open neck, salmon pink shirt.

She instinctively held up her hand, and he did the same. Embarrassed, she glanced down and doodled symbols in the sand.

When she looked up again the launch had moved on down the coastline and further away from her. It then doglegged in from the ocean, through a causeway someway down the beach, into the lagoon behind.

Kayte collected her shorts and top and slowly headed back down the beach, dawdling in the shallows. She found a small shell, not at all dissimilar to the stamp on her original invitation, but with a fabulous purple interior. She put it in the pocket of her shorts as a talisman, a lucky charm.

Before she joined the others, who had all decamped to the beach bar, she went through the gap between the dunes as she wanted to know where the launch had gone. She could now see it being moored up to the pontoon of Omar's monolithic house. The pink, salmon shirt man hopped deftly out of the boat, walked along the jetty and disappeared into manicured foliage below the house. For some reason, her heart fluttered, she was sure it missed a beat.

In slight shock, and awed by the impact of a single, silly moment, she turned and skipped up to the bar to join Chuck and his crew who were clustered under one of the outside umbrellas. She must still be a little jetlagged, she reasoned.

Chuck had sprawled himself on a leather lounger like an emperor with his court around him. The local press were milling around and she could see Jim at the bar, up on one of the high stools, laughing and joking. He was in his element on this all expenses jolly to the Indian Ocean. To her dismay, Steve was there too, perched alongside Jim and partly obscured by a post. Her green eyes, more often than not playful, fell exhausted on him. When he eventually noticed her, Steve turned and goofily held up his jug of beer, as if waving to say, 'look at me mum! Aren't I clever? Like a cocky little school boy. Her look said it all.

'Hey Kat, shouldn't be long now. Hey hon?' Chuck called out. She turned. 'I'm getting the vibe we can have a bash real soon, whaddaya think?'

She looked up at a small skull & cross-bone pirate flag stuttering in the breeze on a pole high above. As she got closer, she replied, 'Yup, I think so. It's definitely getting there. Better give it another half hour though, to be sure. I really want to make it good.'

'Yeah, babe, to be sure, to be sure!' he replied, mimicking an Irish accent. 'I'm just bustin' to get out there. We ain't gonna break any records, but it'll be a start.'

'It's picking up all the time, you never know. Are the time trial guys happy with their setup?'

'Yeah, they're cool. They want us to test it out as soon as we can.'

'Excellent can't wait.' Kayte noticed Papa Jon seated up near the bar, waving at her frantically. 'Hang on, I'll be back in a bit,' she said, and went to join him.

Papa Jon was talking to a wavy blonde lady, a little older than Kayte but with a lovely fair, full moon face, and huge starry blue eyes. It was a tough face though, pockmarked and hard lived-in. When she got to his table, he hopped up. 'Miss Kayte, please let me introduce you to Miss Sonia, she and her boyfriend, Mr Kirk, own this bar.'

'Oh hi, I'm Kayte. Good to meet you. Fab place you've got here.' Kayte leant over and shook her hand. 'D'you mind if I join you?'

'Ya, do, please,' Sonia replied, with a soft German accent.

The moment she'd sat down, Omar's uniformed launch driver, who she'd noticed ten minutes ago, appeared and was leaning down to Papa Jon whispering patois in his ear. He stood up. 'I am so sorry ladies, Mister Omar would like to see me now. I have to go. I will be back soon. Please excuse me.'

Kayte watched the two local men walk deftly down the dune to the waiting boat. 'Papa Jon said it was you and Kirk who suggested getting us out here in the first place,' Kayte said dreamily.

'Ya, we did. Well, it was Kirk actually, he has been here longer than me. He realised last year that, around this time, the strong winds that came down every day would be fantastic for kitesurfing. He told me it is a low pressure system or something, which hangs over this part of Africa at this time of year. This attracts big winds and, ya, it happens all the time, we get cyclones or tropical storms.'

'Blimey, tropical storms,' Kayte repeated, turning back.

'Ya, they come so quickly, it's crazy. You look out one minute and the sky it is blue and all is calm, then the next moment black and pouf, the storm is here. Anyway we discussed this with Roger … ach … he is called Omar now. We thought it was a good value way to promote tourism here on the islands, you know, you guys coming. If we can get some good press then people, tourists like you will come. Perhaps we can clean up the old guest house there to keep it cheap. But we'll see. The main thing is for you to break some records, ya?' she said, smiling.

'Oh yes, of course,' Kayte replied. 'But this is our first day, so we're just getting our heads around the place. It is an ideal beach though for sure, and I can see the wind's getting steadier and steadier. It should be good. We'll be doing our best.' Kayte thought of the prize money. 'And Sonia, who actually paid for us to be here?'

'Omar did of course, ya, he pays for everything. That is his new house.' She pointed back. 'And he is paying for the hotel being built here too. He pays us too, ya.'

'Hungh!' Kayte's thoughts drifted as she gazed across at the elegant launch wafting back over the dappled lagoon. She then glimpsed her boyfriend sink his beer and promptly order another. 'Who exactly is this Omar guy, Sonia, what's he like?'

'He's English, you know?'

'Oh, really.'

'Ya, he's a real nice guy, real cool, good looking guy ya, easy to talk with. I like him, but the men with him are vankers, all vankers,' Sonia replied matter of factly. She looked around furtively. 'He comes here all the time and just likes to sit there, alone.' She pointed at a solitary chair at the edge of the dune. 'But, now that his house is nearly finished, maybe he won't come so much.'

'Oh.' Kayte was distant. She looked around at Omar's empty seat. 'Strange.'

'You know this beach here, Kidd's Beach, it's named after the famous British pirate who ruled this place once, called Captain Kidd. Maybe soon they'll call it Omar's Beach no?' Sonia said, smiling again.

'Maybe,' said Kayte. 'Pirates, hungh, sounds interesting. When was that?'

'Oh, about two hundred years ago I think. I read that that this Captain Kidd originally sailed here from New York. He was sent out by the British Government to hunt the pirates down but ended up joining them. A pirate hunter turned pirate. This is the beach where they hung out, repaired their ships, partied and hid their treasure, apparently.'

'Oh wow, fascinating,' Kayte said. Again, Sonia pointed to the ridge behind. Kayte turned and looked up at Roger's house.

'Yah, yah,' Sonia said smiling. 'There is a big pirate cemetery, in the woods, just behind his house, ya.'

'Wow wee,' said an ignited Kayte. Her imagination lit up. 'Have the gravestones got names like Long Jon written on them, or Bluebeard RIP, or … or …?'

'Ya, people say there is much treasure buried up there too,' Sonia interrupted, 'but really Kayte, this place, The Martinez Islands, is a dangerous place still. Seriously, you all need to be careful here.' She now gestured towards Jim and Steve, acting as if they owned the place. 'I am not interested in politics, I just keep quiet, be polite and do my own thing. But I tell you, the mood can change very quickly here, like the weather, ya.'

'Yeah, I can imagine, it does feel a bit tense out there. We had a bunch of young lads swearing and cursing at us as we left town earlier.'

'Ya, the people are not happy, but it's better now, I think. This place was crazy before, run by the young kids. Then Omar and Prince Jaffa took over. But I have only been here six months so I didn't see it.'

'Yeah I heard, but this Omar chap, Sonia, what does he actually do?' Kayte pressed.

'He's a mercenary, Kayte, or was one. You know what that is?'

'Oh, my. Really?'

'Ya, for sure. In Africa you know, ya, this is normal. Anyway, he is here training police, building this hotel, his house, the roads and I hear he is even paying all the government workers. And then, I guess, when the islands start to make money he will get paid back. He has even bought a big farm at the back here and he has brought experts, you know scientists from Europe, to develop the best crops for the islands. He has big plans. It is good, but there are problems with money I hear, all international aid has stopped because he and his men remain here. When his money runs out, then,' Sonia drew a line across her throat, 'finito, there will be problems, for sure. Anyway, when the hotel opens next month it will get busy for us, which is the main thing.'

'Oh, right, I see,' Kayte lied. 'Nothing's changed then?'

'Ya, that's life. Same old, same old,' Sonia continued, with a knowing shrug. 'I am a bit pissed with Omar, Kayte, because he ordered all the dogs to be shot here on the beach. Every night last month, his men would come down in Land Rovers from the other side, driving about with big search lights. We would hear the rat-a-tat of guns. All the dogs have gone now. They were here all the time, and vicious too. No more.'

Sh-t, I didn't need to hear that. Human to human violence, to Kayte's English sensibilities, was one thing. But human's inflicting any cruelty whatsoever on poor, helpless creatures was completely off limits. Even on vicious dogs! She had seen it first hand yesterday. *I really want to like this place.* Looking around at the wind swept beach, even the sea seemed to be shivering.

'This is his way. If he wants something done he just does it. You see Kayte?'

Time to get kiting, I think. *That'll clear my head.* 'Oh, one last thing, Sonia, who's this Prince Jaffa chap? I'm just trying to put it in some sort of order.'

'From what I know, these islands are made up of only a few small families, tight knit you know. He is one of the old head families. But everyone thinks that Prince Jaffa is really just a playboy, a puppet. He does drink a lot and takes drugs I hear. He leaves the running and management of the islands to his cronies and Omar, but he's a smart guy, I'm sure of it. So the people are scared because they are told in the newspapers that Omar and his men are just here to train a new police force. What they call a Home Guard, whatever that is, but really they know that they are running the islands, that they *are* the government. It's funny, Kayte, we saw some photos of Jaffa last week in magazines, one of him in Paris at a fancy dress party, another of him in the South of France dancing at a nightclub and, I think, one of him in London at a film premiere with, how-do-you-say in English? Ya, in all of them, him wearing a world wide grin,' Sonia said, happy to be talking to a European female for the first time in weeks. 'To begin with I think people find all this funny. But now when they see these mercenaries patrolling the streets, beating people … some people I hear have disappeared completely … they are very angry and don't want to live in a police state, they really want Prince Jaffa here and this Omar to go. But as you can see …' Sonia pointed at the shimmering mansion on the bluff behind, '… I think he is here to stay.'

'Wow, what a mess Sonia, a bit scary isn't it? Nothing seems stable at all here. Bizarre,' Kayte replied.

'Ya, Kayte, this is it, welcome to Africa. This is what it's like here … very fragile. Things can change any second.' Sonia held out both arms, and shrugged again. 'Just enjoy the moment.'

Kayte stood up and stretched. 'Come on Chuck, surf's up,' she called out.

'Yeah, babe, let's get to it.'

'What shall we start with, seven metres?'

'Bit lame, babe, but OK.'

She walked up to the bar.

'Steve, we're going to get going now. I'm going to start with a seven metre kite, and I'll just use my freestyler for now.

'Gimme a minute, OK?'

To his obvious surprise, she answered: 'No, Steve. Now.'

Chapter Seven
Surf's Up

Kayte didn't wait for Steve and headed straight up to the other shack alone. *I may as well just do it myself.* She picked up two boards, one under each arm, and went down to the beach.

Having done a couple of runs back and forth to the shack she was soon joined by Chuck and his buddies. Setting up took them ten minutes in the now strong breeze. The first job was to inflate the leading edge and struts of the kite with the pump and then lay out and untangle all the lines that attached to the bar. This is what's used to steer and control the kite. Steve eventually joined her and begrudgingly began to help. The beach seemed to be made of quicksand to him.

The gathered crowd gasped in amazement at the size of the kites, which appeared out of tiny bags. The kites popped into life like two Jack-in-a-boxes and launched skyward. The appearance of the dynamically painted, tent size structures seemed like a magic trick to them.

Chuck's standard joke when they were about to set up, was to repeatedly say, 'let's get pumping,' in silly accents, and it never failed to amuse him. It was a boy thing.

Kayte and Chuck had agreed to try and hit the water as one, to christen the beach in unison, an alchemical male-female thing. When they were both ready, harnessed up, kites vertical and high in the sky, they called out the photographers and local news crew to get in position to record this pocket sized historical moment.

'OK, babe, let's do it.'

They rushed forward and simultaneously cranked their kites back to create lift. Right at the water's edge they jumped into the air together and, propelled upwards by their kites, slipped their feet into the straps mid air and landed gracefully onto deeper water at full speed.

The instant Chuck had said go, magically, the wind speed and constancy increased perfectly to give them the precise boost to get vertical, which they did to a huge cheer from the small crowd at the water's edge.

The familiar feelings of exhilaration surged through Kayte as she broke out through the surf to open water. Spray showered her face with a thousand kisses. The warmth of the sea and air, tasting salt on her lips and seeing the azure open blue ocean before her made her heart pound a dozen beats of joy per second. She was lifted up and surged forward towards the powder puffed horizon.

As she powered on, she could see Chuck edging hard behind her. He was fully maxed out and looking for any available wave to ramp off, grabbing every opportunity to show off and please the crowd. Desperate for huge hang times in the air, he'd come in as close to the shore as possible, for maximum impact.

Everyone on the beach was loving the spectacle. His kite swept across the shore in huge whooshing sweeps and he moved out to join her. Kayte and Chuck called out, yelling encouragement to each other as they competed for the crowd's attention, egging each other on.

The two brightly coloured kites, one predominately pink the other silver, rose vertically into the sky and then swooped down to propel Kayte and Chuck forward in huge rushes across the wind chopped swell. Their bodies dropping in unison was a wonderful sight for the islanders who gasped and clapped at every manoeuvre. The wind was now very strong and constant enough to give them amazing speed, allowing Kayte and Chuck to pop huge airs and get massive lift.

Kayte stalked the coastline to test the water. As her brightly coloured kite waggle danced to the rhythms of nature, Kayte could just glance the crowd on the foreshore, the beach huts raised up on the dunes behind, the hotel beyond, and Omar's pleasure palace pulsing like a lighthouse, still dominating the ridge behind the lagoon. The newly stuccoed edifice shimmered a soft pink in the lowering sun, making the French windows, which were open to the warm afternoon, glow with reflected gold, inviting the mind to only imagine the wonders within. She really wanted to allow her imagination to wander in, but her mind was too busy concentrating on the here and now. She was having too much fun, immersed in herself, showing off and not wanting to be outdone by Chuck. She could only glimpse through spray at life beyond the moment.

Here they were. A pair, soaring on the breeze. Kayte felt the soft hand of sun on her neck, smelt sea in her nostrils, and felt the dancing wind in her hair. Perfect ingredients; the kiting cocktail.

They'd stopped displaying and were now enjoying the space between one another, sculpting it into all sorts of wonderful chords and distances. A quick flap, and he'd surge off to the west, and then slip back, fast, like a carving knife scrawling sharply around her. She'd dip a wing and they'd soar apart again. Like a pair of feather-tipped quills they drew symbols, letters and unknown words on the surf.

She was the first to come in. Chuck stayed out to test the time trial gates, spaced between buoys 100m apart. Kayte immediately flopped down on the beach. As she lay recovering, her chest heaving violently, Steve packed up her equipment. Sonia floated towards her.

'Oh, Kayte, that was absolutely fantastic. Thank you,' she said, as she approached. 'Come up to the bar now, get in some shade and have a drink. You mustn't get too much sun too soon, it'll make you ill.' She held her hand out and pulled Kayte up.

As they approached the bar Papa Jon appeared from nowhere and rushed at her, congratulating. 'Miss Kayte, Miss Kayte, thank you, well done, a truly wonderful sight.' He paused, catching his breath too. 'We saw you on the water from Omar's verandah. I hurried back to tell you that Omar sends his very best wishes to you. He wanted to be the first to congratulate you.' He hardly paused. 'He say he looks forward to saying hello to you very soon.'

Kayte hadn't noticed any people on the high bluff, thank God! Papa Jon was beaming again, sky high as a kite himself, obviously relieved that the kiting event was under way after the weeks of planning. 'Excuse me,' he said, and gave Kayte a quick, unexpected kiss on her cheek. The girls looked at each other and couldn't help laughing.

He turned and skipped off down the dune to be interviewed by the local news crew, who were waiting patiently for him on the beach below.

Kayte flopped down on Omar's part shaded solitary seat, while Sonia fetched the drinks. She could see Chuck out at sea, circling. First, he'd edge hard to get upwind, then turn and dive his kite towards the surface to create maximum pull. If he caught the wind at just at the right angle, he'd hit tension and blast forward, through the 100m apart time trial gates, parallel to the beach, time and time again.

She reclined, exhausted in sun-soaked bliss. Although she had noodle arms and her stomach ached badly, she had warmth penetrating her entirety and the lovely crinkling of salt on her skin and eye lashes made her lick her lips and bask in contentment.

'I'm sure you're thirsty Kayte, so I put some soda on top, to make it long,' Sonia said, as they clinked glasses. 'Cheers! This is our house cocktail, rum punch, in homage to the pirate history of these islands.'

'Well, cheers to them,' Kayte said, as she sucked the delicious long drink through a straw. Sonia pulled up a seat and they sat back in silence.

Every mouthful of the strong cocktail helped Kayte truly soak up the reassuring neverness of Kidd's beach. It was one of those places that had looked the same for millennia, and would do for millennia to come. The deep blue of the sea glittered with silver flecks, the wind whistled it's eternal *shanty* and the waves cascaded in their timeless rhythm. It wouldn't matter what development happened around it, the beach, this view, would always remain the same.

Kayte's spirits were well and truly lifted by the time everyone came up from the beach to congratulate her. They took photos and generally made a fuss, leaving her positively floating in the afterglow. Someone had turned the volume up and Balearic beats began to drift across the bar area. The breeze caught the music, took it off in gusts and then returned it, the volume rising and falling like her kite in the currents. The combination of lying back and sipping a cocktail on this wonderful windswept beach, having just had an amazing kitesurf session, was absolute perfection.

Chuck came in from the surf to similar applause and entered the bar a few minutes later. Chuffed, he went straight up to Kayte and high fived. 'Hey, hey, not too shabby out there, hun.' He collapsed down. 'I just had a quick word with the recorder guys and they said our times weren't too sloppy either. That one pass you did averaged 18 knots and I got up to 22 on one.'

'Wow wee, that's amazing. I don't believe it. I felt we were going a good lick,' Kayte enthused, 'but it didn't feel that fast. The water surface must be smoother than it felt. When the guys get the course set up properly tomorrow and we hook up bigger kites, we could do it, Chuck. We can really do it.' $15,000 flashed across her mind.

'Yip, we could. It's goddam perfect here. I can't wait to get a fatty-up tomorrow. We're gonna fly baby.'

'Yes siree!'

*

Just over two years ago, Kayte had gone down to Leucate in Southern France for a competition. She surprised herself. She'd put herself in the right position, at the right time. Breaking through the time trial gates on a perfect gust of wind, she was taken skimming, virtually flying across the Mediterranean Sea to achieve a women's world speed record of 26 knots which amazingly still stood after all this time. Chuck had broken his own record last year on the Skeleton coast off Namibia.

*

Fifteen minutes later all the locals had simply vanished into the golden ether of fading light and Sonia and her team began to close the bar down. Fuel supplies were cut off and bottles were packed up. Papa Jon clapped his hands furiously.

'It is going to be sunset soon,' he said in a panic. 'We must get back to the hotel before it becomes dark.' He dashed around urging. 'Please, everyone come now, please.'

'Get back before dark … ' she heard Jim, echoing sarcastically, '… spookie!'

At last they'd loaded up the vehicles. Before jumping aboard, Kayte stood still for a moment and noticed how incredibly calm it all felt on the other side of the lagoon. Omar's palace, through the course of the day, had gone from bright white to pink and now sat peacefully glowing a straw gold colour, perched like a bird of paradise in a gilded cage. The launch had slipped away unnoticed. Although there were some bright patches along the ridge, the shadows looked increasingly dark and impenetrable. As though a dense silence was closing in.

They were soon off around the lagoon, unsettling the egrets once again, who flared up a brighter white against the darkening background. The roads back in to town weren't busy; the only traffic seemed to be on the other side of the road, leaving St Martin.

Chapter Eight
All Becoming Clear

As the minibuses pulled up outside The Splendid, Kayte could just make out, in the fading light, more patches of cleanliness had appeared on the upper floors. It had been a busy day. The painter had managed to decorate umpteen more squares on the fascia of the building in his attempt to resuscitate the hotel back in to life again.

'Come on, wake up Steve. You've got a job to do,' Kayte said, shaking her sprawled boyfriend. She'd done it a few times on the journey back, his snoring was embarrassing.

Kayte waited in the foyer for Steve to haul her bags and boards in when Papa Jon appeared with a rather tall, healthy looking fair man who smiled, and introduced himself in a clipped English public school accent.

'Good evening Kayte, I'm Alistair. Alistair Fortesque from the British Embassy, your mother wrote to me.'

'Oh yes, that's right, quite. I remember. Good to meet you.'

'How was it out there today? How did you enjoy Kidd's Beach?'

'It was absolutely fabulous, thanks. Really great.'

'Wizard. Super news. And the kitesurfing?'

'Amazing. It's perfect for us. We got some really encouraging speeds up, which we'll build on tomorrow, weather permitting.'

'Well, the forecast's good, should be fine. Well done,

excellent news. Up and running.'

'Thank-you.'

Kayte thought Alistair Fortesque looked and acted more military than diplomatic, sort of like an aged ex-Royal Marine. There's was nothing like the man from the ministry, pen pusher type about him.

Papa Jon managed to mobilise Steve and Jim towards Kayte and Alistair Fortesque, completing the British contingent.

'Why don't you take your bags up to your room then come and join me for a drink?' Alistair said. 'Oh, and come back down as soon as possible please. I'd like to have a little chat with you all. Just a little chat mind, nothing to worry about. I'll meet you on the veranda, what would you like to drink?'

'Please don't drink too much tonight,' Kayte pleaded to Steve up in their room.

'I'll do what I want, Kayte, don't tell me what to do.'

'Steve, Steve, please. You're out here to help me and all you're doing is drinking.'

'Kayte, I've been sweating away in that damn kitchen for six months. This is the first holiday I've had. You haven't paid a pound in rent or bills or anything, this is the least you can do. What do you expect me to do? Just be your lacky or something?'

'No, Steve, I don't. I just want us to enjoy this trip together, that's all. It's important.'

'Well, you're kitesurfing and I'm not, OK?'

'I know it's hard for you Steve, but the drinking isn't really going to help is it?'

'Well, whatever, Kayte, it is what it is. Come on let's go down and see what this posh git has to say.'

When Steve and Kayte got back down, Alistair Fortesque and Jim were locked in close conversation. It wasn't until the couple approached that the two men actually noticed and jumped up in unison, as if disturbed from something serious. Jim's expression changed briefly. The intense concentration from his dialogue with Fortesque had squashed his sharp features in to such a narrow space that there seemed to be hardly room for his own two eyes. His normal ratty appearance had mutated and elongated into one resembling a fox. On seeing Kayte and Steve, he turned rodent again.

After the awkwardness had subsided, they all settled and drinks arrived. Alistair Fortesque began his lecture, 'Look, I'm afraid there are a few ground rules you're going to have to obey here on The Martinez Islands. It is a very safe place as far as Africa goes, believe me, but it is still a bit edgy, politically, as you may be aware. Anyway,' he dragged out the word, 'I'm sorry to inform you that the locals seemed to have bubbled up over the last 24 hours, since your arrival, for some reason. We're not quite sure why. We're in the dark a bit,' he seemed to yawn the last words, 'but we trust the return of the President, Prince Jaffa, in a few days will calm things down.' He coughed. 'There's a sort of curfew being imposed as we speak. The new police force, the Home Guard as they call themselves, do the patrols and are all novices, new to the job, if you get my gist? They'll be on edge, nervous ... and consequently ... dare I say it, potentially ... how do I put it ... trigger happy.' They all took furtive sips of their drinks. 'So, I want none of you to leave the hotel grounds for the time being. Just go to the beach during the day and stay in during the evenings. Am I clear?' Kayte and Steve nodded. Alistair brightened up, and leaned back. 'Good, well that's really it. I'm sure it'll all blow over and come to nothing. It usually does. So, just enjoy yourselves. It's such a beautiful place, isn't it?'

'Yes ... it is,' Kayte mumbled. Steve gulped his drink.

'There really isn't very much in town to do anyway so ... sorry to repeat myself ... it's Kidd's for surfing during the day, and then supper and bed here. All will be tickety boo. Are we clear on that? Has anyone got any questions?'

All three shook heads.

'Christ!' Alistair suddenly exclaimed, looking at this watch. 'I'm sorry but I've got to get going myself, it's nearly 6.30 already.

Any problems, just give me a call and I'll be straight round.' He stood up and handed them each a business card. 'Good luck with kitesurfing, Kayte. Have a great time and I'll try and pop out to Kidd's one day, I'd love to see you in action.'

He shook their hands firmly and strode off across the expansive foyer, as if marching on a regimental parade ground.

In the furthest corner of the bar the American contingent had pushed two tables together and were huddled closely, receiving a similar talk from a ginger haired, middle aged man who, with his flat-top and finned haircut, also looked more like a military attaché than an embassy official in a remote outpost.

'This place is just wrong,' declared Steve, smugly. 'I told you we shouldn't have come.'

'Shut up Steve, will you? Stop being so bloody negative,' Kayte snapped, unable to hold back. She turned to Jim. 'It's a bit odd we're having this sort of pet talk from our embassy officials, don't you think?'

'Na, na, na. It's standard stuff, don't worry about it, let's have another drink. I'll get them, same again?'

'Nice one mate, cheers.' It was Steve.

Kayte thought it peculiar - Jim seemed to be more interested in the potential for a good story, if the solids hit the fan, than asking her any questions about the day's kiting and concentrating on the assignment he was supposedly here for. He hadn't asked her about her times or anything yet. God only knows what the hell he's here for, she pondered. Not for free drinks by the look of things, he's going to have to pay for them. He's pissing me right off whatever.

While Jim was up at the bar, Kayte pleaded again, 'Just have this one drink, Steve, and then let's get something to eat and go to bed.'

'Why?'

'Oh come on, Steve, because you've had quite enough today. You look wasted.'

'I'm alright.'

'No, you're not, Steve. You've been topping up ever since

we got here. On top of your medication? Just give it a break will you?'

'Kayte, leave it out. Stop telling me what to do, OK?'

Jim returned, weighed down with goblets of adorned punches. Goblets of fire more like.

'You know guys? Sonia, the bar owner, said there's a big pirate graveyard on the other side of the lagoon, up behind the new hotel somewhere,' Kayte said, looking for a solution and a lighter conversation. 'Why don't you both go and have a look for that tomorrow, while we're kiting? That'll help pass some time.' Wayhay! It was starting to get a bit too much for the boys now, way too exciting - pirates, riots, rum and mercenaries - a helluva troublesome cocktail. They started to sing, 'it'll be ho, ho, ho, and a barrel of rum, and then looked at each other, ignored Kayte and clinked their glasses. 'Ha-harr, me hearty!' they bellowed in unison with theatrical pirate accents. Kayte couldn't help but collapse with laughter, starting to feel the effect of a second rum punch storming through her.

'Apparently, so. Sonia also said there's loads of treasure up there too.'

Ye Gods, that was one ingredient too many. The boys were off. There was no stopping them. 'It'll be ho, ho, ho, and a barrel of rum,' was all Kayte could hear, as she slipped anchor and tacked off for a quick supper alone.

Having sobered up a bit, she got back to the bar as quickly as she could, to rescue Steve before his fourth was ordered. No luck.

'I'm gonna' have one more,' he slurred.

'Whatever, Steve. I'm going to sleep in the other room tonight, OK?'

'Whateva.'

Kayte, misty-eyed, could still hear Jim and Steve guffawing in the background as she pressed the button for the lift.

She jumped straight in to bed. I'm going to get that $15,000 prize. I'm going to beat my record, she resolved. To hell with Steve. I'm going to get a flat of my own too. She shuddered at the thought of her dingy flat in the old tenement block sitting in the grey murk that she'd be back in next week. Her heart sank. *Why couldn't I have brought someone else? If Lisa was here we'd be having such a laugh; Sh-t, sh-t, sh-t.*

Her last thoughts before she switched off the light was of when she'd torn open the invitation letter for this trip three weeks ago. She'd called her pregnant best friend straightaway.

'Lisa, it's me,' she'd squealed excitedly. 'You're not going to believe this, I've just received this random letter inviting me out to somewhere called The Martinez Islands, to go kiting. Have you heard of them? Anyway, I can't believe it. Let me read it to you ...'

'Kayte, Kayte. Hold on. I'm busy right now, but that sounds amazing,' her best friend had said. 'Just what you need. Look I'll phone you back in a bit, I'm in the supermarket.'

'OK, sorry hon. Come up to Tiffin's for a coffee? I'll be there in an hour.'

'Yes, OK. See you there. Wee, how exciting Kayte, great news.'

'Heya,' a drenched Kayte called out, brightening up as she saw her oldest and best friend sitting at a table in their favourite café sixty minutes later.

'Oh, hi me dear,' Lisa said, turning. 'God, miserable day. Poor you, you're soaked.'

'I know, it's foul. Are you OK? You look exhausted hon.'

'I am, I'm shattered. I'm just not sleeping well, that's all.'

'Well, not long to go now. You'd better get used to it! It's only the beginning,' Kayte said, smiling.

'Do I detect you getting broodie yourself?'

'Me broodie! You've got to be kidding. Your life's over girl!' Kayte declared. 'And have kids with that arse Steve?' she'd added, 'No way.'

They both laughed.

'Is he still being awful?'

'Awful!' Kayte exclaimed. 'He's being horrible. All the time. I hate him.'

'Hip, hip hoorah,' Lisa chimed. 'At last you've seen the light.'

'See what you think of this while I get the coffees,' Kayte said, handing over the envelope.

'I'll have a hot chocolate actually, Kaytie. Wow, lovely stamps.'

Kayte went up to the counter to order and came back.

'It sounds amazing Kayte. Just what the doctor ordered.'

'D'you think it's genuine?'

'Yes, I do. If you guys can help promote tourism there, then why not? It's a good idea.'

'Steve is adamant it's a joke.'

'He would, wouldn't he? Miserable git!'

'If you hadn't been in such a rush to grow up I could have taken you, you silly girl. He's being so horrid all the time Lees, I don't know what to do.'

'Dump him,' Lisa said, matter of factly.

The waitress delivering their drinks momentarily interrupted their conversation.

'Anyway it sounds wicked. And all that money too. You can get a place of your own if you want.'

'It's just what I've been dreaming about Lees. Seriously, I have. I think this is my chance to beat my record too. I've got this funny feeling I've been there before. I can picture it.'

'Mmm, alright.'

Kayte knew that quite a few people, including her boyfriend, thought that her world speed record was simply down to luck. Yes, it was lucky to be in the right place at the right time, but that's the magic in life; she'd *carpe diemed* it – she'd seized the day.

'I can't wait to get out of this sh-t hole. And hey, hey, hey, yes the five thousand dollars attendance fee, let alone the 15 grand prize money. I've never had so much money.'

'Look, calm down now Kaytie. It may not come off. Don't count you're chickens before …'

'… your eggs have hatched. I know, I know.'

'I just don't want you to get hurt, that's all. Kaytie, you really deserve this hon, you've worked so hard.'

'Yeah, yeah thanks. I know.'

Kayte was fast asleep. She didn't hear Steve stumbling in next door hours later.

Chapter Nine
Six Degrees West

In the cool of the early morning, Roger MacGill took his time. He wandered leisurely through beautifully laid out nursery gardens in an idyllic valley. He'd stop and scrutinise squares of greenery with his white overalled, South African, farm manager and then move on. They plucked leaves, crushed and sniffed them and then continued onto the next experimental block of plants, shrubs and flowers.

'So, John, you've been here a year, pretty well to the day,' Roger said. 'I trust you've got your head around the place now?'

'I think so, sir. Pretty sure.'

Roger ran his hand through the foliage of a heavily scented sapling and then leant forward and inhaled the exotic fragrance of its spidery, bright yellow flowers. He seemed drugged by its heady scent when he stood back up and looked directly at John Hawley. John was in his early sixties with an incredibly well weathered, gnarled up face. His deep wrinkles resembled the harsh African lands he'd worked for the past fifty years. Bright grey blue, bleached by the sun eyes peered out from this rugged facial terrain.

'Well look, John, I need a plan from you now. A plan of action. Have you worked out what the most suitable crops for the farm are yet?'

'Yiss sir, I have. If you come up to the house, you will see that I've fully mapped every square metre of the farm. I'll explain my proposal to you there, if you've got the time?'

'Yes, sure, I'm all ears. Come on.'

The two men sauntered towards the neat single-storey colonial farm house, set back on a slight rise of immaculately manicured lawn. The old farmstead was propped up on short stilts and had a red tin roof, with a long verandah spanning the whole width of the house. As they ascended the broad central steps to the cool balcony, designed to filter any available breeze, two of Roger's heavily armed bodyguards came into view and followed casually behind.

Roger sat down outside on a comfortable wicker chair. John placed drawings, charts and maps in front of him. One bodyguard stood out of earshot in the garden below, the other patrolled the property. All was silent and deeply peaceful. The only audible noise was from the bodyguards armaments clinking as they moved. The rising sun, like the brightest of bloodshot eyes, peeped through gaps in the mountain peaks ahead, fluttering its pink lashes across a cobalt sky.

'Would you like a drink, sir?' John enquired.

'That'd be grand, just a coffee and a glass of water,' Roger replied.

'I've got some rather tidy brandy I brought over from home last month. How about a nip of that? Medicinal like,' the farm manager said with a glint in his eye.

'Ach! Go on then,' Roger said. 'How can I refuse! Just a snifter though, I've got a long day ahead.'

'Shall I put some 'arse in it for you?'

Roger knew exactly what he meant. 'One cube, thanks John,' Roger answered, smiling.

The old farmer went inside, leaving Roger to gaze out at the wonderful piece of real estate he'd acquired the year before. He'd bought the farm legitimately, albeit at a ridiculously over-inflated price; it was an offer the previous owner couldn't refuse. It was the finest estate on The Martinez Islands and Roger just had to have it.

The weary mercenary sat back in a comfortable rattan bucket seat and stretched out his legs. He flipped his shoes off and rotated his feet as he gazed across the rolling fields in front of him to the high peaks in the distance, which were back-lit and purple hazed by the early morning sunshine. On the other side of the mountains lay the vast Indian Ocean, sprawling towards infinity. On the beach below, Roger pictured the workmen arriving to finish his beachside home. When the joints in his ankles clicked he put his shoes back on.

For the first time since he'd set foot on the islands eighteen months ago, it crossed Roger's mind that he may just have finally arrived. Although he'd bought this farm and his seaside home, he didn't quite feel as if he owned them for some peculiar reason. They didn't feel his. Somehow the ownership was tenuous, possession wasn't real. To all intents and purposes he'd reached his promised land, and he was lord and master of all he surveyed, but he didn't feel secure here at all. He didn't feel at home. That was it. Perhaps I will in six months, he reasoned. It always takes a couple of years to feel at home anywhere.

'Tobacco is definitely the way forward, sir,' John said, putting a tray down. 'We have perfect loamy soil here, here and here.' He pointed at large swathes of terrain on the map laid out on the large coffee table in front of them, and gesticulated to the distance. 'And it has to be Burley, that'll be the optimum variety for your land and we'll get the best return. We can continue with ylang-ylang here and here for sure, but what we'll need to do is plant a hell of a lot more trees, a forest of them, to dry the crop. We must get going on that immediately. I suggest there and there, it's the least productive land. Eucalyptus will be best, it's the fastest growing.'

'Mmm, beautiful. OK,' Roger replied dreamily, sniffing his brandy. 'We can get some game birds in there for a bit of fun too, eh? Partridge or something. What do you think?'

'Definitely. But I'm afraid that curing tobacco ourselves - it has to be done onsite, otherwise the leaves will rot - I'm sorry to say this, but it will mean building a drying shed, which is not going to be cheap. Also, sir, at certain times, we're too late this year, for sowing the seeds and planting out we'll need labour - 40 odd men for three months from February to April next year.'

'No problem, that'll be good for the local lads, get them off the streets. But right now, John, what you need to do is to give me costings; on what we need to do now along with a timetable, a schedule for it all. Judging by the acreage you intend to plant on, give me estimates on the income the baccy and the ylang-ylang will bring in next year too. That's vital. I need to know what the income will be.'

'Of course, sir. A business plan?'

'I guess so, but do it as soon as possible. It's going to take some planning to get all the equipment shipped over, I assume. I must have an idea of income though, d'you understand?'

'Yes, sir, I do, I do. I'll get it to your office as soon as possible.' He raised his glass. 'Cheers.'

'Cheers to you John, all the best,' Roger replied, picking up his charger.

'How's your house coming on?' John enquired.

'Fine, thank you, we're nearly there. We're decorating and the furniture is on its way. I'm having a house warming party next month, the invites will be going out any day now. It'll be quite a bash.'

'Great, can't wait.'

Roger twitched. 'I'd love to stay, I really would, but I've got a lot on. Be in touch soon. Get that quote and income figures over to the office asap would you?' Roger said, standing up.

'Of course sir.' John also stood up and, trying to sound casual, said, 'I hear there's some trouble brewing in town. Some of the farm boys seem a bit tetchy. Anything I need to worry about?'

'I don't think so, no, John. There's some tension about, yes there is, so we put a curfew in place yesterday. Just to keep a lid on it. But I had a word with the head imam here a couple of days ago and he indicated that it was just family squabbles. I assume some loose ends from Zafir's lot. You know, the rabble we cleared up when we got here.' Roger turned to his farm manager with a sad look. 'There's just too many young men hanging around with nothing to do, that's half the problem, John. Fifty percent of the population here are young men under 30. Recipe for disaster really. I'm trying to get them working, but they're so bloody lazy. Anyway I'm sure it's just a storm in a tea cup.'

'Same problem in all Muslim countries.'

'Yes, you're right. Young men with nothing to do is a huge problem the world over.'

'I'll polish my old rifle up just in case.'

'No harm in that John, no harm at all. Any concerns just call the office. No news is good news from our end though, just bash on as normal.'

The two men shook hands. Roger turned and walked purposefully down the stairs towards the opened door of his black Mercedes, leaving his brandy virtually untouched.

The farm manager stood on the balcony and waved at the limousine, which wafted away in its very own swirling cloud, like a genie disappearing down the drive, back to its bottle. An open-topped Land Rover for his men followed closely behind; a dust devil in hot pursuit. John, completely familiar with the vagaries of Africa chuckled to himself and shook his head. It was only the thought of the $10,000 a month, tax free, that Roger MacGill was paying him, being squirrelled away into his Swiss bank account that made him turn back to the task in hand.

Splendid Hotel 09:15.

Across the island, the kiting group were loading up the minibuses with their equipment. Before Kayte got in, she looked up to see the decorator, who was already hard at work, precariously leaning out from a balcony with his roller extended, urgently administering first aid to the building. In daylight, she could see he was two-thirds of the way through the job, dressing the wounded hotel.

Not long out of The Splendid's confines, a surprised Kayte looked up one of old town St Martin's narrow streets to spy groups of armed soldiers combing the busy alleyways. Oh, Christ, what's going on now? she said to herself. As her minibus stalled she saw one young soldier actually lean back and kick a door off its hinges, and then storm in.

'Hey, Steve, have a look at this,' she whispered.

'Oh don't Kayte,' he replied, groaning from behind sunglasses. 'It's way too bright for me out there.'

Kayte thought she'd ask Papa Jon what they were doing, she could tell he'd seen them too, but decided against it. Best keep silent. Best not upset anyone. He, though, seemed genuinely happy to see the soldiers and even wound the window down to wave.

The convoy rumbled on, Kayte noticed the same street sellers from the day before, laying their wares out on brightly coloured blankets. But as the white-gloved traffic warden ushered them through St Martin's central square, he suddenly brought them to an abrupt halt, jumping off his podium and slamming his hand out emphatically right in front of the vehicles.

'What the f-k!' cursed Chuck, as he sat back upright after the jolt.

'Oh look, oh look, it is Omar,' Papa Jon called out from the front, winding his window down again and waving frantically.

Roger's dusty black Mercedes, which no longer gleamed, whisked past in front of them, followed by the bristling armed jeep.

*

Roger, in his cool plushness, sat impervious to his royal treatment. He saw Papa Jon waving at him, but didn't respond. His car hurtled on through town, arriving in St. Martin's exclusive coastal suburb, Royalton, five minutes later. The two vehicles squealed to a halt outside a villa's gates. The Mercedes hooted and an old retainer appeared to open up. The metal creaked and scraped the ground, as though they hadn't been opened for years. Roger's car waited. The jeep swung past precariously, heading in first, and pulled up rudely in front of the large bungalow. The Mercedes tucked in behind. Two armed guards jumped down, one rushed through the open front door, the other took up a position to the rear.

'Oi, hello, anyone there?' the mercenary yelled from inside. He could see the open plan hallway was empty. He walked through a passageway, engaging his semi-automatic MP7 as he went. Not a soul around. He went back out and knocked on Roger's car door. The electric window slid down.

'There's no one there, sir.'

'What! Are you sure?'

'Yessir.'

'I don't like it, get some more boys down here asap,' Roger snapped.

The window went up. Roger got on his satellite phone, as the guard got on his walkie-talkie.

A stillness descended on the walled compound. All that could be heard was the incessant chirrup of crickets. The minutes of calm were interrupted by the occasional crackle of reverb from walkie-talkies.

Twenty minutes later all peace was shaken by the arrival of a truck full of Roger's army steaming into the cramped driveway. Once he saw his armed men spilling out in all directions, Roger got out.

'Frank, come with me,' he said to his loyal personal bodyguard. They walked into the empty villa. 'Put a man there,' Roger continued, pointing to the only internal doorway. 'And two on the front door. Spread the rest around the garden, driveway and gate.'

'Will do sir, straight away.'

'And Frank, we've got this Ishaq muppet coming any minute, tell the guys on the gate to search him and then bring him into me, I'll wait here. You may remember him, he's tall, with a beard, looks a bit like Gandalf. Get my boat sent around here too, I'm going out to Kidd's after this.'

Roger sat on a sofa and picked up a glossy magazine from the coffee table in front of him, *Business Today*, and flung it straight back down, it was three years out of date. He tucked a cushion behind him to stop his pistol, posterior positioned, from digging in.

He didn't stand up as the proud Ishaq was brought before him minutes later.

'Excuse me for not being here to meet you … Omar, sir,' Ishaq said, coming forward.

'OK, guys, thanks,' Roger said, flicking his hand at his loitering men. He sighed in annoyance and skipped formalities. 'Sit down, Ishaq. Here next to me.'

'Would you like a coffee, Omar, sir, something to drink?'

'No, no. Don't worry about that, man. Where is everyone anyway? I thought this is the Ministry of Finance for crying out loud!'

'Yes, sir, they are coming in soon.'

'But it's gone ten o'clock in the morning.'

'I know, I know. I am sorry. It is just the way it is.' He shrugged feebly. 'What can I do for you?'

'You know what I want to talk about, Ishaq. We're going to talk about my money. That's what, as you very well know.'

'Of course, of course.'

'I spoke to my Accountant in Switzerland yesterday and he says I've pumped 30 million plus US into the islands to date. $32 million, two hundred and seventy-five thousand to be precise, and counting. As you well know, I've seen nothing back. The agreement we had when you, Prince Jaffa and I put it in writing was that the re-payment programme would commence exactly twelve months after Prince Jaffa's coronation, and that hasn't happened has it?'

'No, sir.'

'And that anniversary was over three months ago, wasn't it?'

'Yes, sir.'

'Whenever I speak to Prince Jaffa about this matter, he refers me to you. You've been avoiding me for the past two months, he's been in Europe for the past six weeks so here we are. What exactly is happening? Talk to me.'

'Well, I am delighted to inform you, Omar, sir,' Ishaq said, brightening up, 'that we are now in a position to start repaying you. Only yesterday I instructed our National Bank to commence the monthly repayment programme for you. A coincidence, no?'

'Quite. Carry on.'

'It will begin on 1ˢᵗ April and we will transfer $1,000,000 per month to your Swiss account.'

'Right, and that'll run for the next three years I assume?'

'Indeed, sir.'

'So, I can inform my accountant to cease all payments to the Ministry from now on?'

'Yes, indeed, sir. We have received your donation to support the state for this month and we have sufficient reserves to continue unaided from next month.'

'I want to see paperwork to prove this arrangement has been setup. Something I can send to my accountant.'

'Yes, of course. I will send proof over to your office.'

'No, you'll go and get it for me now.' Roger looked up. 'Frank,' he called out, snapping his fingers. Frank appeared.

'Yes, sir.'

'Take this man to his office and wait with him. He's getting me some paperwork.'

Roger sat back as the two men walked off. The cushion had slipped so the butt of his pistol pressed cold and hard into the base of his spine. The overwhelming relief from the financial haemorrhage he'd suffered over the past eighteen months finally coming to an end was evident, he felt drained. With both palms he rubbed his cheeks vigorously, sighed deeply, craned his head back and ran his hands tightly across his forehead and back through his oiled hair.

Chapter Ten
Seven Degrees South

The subdued group hadn't noticed the sparkling launch cruise past the beach bar, just offshore, sedately enter and moor up on the lagoon opposite, not even Kayte.

It was gone twelve thirty by the time they had arrived, an hour and a half earlier, on the extraordinary, non functioning project that was the new road. They'd flashed past already tired looking billboards advertising hotels and banks that were yet to be, with no sign of work progressing. They went across the ridge where the hillsides looked liked heads, partly razed in readiness for surgery. Beyond, the expansive sight of the eternally rhythmic Indian Ocean, stretching far out towards the morning sun, swept all thoughts of dystopia away. This is what you are here for, the sea was saying to Kayte, not your human politics, leave all that behind. The pristine coastline, embraced by lush vegetation with palm trees poking up and out was all that should be of any importance to the kitesurfers.

When Kayte stepped out of the minibus, she looked across at the fast-becoming familiar sight of the lagoon and the marsh birds settling back down. She hardly noticed the teams of people working on the hotel behind, some on the building, others in the gardens or on the lodges.

By the time they arrived, blustery weather was starting to bristle and brush the surface water. The wind wasn't quite forceful enough to kitesurf yet, but the day was looking promising. The time recorders were soon out in front on Sonia's boat and the time trial gates were reassembled to the optimum position, tweaking the setup from the previous day. Sonia's team had set the bar up for the day. The bottles glistened. The whole group, being the only customers, gathered furniture around one umbrella.

'OK everyone, as we know from yesterday I recorded 18 knots and Chuck got up to 22. So today we're going to hook up bigger kites and ramp it up,' said Kayte taking control. She looked around. 'Come on everyone, cheer up. We could be recording new world records today.' Kayte sat back down and leant across to Chuck. 'What's up?' she whispered.

'Ah, just that shite our embassy guy said last night,' he replied quietly.

'And what was that?'

'He said there's some trouble around and we may well all have to leave the day after tomorrow.'

'What! Why didn't you say. Our chap seemed to suggest something minor was going on and to be back at the hotel by six. No big deal, he said.' She turned to face Chuck. 'Anyway, look … come on, we're here to kitesurf, let's just do it. Let's aim to be ready to go in about an hour, then we've got a few hours of high winds before we have to pack up and get back by six.'

'I know babe, you're right. Just look at it. It's so frickin' beautiful here.'

'Exactly Chuck. I know it's hard, but just relax, there's nothing to worry about here. Let's just enjoy ourselves and try and beat our records and get the prizes. It's a ton of money too. Come on.'

'I know, I know. You're right.'

Sitting on this intoxicating, unspoilt beach, it seemed impossible to picture the world as being anything but stable and safe.

'My story is combining the political tension on the islands with Chuck and Kayte's struggle to master the beach and beat their records,' Jim piped in with. 'I'm going to weave those two stories together.'

'Whatever,' said Kayte.

'Sounds cool,' said Chuck. 'Ramp up the tension.' He stood up. 'Come on guys,' he said to his group, 'let's get down on the beach with the hacky sack and spin a Frisbee.'

'Woah! That's a bloody relief they've cheered up,' Kayte said to Steve and Jim when the American contingent had decamped to the beach a few moments later. Kayte could see them begin to kick the little bean bag to each other without it touching the sand. One of them even had a bungee out and was using it as a catapult, flicking scrunched up balls of paper at human targets.

'Hey, look at that guy,' said Steve, 'it's like a grownup version of the paper missiles I used to flick around the classroom with an elastic band.'

'Grow up, more like,' said Kayte smiling.

'Anyway Kayte, well done geeing them up,' said Jim. 'The Americans always freak out at the slightest thing and just want to run home. They're pathetic actually. They live under the illusion that America is so safe but it's got one of the highest murder rates and some of the most violent cities on the planet. 35,000 deaths a year are gun related. There's more chance of being murdered or robbed on home soil than anywhere else. It's actually worse than a war zone over there.'

'Funny old world,' said Steve.

'Topsy-turvey, more like.'

Papa Jon came across from the bar.

'I am going to go back into town now my friends,' he informed them. 'But please, if you need anything, anything at all, please ask for it at the bar. We have put your packed lunches in the fridge. Have a good day, I will see you all later. I will return by three o'clock at the latest.'

'Why don't you guys go across and have a look for the pirate cemetery? I see the boat coming back, it can take you over,' said Kayte, standing up and looking around.

A speed boat was making its way towards her. It had stopped at the hotel's pontoon and picked up Sonia and a dark-haired man. The slim craft then slid across the lagoon, bisecting it with a single white line that sent echo waves out across the glassy surface, breaking up the clear reflections of the ridge. When the ripples reached the crisp reflection of Roger's palace the building shattered and fragmented into a million pieces, temporarily making his home a marbled mess on the water's surface.

She saw Sonia kiss the dark-haired man farewell, join Papa Jon and drive off in one of the minibuses. Kayte turned back to Steve and Jim but, unnoticed, they'd slunk off back to the bar. She snatched up her beach bag and stomped off to Roger's untouched seat and opened her book.

All she could hear was the two Brits at the bar, clinking glasses and laughing away as they, *ha-haarhed*, talking loudly of pirate treasure. Kayte was loathed to admit that they were helping to lighten the atmosphere up somewhat. Whether it was British stiff upper lipness, she wasn't sure; whatever it was, they didn't seem to have a care in the world.

The Americans continued to play. The wind started to gust with purpose. Kayte looked out to sea, ignoring the book beside her, and tried to block out the waffling of the two juveniles behind her.

'Hi Kayte, I'm Kirk, sorry to disturb you. I just wanted to come over and say hello,' said the bushy haired guy Kayte had seen hop on the boat and kiss farewell to Sonia. 'I am sorry I couldn't come over yesterday, but we were working on our new shop and if I'd left, something would go wrong or the guys would just vamoose. But I could see the kites over the dunes. It was beautiful to watch, really fantastic, you're bringing the beach to life at last.'

'Oh hi, I was miles away. Good to meet you. Yes, it is a great beach for kiting Kirk, really superb. I hear it was you who suggested getting us over here in the first place.'

'Yes, that's right. I was here this time last year and for these two months only, it is incredibly windy. The rest of the year is calm, but now it blows. I thought getting you guys out here would be a great start to promote tourism. You know, grass roots up. Anyway, come up to the bar and have a drink.'

'Thanks, I will. I'll be up in a minute.'

She glanced up at the skull and cross-bone flag and could see the wind had truly picked up. Blasts were sweeping in and ruffling the sea's surface perfectly. She looked behind. The profuse vegetation on the ridge side looked as though it was actually steaming in the early afternoon sun. The haze had produced a net curtain effect that made everything look distant, as if it was all within another world altogether. Kayte couldn't help but gaze at Roger's house, mesmerized. It looked like a mirage, worthy of Kublai Khan, shivering behind the mesh like screen.

'I'm going to setup in a minute, Kat,' Chuck called out from the beach below.

'Give me ten minutes, I'm going to have a quick drink,' she called back.

Kayte approached the bar. She could see Kirk leaning forward, talking to Steve and Jim.

'Catch-22,' she heard Jim say, as she neared.

'Ya, exactly, a catch-22 situation. It's a shame because he's such a cool guy but hey, we'll see what happens. I just want there to be peace and my project here to work. I really hope it works out for him too. He's like a hippy really, he's got a beautiful heart. He just wants the best for everyone I think. And boy is the guy generous. He never quibbles. He gives you what you want and more. You know, he's paying for all you guys to be here?'

'Yeah, we heard,' said Steve.

'How did he get all his money?' Jim asked.

'He's worked all over Africa. I heard he made most of his money in Angola. He put a leader in power there and got all these incredible mineral rights, which brought in tens of millions. I also heard one of his men say that they'd been paid to protect some diamond mines in Mozambique, and you can imagine what went on there.'

'What did?' said Jim.

'They helped themselves of course. Wouldn't you?'

'Probably.'

'Damn right, I would,' chimed Steve.

'Oh Kayte, sorry I didn't see you there, what would you like to drink?' Kirk said, looking up.

'Just a coke for me.'

'Oh hi, Kayte. Are you OK? I didn't see you there either,' said Steve, turning around.

'We're going to setup in a minute Steve. I'm going to give my 14m kite a go.'

'Cool, go for it. Better you do it now, get a feel for it before the wind really picks up.'

'Yes, that's what I thought too.'

'I hear this Prince Jaffa is due back in a day or two,' Jim continued. 'I imagine he's been talking to the next bunch lining up to invade!'

'Yeah, he probably is,' Kirk said, laughing. 'That's probably exactly what he's been doing. From what I know of him, I bet Prince Jaffa wriggles like a snake. The islanders here are so two-faced that I wouldn't be surprised at all.'

'Yeah, I heard there's been 15 different leaders here in the past 25 years. So that's one every year and a half. Time for a new one, eh!'

'Crazy no? These islands have always been invaded and governed by foreigners, going back to the British pirates in 18th century. Even back then, I believe you English sent quite a big force here to stop the islands doing business with the pirates, but the locals continued, you know dealing in the stolen goods. By the way there's still the old English fort about 20km over there. In the islanders minds, everyone is an enemy, so there's no real difference between one nationality to the other. And they don't like to put all their eggs in one basket. So we'll just have to see what happens when the boss … haha … Jaffa, gets back.'

'Come on Steve, let's go and set up, I'm ready.'

Twenty minutes later, having hurried to inflate the tubular edges and struts, Kayte was rigged and ready to go. She stood five metres from the shoreline, feeling the power of the kite jerking her forward, urging her out to sea. With the wind tugging hard at her arms, and with a few loud cheers of encouragement from the beach party, she swept forward, breaking through the surf and skimmed out towards the horizon beneath her brightly coloured banner to join Chuck. The exhilaration of the frenetic action always caught her unaware. One minute she was solid and stable on the beach, the next minute she'd be fighting for buoyancy, flying on water. The rapid, pneumatic movement of her legs and arms at speed, combined with the blinding spray in her face, demanded enormous concentration just to stay upright.

Soon she glimpsed Chuck's kite heading towards her like a charging bull, full of menace. He pulled his kite back and braked just before impact then pirouetted on the spot. They twirled together dancing around each other like mating butterflies flapping together and fluttering down in a tumble. The next moment the two kites were poised apart, erect, perfectly still, imperceptibly vibrating on the breeze and then they'd pounce upon each other like fish eagles in perfect diving arcs, stretching around each other and back up to verticals in easy, fluid motions. Now they were like mating swans, necks intertwined. The two kites snaked around each other surging the two wave dancers forward in bursts, occasionally breaking out, like slingshots flying above the shimmering surface. They were tuned in. One moment Chuck led and instinctively Kayte would follow, the next Kayte would lead and Chuck followed in forward and backward rotations landing toe to heel or just blind.

Having had their fun for fifteen minutes, Chuck and Kayte turned their concentration to the business in hand. From the beach, anyone watching closely would clearly see each sinew on their bodyies flex under the tensile forces of their kites greater wingspan. They'd both drop their kites low for maximum pull, sending up great draughts, which ruffled the surface water and then, whoosh, they'd sweep forward through the gates. They both tacked hard to get themselves in the right position at the right time, trying to break between the time trial posts on the perfect gust of wind; gunning to get their bodies dropped at the optimum angle. They'd edge as hard as they possibly could to hold their lines and then, with a split second flash, they were blasting, slantwise across 100m of Indian Ocean. And then they'd circle around time and time again, taking turns.

After less than an hour, Kayte powered back to the beach. Steve rushed up to the shoreline, unclipped and took her kite.

'How you feeling?' he shouted above the breaking waves and ferocious flapping kite.

'Shattered, that was intense,' Kayte called back. 'How did it look?'

'Fast.'

Seeing Chuck come in, the official time recorders leapt onto the launch and rushed out to sea to dismantle the course. He joined Kayte up at the shack.

'How'd we get on?' he asked immediately.

'Pretty good, pretty good,' said Kayte. 'Apparently you got up to 26 knots and I got up to 23.'

'Hey, hey, babe, not too shabby.'

'Yeah right, you equalled my record, you bastard!'

'Ha, if I can push it, babe, you can too. Strap your twin-tipped board on tomorrow and go for it. I don't know if I'm gonna' get there to be honest. Another seven knots for me to beat mine is a big ask. I don't know, I just don't know. But you Kat, you can, for sure.'

Clap. Clap. It was Papa Jon from the gap below.

'Come now, everyone. Please pack the minibus up. Let us go now. Chop, chop.'

It was three thirty when the small convoy rumbled back to St Martin, through untroubled streets to The Splendid Hotel.

After a good long chill in their room, Kayte and Steve had an early supper and went straight to bed.

Chapter Eleven
Lulling

The following morning they were running late again. The vehicles had to be repacked. It was gone ten thirty by the time the two minibus convoy eventually rumbled out of St Martin.

'Everyone seems to be in a brighter mood this morning,' Kayte said to Chuck as they hit the smooth tarmac.

'Yeah, definitely. I dunno if we were all still a bit jet-lagged from the trip over or whatever yesterday. The guy from our embassy the night before obviously didn't help either, he really put a big downer on us.'

'Nah, it all looked fine out on the streets back there today. Bit quiet though, there were no street sellers. Maybe it's a holiday or something? I could see them putting up loads of bunting and stuff. Did you?'

'Yeah, I did.' He then called out. 'Excuse me, Pappie, what were they doing back there?' He looked at Kayte and flicked his eyebrows. 'Setting up for a party or something?'

'No, Mr Chuck, not today. We are preparing for Prince Jaffa's return tomorrow.'

'Hey, cool bananas.'

Walking past the beach bar two hours later, Kayte overheard Jim talking.

'Hey Kirk,' he was saying. 'I'd like to go and have a look at the hotel, if that's OK? Do you think your boat can take me over?

I'll write about it in my articles, it looks superb.'

'Yes, sure. I don't see why not,' Kirk replied. 'No problems, ya.'

'Sonia told me about an old pirate graveyard behind the hotel,' Jim added. 'I wouldn't mind having a look around there.'

No, Jimbo, it was me who told you actually, Kayte said to herself.

'Hey, I'm going to come too,' said Steve. 'How do we find it?'

Yes! Kayte yelled to herself, result. No boozing today.

'Sure, ya, that is up there too. You'll see a path through the forest, right opposite the entrance to the hotel. It climbs maybe 500m to the top of the ridge,' Kirk was saying, gesticulating directions. 'Then there's a fork on the right. Go across another 500m or so and you'll come to a clearing, ya, with the crosses and an old rotting wooden shed, which I think, ya, it was their church. And that's it, you can't miss it.' He was now pointing vaguely towards Roger's home. 'It's right there.'

'I'll have a quick drink first,' said Jim.

'Steve, we're going to set up now,' Kayte interrupted.

'Come on then, which kite are you going to use today?' Steve said as he swung off his stool. Before walking away with Kayte he turned to Jim. 'Hold on for me, I'll be back in a minute.'

Jim was perched head down, swilling his straw through ice at the bottom of his glass, deep in thought. 'Sure, no probs,' he said as if to the glass.

'Good luck Kayte. I hope you break your record,' Kirk called out.

Chuck was already on the beach strutting around, confidence regained, repeating his mantra. 'Let's get pumping, yeah baby,' again and again whilst looking at his caddy thrusting hard to inflate his kite.

Kayte could see Steve hunched over, sweating freely as he feebly began to pump up her kite. She was amazed at how sick he looked. He hadn't got any sort of tan at all. I wonder if he's ill? she said to herself. Maybe it's just the painkillers he's taking or, of course, the drinking … the damn drinking. Maybe he's not drinking enough water? she thought. He just looks so unhealthy. Standing next to Chuck didn't help, it only highlighted it further. She realised, it was glaringly obvious now, this wasn't the man she'd met and fallen head over in heels in love with. She stood awkwardly, half in a trance. 'My God,' she exclaimed to herself. Reality had dawned. The brutal truth had leapt upon her, on the other side of the world without warning. Another hemisphere of her brain had suddenly woken up and popped alive in the new environment. It was as if half her brain had been asleep forever. Poof! There was clarity. It was that simple. I don't love him any …

The wind began to hiccup and falter as Steve and Jim boarded the small launch ten minutes later. Jim wobbled under the weight of the bulky camera dangling around his neck.

They approached the beautifully designed hotel from the lagoon below. The sleek, empty structure slept harmoniously above them, tucked up within the ridge, just peeping out of the jungle.

Steve and Jim clambered onto the solid jetty and slowly walked up towards the hotel in the intense tropical humidity. The ridge had been landscaped into two terraces. The first one they reached hid an unfilled infinity swimming pool, fully paved with sun loungers and chairs piled up neatly at the back in their cellophane wrappers.

They turned around and looked down at the jetty where their boatman was polishing his craft. The lagoon stretched out lazily below them, dark and thick, viscous, like mercury with pearly glints in the shadows. Beyond the shimmering sand dunes, on the far side, the two brightly coloured kites beat and tacked behind them. All was deathly still though, heavy and peaceful. The only movement before them was from the two kites in the distance and the faintest of ruffles on the lagoon's surface, otherwise all around them was silent and motionless. They were in a pocket out of the wind, it was almost eerie. The workmen had retreated into shady corners. A few had melted into the darkened canopy beneath the trees dotted around the garden's perimeter. Dark limbs, like gnarled roots poked out from scraggy borders.

Jim put the camera to his eye, extended his telephoto lens and began to take photos of Kayte and Chuck's kites through the dunes. The alien, mechanical, rapid fire clicks shot through the stillness rudely, scattering across the paving like loose marbles.

The two visitors then walked in silence up broad stone stairs to the level above. A wide patio ran the whole length of the building, completely unencumbered and partially shaded by the long balcony above. Again there were neat piles of rattan furniture stacked against the floor-to- ceiling smoked glass windows that led to the hotel's empty interior.

Turning back Steve and Jim noticed that both kites had suddenly collapsed and were now floating limply in the breakers near the shore; lifeless without wind.

'Oh shit man,' said Steve. 'I'd better get back and give her a hand.'

'Na, na. She'll be fine, there are plenty of people to help her,' said Jim. 'Come on.'

He bolted inside the building, through a glass panel that had been left ajar.

'Yeah, I suppose so, she'll be fine,' Steve muttered, more to himself. He turned his back on his girlfriend, flaying in the surf below, and followed Jim into the empty shell.

They wandered through the hotel's bare carcass until they stumbled across an unfitted large atrium, as damp and musty as a neglected World War II bunker.

'God knows how on earth they're going to get this ready to open in a month,' said Jim, his voice echoing. They slowly walked towards the entrance, staring around. 'Argh, the cold's getting right into me.'

'Yeah, me too. Surely the workers out there should be trying to cool down in here, not out in the sweltering heat.'

'It's just got such a rank feel about it. Unhealthy. Stale.'

'Pissy, more like. Come on, let's go.'

Out in the forecourt with a silent fountain, the two amigos walked towards the main gates with the hotel behind. The air was no fresher outside, just different. In the enclosed by foliage driveway, breathing was laboured, seemingly devoid of oxygen in the ozone filled lushness. Even their eyeballs seemed to be sweating.

'There it is,' Jim said, pointing ahead. 'Come, on me hearty, there'll be treasure in dem dere hills.'

'Ha-haar,' gasped Steve.

Clearly visible was the gap in the jungle Kirk had described. A narrow but definite path led into the humming morass beyond.

Back on the other side of the lagoon Kayte and Chuck had swum back to the beach and dragged their sodden kites ashore. Frustrated, Kayte quickly and unceremoniously dumped her kit in the storage shack and tramped up the beach to cool off as Chuck and crew headed over to the bar.

Soon the mass of people were just vague movements on the dunes behind her, more like little black termites busying around their mounds. At last, alone with nature, every lonely step forward she took, taking her further away from humankind, helped her flagging spirit charge up and regain its strength. By the time she reached the curving quay of rocks that she'd discovered the day before, her irritations had ebbed away completely. She tore off her shorts and t-shirt and left them casually strewn on the beach again. She waded into the calming shallows of the aqua blue natural pool.

Although she'd only been out in the sun for a couple of days, Kayte's naturally dark complexion had rapidly bronzed over the past 48 hours. Gone was the pallid whiteness from being covered up for six months, which blurred the definitions of her fiery red bikini. As she stood, thigh high and poised to immerse in the calm water, resembling a ravishing siren about to mount the rocks and lure men to their deaths, a strange voice called out.

'Hello,' it said.

Startled, Kayte turned around to see a deeply tanned, dark-haired, middle aged man standing in front of her wearing a pair of white swimming shorts with blue trim and a rolled up white towel tucked under his arm. He looked like a old matelot, something out of a Dolce & Gabbana advert.

'So, you've discovered my secret spot,' he continued, his eyes twinkling in the sunshine. She looked at him silently, forced to squint in the blinding brightness. She looked confused. He was forced to ask her, 'Do you speak English?'

'Yes, I am English,' she managed to reply.

'Oh great, hello, I'm Roger, Roger MacGill,' he said coming forward. He threw down his towel and waded in.

'Kayte, Kayte King. Nice to meet you,' she said quickly and held her hand out as she stepped back.

'Ah, Kayte, the champion kitesurfer,' he said, wading forward. 'Good to meet you. I've seen you at it over the past couple of days. It looks absolutely fantastic. I must learn myself one of these days. How are you getting on?' He reached forward and took her hand.

'Oh, fantastic, thanks. Well, up until just now when the wind died off.' She wanted him to let go but he held tight.

'Near breaking any records?'

'Yesterday was great. We did pretty well and I was hoping to better it today. Getting closer anyway.' She tried to tug her hand back and he released it. Kayte stumbled back slightly.

'That's great news. Well done.' He was smiling.

As he'd neared, strangely for Kayte, the tension was immense; it was as if a force field pushed her back with every step he took towards her. *What was he doing?* She'd had to hold a hand out to stop him, not to shake his hand. She noticed there was no wedding ring, only a thin gold signet hoop glistened on his little finger, just like her father's.

He was average height, toned and muscled and tanned all over with very little body hair. Just the faintest hint of a black tuft on his chest. His black hair was oiled and brushed back, making his bold, rugged features stand out all the more. Kayte couldn't quite equate the homely English accent here on the empty tropical beach. She hadn't noticed anyone else around and he seemed to have just appeared out of the blue like a mirage.

'I trust you are enjoying The Martinez Islands,' he continued. 'Is everything OK for you? Are you comfortable at The Splendid? Is there anything I can do to make you more comfortable?' His authoritative voice, slightly drowned by the sea song, forced her to lean forward. It was the waves slapping onto the rocks and wind whistling through them. 'The hotel, and setup here on the beach I mean?'

She was very close to him. She leant back. 'Yes fantastic thanks. It's all superb.' Her arm flopped into the water with a splash. *Say something, fast.*

'It's the first time I've ever kitesurfed on the Indian Ocean, so still getting to grips with the currents,' Kayte was blithering. 'But it's really fabulous here, really lovely.'

'Yes it is, it really is … a paradise,' Roger said dreamily, looking around at the unspoilt beauty and cynically added, '… of sorts.' He snapped out of his reverie, took Kayte's hand and said playfully, 'Come on then.'

They rushed forward together. Laughing, and ploughing through the surf they plunged into the gin-clear pool. After a few strokes Roger, flipped over onto his back. He lay still with his arms outstretched, horizontally crucified, staring up at the sky. Kayte, who was following, bashed into him and instinctively rolled onto her back too.

'Oops, sorry,' she said cheekily.

They lay on the calm surface in silence; water gently flapped the rocks directly behind and the faint, ever present, thunderous rumbles of waves hitting the offshore reef were the only sounds to be heard. At that moment, lying prone, suspended and still on the ocean with her arms outstretched, Kayte felt as if she was flying. Her imagination took hold and sent her surging forward, soaring upwards towards romantic settings and love and happiness. At that moment The Martinez Islands felt like they could truly be 'the isles of serendipity', a magical place, a perfect setting for poignant coincidences to occur. The sort of land where dreams become real. Roger's mental wonderings went elsewhere. Neither up nor down, neither forwards nor backwards. He simply wanted to be elsewhere.

Chapter Twelve
'Check, Check, One, Two...'

Life, for Roger MacGill, had been meteoric. Since he'd left the confines of home and had gone off on a military secondment to Cyprus 23 years ago, he'd been on a rollercoaster. He'd gone back to England only a handful of times in all those years, the last being just over two years ago for his parent's funeral.

It wasn't so much a car crash that had killed his elderly parents in an accident; no one else was involved. They had stopped their car at a beauty spot and Roger's father, it was discovered, had forgotten to put the handbrake on. The car had simply rolled forward and dropped over a steep ridge, falling into a ravine, killing them both instantly.

On hearing the shocking news, Roger had immediately left his men in the bush, protecting private gold mines from furious rebel attacks and flown back to England.

Alone at his parents home after the funeral, the huge gulf of what he'd left dawned on him. The fact so little had changed in all those years was the real shock for him. Roger wandered around his recently deserted family home a little lost, gazing at every thing. He wasn't sure if he was looking at everything for the first time or the last time. He furtively picked up familiar objects, opened doors and peeped in cupboards. The décor, the paintings on the walls, even the street outside ... all the same. As if the whole place had been held in aspic. He wandered, ghostlike, around his childhood home, as that's what the place still was to him, and he wasn't sure if he pined for this sort of security or he still detested it. He felt like a trapped little boy again, someone who hadn't really grown up at all, a Peter Pan. He'd never addressed any emotional scars from his childhood, which lay buried, but were torn open as he stared at photos of his parents. For some reason the 'his n her's' coffee mugs by the kettle really got to him.

He dashed out of the house and headed straight up to Billkicker Fort. He scrabbled up the muddy embankment and stood over the Solent in the rain, staring wildly down at the entrance to the cell like recess where he'd cocooned himself for endless hours as a child, peering out to sea. He stumbled down and cleared the brambles that covered the alcove, kicking them down frantically, flattening them as best he could. Roger looked around, thanked God no one could see him and then squeezed feet first into his moist, grimy sanctuary. Panting hard, he stared out at the familiar, utterly unchanged, scene, and broke down, crying for his loss and loneliness. It was just him now, back where his journey had all began. He sobbed and shook in the enclosed, womblike space. This was the one and only place he felt secure enough to cry in. This was his childhood home, his private space. It may have been the only spot on the planet where he did feel safe … this grimy black hole. His huge teardrops exploded onto the slime covered stone.

When he finally calmed down and regained some sort of composure he crawled out, all mud and grime, and went straight home. There he changed, packed his bag, locked the door and left.

It was only when he'd returned to Mozambique the following day and resumed his dirty business in the bush that the collapse happened. It may have been exacerbated by the transition from hot tropical chaos to the cold civilisation of England, and back again, in the space of a few days which was too much for his mind, body and spirit to take. He wasn't sure, he'd just collapsed into a catatonic state. He hadn't given himself time or space to grieve, to come to terms with his parent's sudden death, so he'd combusted. Roger had a mental breakdown, a meltdown. He was delirious and lay confined in a confused state for five days.

His epiphany moment happened a week later when in recovery. It was while he was lying on his back, fevered in oppressive humidity and being cared for by a ruddy faced, unwashed priest, on an isolated mission station, hearing machine guns crackling around him, that the light shone. It was a crystal clear moment. An epiphany. Roger realised this way of life was over for him. Fighting someone else's wars for money was finished, that was it. He was in no way addicted to that sort of adrenalin rush or killing as many of his soldiers were. He was simply doing it for money and adventure, and he'd had his belly bloated full of it. It all had to stop, and now. Belatedly, in honour of his dead mother and father, he pledged to change his way of life, once and for all. The priest would be his witness.

Roger's father had taken a rigid stand against his son's decision to become a mercenary. To his father's sensibilities, military service was about serving your country not simply joining any old army and fighting any old war; being a gun for hire was utterly abhorrent to him. As a result the gulf between them had become an iron curtain. His mother was locked on the other side. Roger did write and phone them once or twice a year, attempting gestures of reconciliation. The calls and letters went unanswered. He always thought he'd have time to make it up to them.

He'd sat up in his campaign cot, weak and delirious and called the priest over.

'I want you to hear my confession, Father,' he'd said.

'Of course, my son,' the drink-sodden priest replied, taking Roger's hand in his pudgy palm.

'Father forgive me for I have sinned ...' He reeled off a litany of horrors to the impassive priest, who no doubt had a sack full of sins he should have been discharging.

Roger wasn't the sort of Christian who went to confession. He detested the notion of being absolved of his sins and being free to repeat them. He was embarrassed even thinking about it now. He considered it weak to seek forgiveness; you do what you do, you do it as well as you can and you move on. You have to live with your crimes or sins or shame, whatever they may be called. You take it on the chin, mend and shut up. You only really need to confess to yourself. He didn't have time for religion, full stop. Doctrines spelt out two thousand years ago and moulded by men in medieval times were laughable. It was only his enfeebled state that drove him to it, he concluded.

The gold mines secured, he disbanded his troops and went on a much needed holiday. It was taken on a glistening 39m super yacht in the South of France, owned by one of his previous Middle Eastern clients. This was where he'd first met Prince Jaffa.

Soon after meeting the Prince, Roger made a brief, low key reconnoitre to The Martinez Islands and immediately fell in love. He found his Shangri-La. Not only could he see the enormous scope for improvement in living standards for the inhabitants, but he could see infinite improvements for himself too - living on the beautiful islands and being very much part of that growth. These islands were the perfect place to settle, perhaps even raise a family, farm, develop tourism, create some businesses for himself and live well for the rest of his life. Importantly, he felt he could make a difference to the islands life, a positive contribution. He would take a depressed state and turn it into an ideal, prosperous, flourishing country. He decided that his mission on The Martinez Islands was going to be exactly that, a divine mission, a devotional exercise. He would be a new man, a modern missionary, and make good of himself in the process. Someone his parents, looking down on him, would be proud of at last.

Two years later the reality was, he was drained - financially and emotionally. He was paying salaries for 80 mercenaries, and had been for eighteen months, plus he covered all the costs of equipping, arming and accommodating them. Added to this was the vast cost of building the new airport, his house, his farm, the hotel, paying wages for Prince Jaffa and his cronies, some road building projects, paying for public services and servants; the list was endless. It was a nightmare. He had seen nothing back from his investment yet, and his originally huge fortune was now reduced to a pathetically small one. The news he'd got the day before, from Ishaq the Finance Minister, about his funding of the islands infrastructure coming to an end, was an enormous relief. Perhaps the tide was finally turning.

He hadn't won the love of the local inhabitants either. Becoming Omar hadn't really helped at all. His mission of divine light had turned into another campaign - plain and simple - and it wasn't going to plan. Nothing ever does he reconciled, I'll turn it around. It's a bitter pill to swallow, people biting the hand that feeds them. But that's life, that's people, nothing new there.

Roger knew that one of the biggest and most difficult lessons to learn in Africa, apart from keeping out of the sun, is to stay calm at all times.

Blissfully floating on the Indian Ocean with a beautiful young woman at his side, Roger did feel calm - the perfect state in which to enjoy Africa or indeed anywhere. Like the original couple meeting for the first time in the Garden of Eden, Roger and Kayte were momentarily suspended in the seemingly complete security of this island paradise; as if nothing would dare disturb them.

They both lolled back in the low humped waves, barely perceptible other than as shrugs of the water, which raised them up and lowered them down as if they were being politely lifted to make way for a tray laden waiter beneath them. Now and then, as they drifted, they'd raise their heads up slightly to see the sparkling crystal sea merge with a clear cobalt sky. The only sound was the swirl of the sea, caressing and nuzzling among the tumble of rocks.

Roger rolled off his back. 'Come on Kayte, I'll race you in.'

Kayte, always up for competition responded immediately. They pounded the surface together, breaking the peace and fast crawled onto the beach, arriving in the shallows together. Laughing, they glanced into each other's eyes. Kayte scrabbled for answers to make sense of what she was feeling, then the look ran away.

She got out straight away and walked the few steps to her clothes as Roger wallowed a while in the surf.

'Use my towel if you want?' he called out, as she turned and sat on the baking sand, pulling her knees up to her chin. She sat dripping, gazing at Roger and out to sea. No sound except the gentle slap and flap of the sea sliding along the rocks in little curls of white frilly foam.

'Whereabouts in England is home Kayte?' he called out again.

'Oh, just a little place near Portsmouth, called Lee-on-Solent.'

'You're kidding!' He was stunned, he'd just been thinking about it. It only took him a moment to recover from the sudden coincidence. 'I know it well, I was brought up in Stokes Bay, just up the road.'

'That is amazing, I don't believe it,' she yelled back.

He came out of the sea, smiling, and joined her. Kayte not only felt instantly familiar with this stranger, but incredibly secure with him. The sigh she released left her feeling a calmness she hadn't had in years, maybe ever.

'I just don't believe that, it's incredible. You come from Stokes Bay, I come from Lee and we meet here. Amazing,' she said, shaking her head.

'I know, it's extraordinary. How funny. My father was in the navy, that's why we were there. I haven't been back for a couple years though.'

'Are they still in Stokes Bay, your parents?'

'No, they're not,' he said slowly, 'but their house is, it's on Marine Parade, d'you know it?'

'Yes, of course I do. Is it near the Anglesey Hotel?'

'Right there. It's five doors down, number 33.'

'Hungh! That's amazing. Is the house empty?'

'Yes, it is actually,' Roger replied, momentarily silenced, surprised by the question. 'You know Kayte,' he continued, 'if it's OK, would you do me a favour when you go back next week? Would you pop down and have a look at the old place for me, it's been empty for eighteen months. Let me know what state it's in? I'll pay you. Take some photos, that sort of thing.'

'Yes, I'd be delighted to, no problem,' she said leaning back and soaking up some rays. She tilted her head right back and could see the white turrets of Roger's palace glimmer above the dunes, upside down. 'It's the most incredible house you've built here, Roger. It really is spectacular.'

'Thank you. Yes I'm delighted with it, it's a dream come true. I'm going to spend my first night there any day now. It's been stressful though, the build. You can't imagine how long it takes to get anything done here, ruddy nightmare to be honest.' He sighed. 'Anyway we're nearly there. You must come up and have a look, the views are to die for.'

'I'd love to, thanks.'

'I'll let Papa Jon know and he can bring you up.'

'Oh, great. I'll give you a kitesurfing lesson if you want? Just for beginners, get a feel for it. Any time you want.'

'Excellent, I'd love that. It really does grab me. It looks so exhilarating. Perhaps tomorrow morning, if it doesn't interfere?'

'No probs, just come down.'

'I don't suppose you learnt to kitesurf in Lee, did you Kayte?' he asked.

'Yes, I did actually. There's a great beach by Hill Head, and Stokes Bay's pretty good too. Up towards the old fort, there's not so many people up there.'

Roger hadn't allowed himself to dwell on his last visit home at all, not until just now, somehow forced to by this conversation. He gazed up and down the coastline. The mere mention of the fort at Billkicker Point triggered more memories of himself as a child crawling into the small, hidden recess. His sanctuary within the lower ramparts. He now remembered wriggling into his den with ease as a child, like a tiny sniper, lying there, spying on the world outside, whilst breathing in the damp and mossy musty aroma. He relished the memories of that cave more than any other; a time when he was invisible but could observe everything. He loved the feeling of not being seen and had brought that forward into adulthood. There was safety in being covert. Invisibility had served him well. When he was the hidden child looking out to sea, he could always spot various naval craft, bristling with armaments, entering or leaving Portsmouth harbour to his left. He recalled that, even as an adolescent in his monk like cell, he would imagine these floating war machines engaged in action, pounding away at enemies in foreign lands. He could picture the destroyers and frigates in actual conflicts, which he saw on the news, and pictured his father heroically leading his men on deck like he saw in old war films. In his youthful imagination he pictured the deadly, sleek grey war ships cruising the African coastline, shelling old desert castles, with turbaned horse riders firing ancient rifles back at the metal monsters. Hidden from the world in his little crows nest, he had powerful visions of himself too, leading his men into armed conflicts … just like here.

'Do you like this place, Roger? I don't mean the beach but The Martinez Islands generally,' Kayte asked.

'Why? Yes of course I do, don't you?' he replied, somewhat ambiguously, coming back to reality. He shrugged his shoulders and gestured at the beauty around them, making Kayte qualify herself.

'Yes sure, it is so beautiful and unspoilt but there's all this aggression everywhere and violence in the air. It feels so unstable. It's disturbing.'

Roger cleared his throat. 'I know it does Kayte, I'm sorry for that,' he said, 'but this is exactly what I'm trying to stop. I don't know if I ever will though. It's a hard place to fathom.'

'I imagine so,' Kayte mumbled.

'Tell me, Kayte, out of interest, what have you heard? I'd

like to know,' he said lightly, trying to mask the serious intent of his question.

'Well, nothing really,' she said, 'just some lads spat at our minibus, then we had a bit of a talking to by Alistair Fortesque, you know, about the curfew? And just the general talk around.'

'General talk around, eh?' he said casually, as if to himself, leaning back on his hands. He turned towards Kayte. 'Tell me, what exactly *did* Alistair say to you?'

'Umm, well he said there was a bit of an atmosphere around at the moment but Prince Jaffa's return over the next couple of days should calm the situation down,' she said, enjoying the little gossip and an opportunity to bond. 'But the guy who talked to the Americans in our party, I didn't catch his name, seemed to have freaked them out. I don't know what he said.'

'I see.'

Their glances met and ran away from each other again. The sun was really beginning to penetrate now and Kayte felt dehydrated and sleepy, lulled by the pulsing waves folding onto the nearby rocks. Kayte was on the verge of saying she'd better get back when their tranquillity was rudely broken by a crack, crack, crack sound shattering through the air.

Roger, startled, thought he may have slipped into some sort of nightmarish flashback, but when the definite sound of gunfire echoed out again, reality dawned. He'd hardly had time to admire Kayte. There was nothing to be done. It ended there.

Chapter Thirteen
Rockin' My Boat

Roger sprung up. The shots were coming from the ridge behind.

'Come on Kayte.' He held out his hand for the second time and yanked her up, forcefully. Kayte found herself pulled along, dashing towards the protection of the dunes. As they rushed up the beach, two armed soldiers appeared ahead of them. Kayte and Roger momentarily froze. Roger's free hand waved them forward and the two pairs converged.

Roger held Kayte's hand tightly saying nothing. She knew their moment of intimacy was over and, for now, it'd been replaced with fear, all warmer feelings abandoned with her clothes, left on the shoreline.

'What the hell's going on?' Roger barked, as the two soldiers approached.

'We're not exactly sure, sir,' one of the armed men responded, in a harsh guttural South African accent, as his walkie-talkie crackled. 'It seems like there were intruders up at the house, at the back. The men and dogs have gone after them, sir.'

Roger calmed slightly. 'Get on the radio again, and find out *exactly* what *is* going on.' He demanded, still holding Kayte's hand. More gunfire. 'Oh sh-t, come on!'

The foursome hurried up to the protection of the dunes as the machine gun fire continued, the sound ricocheting around. Roger now in Major mode, clearly issued another order.

'Serge, you come with me. Midge, you take Kayte here back to the bar and wait there. Don't let anyone move, get rid of the locals if there are any and for Christ's sake, get everyone to stay put. Are you clear?'

'Yes, Sir.' Midge grabbed Kayte's free hand and they tore off.

'Don't worry Kayte, you're in safe hands,' Roger called after them.

Kayte just managed to look around briefly, as the burley Midge pulled her away, and saw Serge passing Roger a chunky chrome pistol, which caught the sunshine and flared alight, before they too jogged off, heading through the dunes towards the lagoon and gunfire beyond.

As Kayte and Midge hurtled back across the beach, they could hear yet more volleying gunfire. The lack of wind made the sound of bullets ricochet around the confines of the lagoon, hemmed in by the ridge and dunes. The white marsh birds were on the wing and their anxious squawks croaked ominously between the shots.

Nearing the bar shack, Kayte could see the kiting group had clustered around the bar area as though they'd all heard Roger's orders. She joined the quivering group as Midge scoured the vicinity below. The swell of exhaustion was palpable, a rip tide of panic unmistakable.

'Hey Kayte, where have you been?' Chuck looked alarmed. 'Give me a hug babe? Thank Christ you're OK.'

'I just went up the beach for a swim,' she said, muffled in his embrace. 'That's all.'

'I dunno what the hell's going on, it's crazy here.' He let go and held her shoulders. 'This is just outta control.'

'Calm down Chuck, it's alright, apparently there's some trouble up at Roger, I mean Omar's, house, that's all, some intruders or something,' Kayte said with authority, catching the groups attention, calming the situation. She was in the know, and she liked it. 'Can someone get me a drink please? I'm completely parched, just some water.'

'Who's that goon down there?' Chuck said, pointing at Midge, who was furiously charging around securing the area.

'One of Roger's men,' said Kayte casually, between gulps. She looked around. 'Where's Steve?'

'Dunno.'

As Chuck responded, shouts rang from the hotel on the other side of the lagoon, punctuating the continuing screeching of the disturbed roosting birds. They all turned to see Steve and Jim pounding down the slope opposite as fast as they could, calling out frantically for the boatman to get the launch going. They both hit the jetty so hard the aghast group, looking on, could hear their thumping footsteps echoing across the still water. Steve and Jim leapt onto the launch, hollering. It slipped its mooring and sped back towards the bar.

Kayte had completely forgotten Steve had gone across to the other side. 'What the hell has he been up to now?' she said to no one in particular.

As the boat sliced the lagoon, their gaze averted to a large group of workmen clustered on the lower terrace of the hotel above. They were furiously pointing out Steve and Jim, who were now crossing the centre of the lagoon below, to four or five armed men in army fatigues and a barking, tethered Alsatian dog. Then the soldiers, in hot pursuit, charged down to the pontoon, causing havoc, shouting and pointing frantically, radioing for their launch to come around from Roger's jetty. The ferocious dog howled, baying for blood, birds shrieked and radios crackled. It was pandemonium.

'Come on Stevie boy. You can do it Jim-bob,' Chuck urged, as their launch neared. 'Yeeha!'

The boat hit the jetty dune side. Steve and Jim scrambled out. Then Midge, running through the gap in the dunes … was there to greet them. He lurched towards the boys, menacingly jabbing his semi-automatic and snarling in his loudest, ugliest tone, 'Get down you two, on your knees, now!' Steve and Jim dropped in unison, as if by remote control. Steve's legs had turned to puddings and he crumbled onto the dirt. 'Put your hands on your heads and stay completely still or I'll blow your f-ing brains out, d'you hear me?' Steve and Jim nodded frantically.

'Jesus H Christ!' exclaimed Chuck, from above. 'This is insane.'

Midge ordered the shaking boatman to go back to the hotel and told his fellow team members via his radio that the assailants had been apprehended.

The drama came off the boil slightly and simmered. Panic turned to tension as the group at the bar stared helplessly, gobsmacked, at the scene unfolding below. They saw Jim and Steve heaving and moaning, prostrate in the dust, as the heavily armed soldiers on the hotel's pontoon opposite, continued to howl like a pack of wolves demanding the launch get back to them as fast as possible. Their dog was up on two legs, snapping at its lead and the frantic birds swirled around in confusion.

As the soldiers clambered onto the launch opposite, one of them pointed and yelled to Midge, who was standing by the pontoon near the supine Steve and Jim. He dropped to one knee and pointed his gun towards an approaching vehicle swirling around the lagoon in a ball of dust. They heard Midge's gun engage, he hissed venomously, 'You two, stay mighty still, don't move a millimetre, right?'

Steve's head wagged.

All weapons on board the loaded launch tracked the approaching vehicle, which stopped just as they landed beachside. The car's dust ball caught up with it and then swept past, dispersing like talc on the arriving pack of mercenaries.

The back seat window wound down and out popped Papa Jon's head, accompanied by his two hands, flapping submissively.

'Mr Midge it's me, Papa Jon,' he called out. 'It is only me.'

Ice broken, the tension dropped another notch and there was a collective sigh.

Midge stood up. Steve followed to all fours, as if saved by Papa Jon, only to feel the hard butt of Midge's gun crash down on his upper back, winding him. He seemed momentarily stunned, out cold and face down, with just the faintest puffs of sand moving near his nose and mouth.

'You, matey boy, are staying right there. D'you hear me? Wait for the boss to come over, just now,' Midge said, still in a high state of alertness, his gun flicking between Steve and Jim.

'Mr Midge, I know these men, they are with the kitesurfing party,' Papa Jon implored, as he approached.

'We've done nothing, I tell you.' It was Jim.

'You shut your f-ing mouth, or you'll get a knock too.' Midge's fellow squaddies swarmed around and the seriously restrained hound salivated, snapping to get at Steve and Jim.

In what seemed an age, but was in fact no more than a minute or two, Roger's beautiful launch thundered into view, churning the lagoon's smoothness into a seething mass. His boat powered to a halt, water boiling and engines roaring in reverse.

Kayte, held back by Chuck, could see Roger standing coolly on the bow, legs akimbo. He wore a light, powder blue shirt over his white swimming shorts and held the silver pistol casually at his side. He gripped the rail firmly with his free hand, his gold signet ring flashing in the sunshine. Roger seemed otherworldly, gazing around, calmly taking the scene in.

Assured that all was now under his command, he unclenched his fist from the rail and raised it above his head, Caesar like. 'At ease men, at ease.' His boat's engine cut off.

With those few words the tension, which had escalated and crescendoed over the past twenty minutes, vaporised and all was silent. Everyone stood still, the relief palpable. It was as though the only sounds to be heard were the twenty hearts present, pumping furiously in the still heat, the waves in the background gently crashing, the last croaks of the birds called out as they settled again.

Roger stepped ashore and approached Steve and Jim. Steve had curled himself into a ball, like a dormouse, and Jim was kneeling, hands on head. Roger turned to his men.

'So, what's been going on?' he said, somewhat lazily. 'From the beginning.' He flicked a finger at one of the five soldiers.

'Well sir, the dogs seemed to be taking a very keen interest in something at the back of the garden and when we went to investigate we saw a man. I think it was this one here,' he said, jabbing at Jim. 'He was pointing something that looked like a gun, and then he ran off into the jungle. We fired shots and followed, firing as we went down round the back through the scrub out to the hotel and here we are, sir,' the young soldier said in a soft Afrikaans accent.

Pointing to the somewhat recovered Steve, Roger asked him, what he had to say about this.

'We just went across to have a look at the hotel and the pirate cemetery behind, that's all. To pass some time,' Steve whimpered, squinting at Roger standing above him.

Roger turned to Papa Jon. 'Are they part of the kitesurfing group, Papa?'

Kayte, who had surreptitiously appeared at Papa Jon's side, interrupted, 'That's my … my boyfriend.' She gestured at Steve.

'Yes, sir. They are both part of the group,' said Papa Jon.

Roger stood for a moment staring around and then said,

'OK, you two get up, off you go.' He turned to his men. 'Right, you lot, everyone, get aboard my boat.'

He put his arm around Papa Jon's shoulder and led him up the dust track, to talk privately. Steve, enfeebled, stumbled into Kayte's embrace. They limped up to the group, Steve leaning heavily on Kayte. No one noticed that Jim, who had trailed behind, didn't have his camera anymore.

Roger returned from his parlay with Papa Jon, boarded his launch and, as it pulled away, and out of earshot from the others, said to his men, 'I'm going to drop you off at the hotel here, retrace your footsteps, slowly mind, back to the house. See what you can find and have a word with the workers; find out what they saw and then report to me when you get back. Clear?'

'Yessir.'

'Good lads.'

As Roger's launch powered off, taking the tension with it, Papa Jon walked up to the bar, stood on a chair and clapped his hands.

'My friends, Mister Omar is very sorry for this little incident, very sorry indeed. He has had a lot of problems with thievery up at his house. Much has been stolen. So be assured there is nothing to worry about, nothing at all.'

Papa Jon tried to end his apology on an up-note, virtually singing, but it did nothing to help the badly shaken group's morale.

'To hell with this shite, man. Let's pack up and go now. And who the f-k is this Mister Omar?' Chuck said shaking his head.

'That's Roger, the mercenary, the guy in the trunks. He's also called Omar,' said Kayte.

'Oh, for f-k's sake. This place is f-kin' nuts. Come on let's go.' Everyone agreed.

The time recorders nervously got on board the launch to go around and dismantle the time trial course as the others packed and loaded the minibuses. Jim stayed up at the bar, preening, empowered by this recent escapade and brush with the mercenaries, whereas Steve perched on the edge of one of the loungers, completely deflated and hunched over as if he'd run a marathon. Jim was shifty, his eyes darted, his fox like features came to life, his nose twitched with excitement.

When the American contingent were close to finishing the loading up process, Kayte had to virtually kick Steve to move. She wasn't going to do all the hulking herself.

'Come on now Steve, let's get my stuff loaded up?'

'I can't hon, you do it,' he groaned.

'No, Steve, get up and help, now. That's what you're here to do, not gallivant off.' Kayte, surprised at her forcefulness, glowered down at him, all sympathy gone.

He obeyed. As she watched him lumber off, she couldn't quite believe she'd found the confidence to face up to him and be assertive.

The journey back to St. Martin was silent. Steve fell asleep with his head lolling on Kayte's shoulder, but as they came into the main square the traffic was gridlocked. Car horns blasted.

'Oh shite, what the frickin' heck's happening now?' Kayte heard Chuck curse from the back.

Crowds of people swarmed past, some staring into the minibus aggressively.

Someone opened the side door to let some air in and Chuck and a few others stepped outside to stretch their legs. A turbaned local man in his thirties had mounted the traffic policeman's rostrum to rabble rouse, shouting and vigorously shaking his fist. Regular angry yells and occasional cheers erupted from the gathering crowd in response to his urgings. Banners waved, cars honked and surrounding residents, who had ventured onto their balconies, waved and joined in the shouting from above.

Kayte leant forward. 'What's going on, Papa Jon?'

'Nothing Miss Kayte, just a meeting, a gathering,' he said nervously.

'What d'you mean? It can't be.'

'It is Miss Kayte, I assure you. It is only the people cheering to welcome home Prince Jaffa, who arrives tomorrow or the next day.'

'Yeah, right,' said Jim, sniggering.

The next thing they knew was that Chuck and the few others who were standing beside the minibus were unceremoniously brushed aside by a stream of young local soldiers charging past, rushing at the madding crowd, followed by older, western, heavily armed men.

Within a few seconds shots fired out, echoing loudly off the surrounding buildings, making the crowd flee for cover. Chuck and the others dived back into the minibus, piling up and lying as low as they could, creating a series of heaps inside, covering all available space.

The atmosphere had changed from a manageable, albeit heated, demonstration to a riot in an instant. People screamed, scattering in all directions, banners were discarded and trampled under foot. More shots fired and sirens blasted, blue lights flashed, flaring off everything; even a helicopter's searchlight sprayed the crowd, it's propellers thudding ominously overhead.

Chuck had landed in a heap in the narrow aisle beside Kayte.

'Shite Kat, this is friggin' outta control man,' he called out, above the din. 'I ain't gonna leave that hotel except to go to the airport. Believe me, I'm done. I'm outta here, this is in-sane.'

And then it was all over. The demonstrators had scattered, vaporised into the warren of narrow streets and traffic began to move. Their driver started the engine and they moved off, crunching over debris. They all got up nervously and peered sheepishly out of the windows to see soldiers searching alleyways in the blue flashing half-light as they made the short journey up to the hotel.

Although relieved to be back in the calm comfort of the hotel, the exhausted, shattered and confused group quickly dispersed and went up to their rooms, agreeing to meet in the bar in a couple of hours. Chuck headed straight over to the reception.

'I'm gonna get that embassy guy down here pronto.'

Chapter Fourteen
White Lies

Kayte and Steve hauled their kit into the lift without saying a word, but the moment they got behind the closed door of their room, Kayte's fury was uncontrollable.

'What the f-k do you think you were doing, Steve? You could have got yourself killed out there today, you muppet. You're here to look after me, remember? Not sit around drinking with that idiot Jim all day.'

'Look cool it Kayte. I'm sorry OK?' It really didn't matter to Steve anymore, now that he was away from the situation. The fact that he was nearly pistol whipped or a nearly dead dummy, who'd been rescued by his girlfriend, went right over his head. 'Come here babe,' he said, pulling her close.

'No, I will not.'

'Hey look, it was you that suggested going over there in the first place.'

'I know I did Steve, but that was only to stop you drinking all day.'

'I didn't do anything alright, it was Jim. He went off on his own. I didn't have a clue we were at the back of what's his name's compound.'

'Whatever, Steve.'

She slid the balcony door open and stepped outside. A gentle breeze blew the long net curtain deep inside the darkening room. It fluttered around, ghostlike in the twilight.

'Steve, can we talk?' she said, coming back in, but he'd passed out, fully clothed. Exhausted herself, she lay down on the bed next door and joined him in sleep. His groaning woke her up an hour later.

'Have a bath Steve and take a couple of painkillers. I'll bring you something to eat and drink, see you in a minute,' she said, stepping out of the door.

As she went across the foyer towards the restaurant, Mr Toyful, the manager, came hurrying across to her in some state of agitation.

'Miss King, I am so sorry to hear about the incident on the beach today with your friend, I hope he is OK?' he asked, genuinely concerned.

'Thank you, Mr Toyful, he's fine,' Kayte replied. 'It's kind of you to ask.'

'If you need anything, anything at all, please let us know. We have plenty of First Aid.'

'No, no that's OK, no need. I'm just going to get some food and take it up to him, he'll be fine,' she said, making to move off.

'Oh by the way, Miss King, I'm sorry to say but it looks as if we have a tropical storm coming in tomorrow so it may well be a very hot night.'

She stopped and turned back, her interest piqued. 'Oh, really? That's interesting. It'll be windy then?'

He looked at Kayte a little perplexed, not understanding that wind was exactly what she was here for. 'Oh, yes, Miss King, there'll be wind.'

'Excellent,' she said and turned, leaving him standing alone.

In the restaurant, she bumped into Chuck by the salad bar, who insisted she join the rather sombre looking American contingent cowering at a corner table in the empty dining room.

She looked around to make sure they were alone. 'Chuck, sure, but listen to this. I've just heard we've got a tropical storm coming in and that means even stronger winds. I don't know how badly off for money you are, but I could certainly do with that bonus, big time.' She looked around again. 'Fifteen grand is a fortune for me, an absolute fortune.'

'Me too babe, me too,' he whispered.

'If we can do just one more day here and get a record, or two, then we've just got to go for it. Haven't we, really?'

'I guess so.'

'Come on, we're here now,' Kayte insisted. 'One more day won't make a difference, will it? I'm definitely up for it if you are?' she said. 'I'm sure the police will get a grip on whatever's going on. Please, have a word with everyone on the table and see what they say. Let's go for it. Do one more day here and that's it.'

'Ok babe, I'll try.'

By the time she'd loaded her plate with spaghetti carbonara and got to them, the mood seemed to have changed. The group she joined were actually having an animated conversation.

'OK, Kat, we've decided,' said Chuck. 'We're all going to sleep on it and see what the situation's like in the morning. Our embassy guy is going to come by too, so we'll see what he says, and obviously see what the weather's doing. Is that OK?'

'Yeah, I guess so.' Then she turned to the group. 'But let's all try. Just one more day,' she urged. 'Please everyone. Let's all be part of getting a new world record. We probably won't get another chance, or at least one that's as good as this. We've got to really try and go for it, please,'

'Don't worry Kayte, we will.'

'Sorry folks, I've got to go up to my room. Steve's not in great shape. I'm going to take some food up while it's hot. See you all in the morning. Let's all meet in here at nine. Sleep well.'

Kayte grabbed Steve's doggy bag then darted back up to the room. She propped him up in bed and left him to eat alone while she went back out onto the balcony, still reeling from her day.

She gripped the balustrade to stay stable as a clammy wind buffeted warm blasts of musty air at her from the sea. The crescent moon, occasionally reflected on broken waves in the distance, resembled a cracked egg. Through the fast moving translucent clouds, it shone a rotten green. The rumble of waves breaking offshore, like rolls of distant canons, created the perfect atmosphere to herald the impending storm. She heard an occasional crack from somewhere. It could have been tree branches splitting, thunder breaking or simply the sound of gunshots echoing in the distance. It was all becoming perfectly normal. Hearing gunfire coming through the evening breeze back in England was virtually impossible to imagine, but here in paradise bizarrely, it seemed to suit the place. It balanced the beauty out somehow.

Although this had been one of the most intense days in Kayte's life, she felt strangely calm, dazed but in control. Here on the balcony, with the hot sweet gusts in her face, surprisingly she felt her essential life force gently pulsating, not racing. For some odd reason, snippets of Kipling's 'If' poem crossed her mind. 'If you can keep your head while all about you is …'

Here, Kayte was in a new, strange, and volatile place on the planet. But she knew she was still on Earth and she was under the same moon as home. With these feelings of amazement and interest, she went back into the room, closing the sliding door as she entered, leaving nature behind.

She was oblivious to Steve and was soon snuggled up in her own twin bed.

'You know, Kayte,' Steve was saying with a mouthful. 'I think there's something fishy about Jim. I think he may be spying or something, I dunno. It's strange. He insisted I stayed at the pirate cemetery while he went off. He really insisted.' And then, 'Kayte are you listening, Kayte?'

That was the last thing she heard before she fell asleep.

She dreamt she was standing in front of an ornately carved doorway, about to knock. She was stopped from entering by the white-gloved traffic cop, who then gestured she go ahead. She obeyed. Then, when she turned back to him, like Alice in Wonderland about to leap, with one hand on the big brass knocker shaped like a clenched fist, he'd turned into a surgeon and was snapping his rubber gloves on tight. 'Can I come in please?' she asked. 'Why, of course,' said the surgeon. She stepped over the threshold and tripped, which made her look down. She found herself staring at varnished planks on board a fully rigged galleon. She looked up to face ... Roger, transformed into a pirate. He wore a bandana, and striped trousers. She was now dressed as a maid, white robed with a garland in her hair. 'So you want to go to the promised land, d'ya?' he said laughing. 'Wanna leave home d'ya?'

She replied, 'I do.'

He laughed again, a horrible roar. ''Tis gonna be a long, long journey young lady. Are you sure you'll make it?'

Kayte opened her eyes, shaken awake by booms at the windows. It wasn't bombs or gunfire but heavy blasts of rain soaked wind from the storm beating hard and furiously, lashing against the big glass panels. The whole building shook violently. The metal furniture on the balcony skipped and jumped to a strange jig, and occasionally screeched across the tiled floor, like chalk on a blackboard. The rain was being thrown at the windows in bucket-loads, making Kayte feel a little more at home; all cosy in bed while the rain hammered down outside. *So, will this be the day for a new kite surfing speed record*? she mused. *Not a chance*, another more definite voice inside her responded. More tubs of liquid flew and thudded onto the window panes as the first light of dawn entered the room.

The rain storm continued unabated when Steve and Kayte entered the hotel's restaurant at nine o'clock. They found the rest of their group sitting exactly where Kayte had left them the night before. Only now they were wearing different outfits and their faces, in the daylight, seemed to have grown longer and more drawn out, which the discreet shadows of the previous evening had disguised.

'They should have stayed in bed, look at the state of them,' a smiling Kayte said to Steve up at the buffet bar.

'It's like a morgue.'

Kayte and Steve squeezed onto the cluster of tables with their bowls of fruit salad. Before they'd even taken a mouthful, the first thing one of the more negative members said was, 'Did you hear all those gunshots last night?'

'Nah,' said Steve, casually slurping a piece of papaya into his mouth.

'I heard *something*. But are you sure it wasn't just the storm? The waves on the offshore reef sounded like canons going off, are you quite sure it wasn't that?' said Kayte, trying to be rational.

Ignoring a more depressing conversation, they finished their fruit silently. Obviously everyone had had a rotten night's sleep. Kayte pictured them all huddled up, lying awake and distorting sounds, their imaginations going ballistic. Kayte called out to Chuck at one point, 'Hey Chuck, I don't know what it's like out at Kidd's right now, but it'd be good to know how choppy the surface water is out there.'

'Yeah it would, maybe we can call Sonia or Kirk and find out.' He got up and came over. 'Look I'm keen to get out there again today if we can, Kat. Believe me. But, we've all decided we're gonna be on the next plane outta' here for definite. Whenever that is, we wanna' be on it.'

'Oh, right, OK.'

'Our embassy guy's on his way over and we're gonna sit down with him and Pappie to sort out tickets or whatever. That's it, finito.' The Americans in the group nodded in compliance.

'Mmm OK,' she conceded. 'Well I guess we'll all have to go then. I'd better call our embassy guy too.'

Even the staff seemed glum, if not nervous. They ambled about clumsily, occasionally bumping into each other.

Next to arrive at the restaurant was Pappa Jon, clapping his hands and beaming as usual.

'It's only me …,' mimicked Steve, imitating his arrival on the beach the previous day, which at least raised a few eyebrows from the otherwise sullen group.

'I am sorry to inform you that, sadly, we cannot go out to Kidd's Beach this morning, my friends,' he said, rushing up. 'The roads are badly flooded just now but it looks as if it is clearing and we should be able to go out later. I have rebooked the minibuses to return at midday. I am so very sorry. I hope that is OK with you?'

'Well done Pappy, that's fine for now …'

'That is good, very good. Would any of you like to go to our local museum here in town and learn a bit about the history of our islands?'

'… Pappy? We'd like a word with you,' Chuck interrupted, holding up a finger up.

'One minute, Mr Chuck please. I will be right back.'

He turned and scooted off as quickly as he'd arrived.

Kayte put her hand under Steve's arm pit and hauled him up, chirpily saying to the group, 'We'll be back in a minute too. We're just going to make those calls.'

'Hey Steve, how ya feelin' this morning buddy?' Chuck called out as they got up.

'OK on the whole thanks, mate.'

Kayte dragged him off to the empty foyer. She went to reception to make the call and took the embassy official's card out of her bum bag.

'Alistair Fortesque. Good Morning.'

'Oh hello, it's Kayte King here, with the kitesurfing group up at the hotel. We met two nights ago,' she said, momentarily hesitating on the words 'two nights ago'; it felt more like a two weeks ago!

'Morning, Kayte, what a coincidence. I was just about to call you. How are you, my dear?'

'I'm OK, thanks, but we had a few very scary moments yesterday and the American lot want to leave right away, as soon as possible basically. I guess we can't be left here on our own so please can you organise the same for us too? Tickets and what not.'

'Yes, I heard about the incident on the beach yesterday with Jim, and Steve is it? Your boyfriend? I'm sorry about that. Is he OK?'

'Yes, he's fine thanks. Just a bit bruised. I don't know about Jim the journalist though, I haven't seen him today.'

'Well look, I'll organise flights straight away. I don't want you to leave the hotel today though, that's what I was going to call about, it's dreadful weather anyhow. Quite unexpected this storm, shame.'

'I know, the weather's worse than in England.'

'Well, not quite that bad, Kayte! Seriously though, I'll call Papa Jon now, I know him well. I'll sort it all out. Don't worry and I'll either call you or drop by at the hotel later. But Kayte, promise me you won't leave The Splendid at all today?'

'Well, actually we're all going to try and get back out to the beach this afternoon, to make use of the wind and go for gold and break my record. That's what we're here for.'

'No, no please Kayte. I don't think you heard me clearly, do not leave the hotel today.' He spelt it out.

'Um, yes, well OK,' she replied, somewhat taken aback. 'Not even to go to the local museum?'

'No Kayte, please. Promise me you won't leave the hotel?' he insisted.

'I promise.'

'Good. Thank you.' She heard a definite sigh through the receiver. 'Look just take it easy there, and I'll see you later.' The diplomat put the receiver down.

'Promise what?' Steve asked.

'Oh, nothing.'

'Oh, come on Kayte, he must have said something.'

'He's going to sort the tickets out, that's all, and he'll call us later. He just made me promise to be careful.'

'Oh, right. That's a bit odd isn't it?'

'No, it's not Steve. Look, I'm just going to try and call Sonia and see what the weather's like out at the beach. Why don't you go up to the room? I'll see you there in a minute.' Kayte's mind was firmly focussed on winning the fifteen thousand. She was so near, and with her twin-tipped board she knew she could do it. This was her chance at a ticket to freedom.

Chapter Fifteen
Oops!

Up in the room, Steve barely had enough time to lay out on the floor and start doing his exercises when Kayte came in. Stepping over him, she flipped on the old television set. The rain falling outside complemented the screen's fuzz. She began to tidy around as dated stock images flashed up behind Steve's suspended legs: fish being netted, men in white overalls inspecting flower harvests, joyous children waving flags, beautiful market stalls full of produce being tended by smiling happy people. Then a live item cut in, catching her eye; it was a white robed sheikh. She presumed it was Prince Jaffa boarding a plane along with some images of St Martin, as she'd seen it yesterday, being dressed for a celebration with bunting and banners, despite the rain and howling wind. There was no report or whiff of the unrest that they'd witnessed the evening before. The programme soon reverted to library images. She lost interest and switched the set off.

'No mention of the riots we saw last night, Steve, can you believe it?' she said a few minutes later.

'Hungh! Oh come on, Kayte, this is a police state. They ain't going to broadcast civil unrest,' he said, getting up and stretching. 'That's better. Look, I'm gonna pop down to reception, and see if there's anyone around to give me a massage. That knock I got yesterday has really bruised my neck and shoulders. Do you want anything?'

'That's a good idea, have a word with Mr Toyful. No, I'm fine, thanks.'

Alone in the room, Kayte lay on the bed. Her thoughts whizzed back to the bizarre encounter she'd had with Roger on the beach the previous afternoon. She hadn't really had time to think about it. It was full of coincidence on the one hand, and menace on the other. It was really quite intense; one moment they were swimming in paradise, the next talking about home on the beach and then gunfire and … Steve! She half-shuddered with incredulousness at the fast-paced, fast-changing memories. What seemed like a dream encounter in one thought, was a nightmare in the next, or both at the same time. Roger seemed perfectly charming one moment and possibly evil the next. He seemed to be able to flit between virtuous and vicious in an instant.

Although they'd never met before, Roger seemed instantly familiar. As if he'd known her intimately, and it left Kayte with an indelible impression. That was what was peculiar. How could she even have a connection with or get on with someone like him? Not only did she like him, she sort of fancied him as well. She immediately felt embarrassed about being attracted to him in any way. An older man and a nasty mercenary to boot. Kayte tried but couldn't brush her feelings aside. As hard as she tried to deny them, to shove them to the recess's of her mind, memories of him came back all the stronger. It wasn't long before she began to feel shamefully aroused at the mere thought of him. The isolated tropical beach, the dark powerful man with gentle authority; these images were just way too strong for her to dismiss.

The danger outside, which Kayte wanted to escape, helped her imagination focus with greater clarity. She sought refuge in her own world, to get away from the multitude of emotions that were tide tugging her. She began to fantasise. She couldn't help herself, she tried to stop it but couldn't. In her mind's eye she began to transform the encounter she'd had with Roger into a love scene.

Maybe he would, she imagined. Maybe he'd pretend she was his girl. That they'd swum to the shallows together, and he'd sat beside her as they stared at the timeless horizon, the water lapping at their midriffs. She pictured him kissing her neck and around her ears gently. She began to tingle. Wow! Stop this girl, she said to herself, but couldn't. She stroked his inner thigh invitingly. His hands caressed her, touching her carefully, yet firmly. She leant back into him. Stop, now Kayte, her inner voice of reason yelled. That voice was ignored. He confidently peeled her swimsuit off. She lay back, her arms stretched behind her, her fingers trying to clutch the loose sand. It ran through her fingers. He rose above, shading her. She could see into his eyes. She welcomed him … and then, no, no, no.

It didn't stop there. She envisaged them both coming into the hotel together, sometime later and asking for her room key. They got in the lift together and it came up very slowly, clicking at all the floors, she could feel him coming, and then it stopped at her floor. They stepped out and walked across the hall. She put the key in the door, opened it and they stepped in. He was here in front of her, he'd arrived. She pictured them both in the very room she was in, naked because of the heat. The balcony door was open, with the net curtain billowing in and swallows screeching over the rooftops outside. And then, when it was dark afterwards she pictured herself going to the window and seeing big bats hunting, close down over the trees. Then they sat up in bed talking with the door locked, with only a sheet over them, loving each other the whole night. That was how Kayte wanted it to be.

She sat up, as satisfied as mystified, and thought she'd better get dressed and find out where Steve had got to. She went down to reception, and low and behold there he was, not at the desk but, surprise-surprise, he was perched on one of the zebra skin bar stools with Jim; laughing and no doubt embellishing their adventure from the previous day. She approached with stealth and, catching them by surprise, enquired sharply, 'Any news on the massage then Steve?'

'Oh wow, hi babe. Yeah, they're making a couple of calls and are gonna let me know.'

'Is anyone else around?' she continued.

'No, I don't think so, I haven't seen a soul. It's deado. Have you Jim?' Steve said, turning to his Tonto.

'There was a bunch sloping around earlier, but they seem to have disappeared,' Jim replied, feigning interest.

'D'you know if they went off on this museum trip?'

'Nah, it was a washout, no one went. Shame, because I would have liked to have got some background on the islands, but there we go,' Jim said. 'Do you fancy a drink Kayte? Samoza here does a fabulous Pina Colada.'

'Oh no, no thanks,' Kayte declared and, not wanting to sound prudish, added, 'maybe later.'

'I'll come up and bring the kit down in a bit,' said Steve.

She half stumbled, half marched away awkwardly, hearing Jim say, a little too loudly, presumably so she could hear, 'Two more rum punches Samoza, there's a good man.' As she got to the lift, Kayte could hear their piratical laughter and giggling resume. 'There we go, me hearty, it'll be ho, ho, ho and a barrel of rum!'

It was about one o'clock when Kayte next appeared, having had a disturbed snooze. She had a peep outside on the way down. She thought she'd noticed flickers of lightning and heard faint, yet ominous rumbles of thunder or shots somewhere out there. Perhaps in her dreams, she wasn't sure. She went out onto the balcony, the long net curtain burst into life again, blasting into the room behind her, dancing wildly on the gusts. She clutched the railing and peered about. It dawned on Kayte that her day under a warm cloth of gold may have gone, replaced by a shroud of black angled rain. She could see the squalls, being discharged from ferocious looking clouds, raining down on St Martin like arrows unleashed from a marauding army. This is actually bleaker than home, she thought. More menacing, definitely.

Kayte crossed the hushed, empty foyer and could see Steve

still in the bar, but sitting at one of the tables now, with his back to the wall, one leg up on a low stool and his right hand cradling his chalice of rum punch. He was with Jim and two men she hadn't seen before. As she walked to the reception desk, she looked around and caught his eye. They both casually held up a hand in recognition, like acquaintances might do.

'Hi Sonia, it's me again, Kayte. How's it looking out there?' she said into the phone.

'Oh hi, ya, Kayte. It's not too bad at all. The storm's blown over ze mountain. It's much calmer, ya.'

'Oh great, but not too calm is it?'

'No, no, it's certainly much windier than it has been for you.'

'That's good, and the surface water?'

'Actually, it's quite smooth.'

'Fantastic. Sounds perfect. Hopefully we'll be out in a couple of hours. See you then.'

Inside the restaurant there were a few of the American contingent who informed her that their man from the embassy had been down and they were all booked on a flight out the following morning. One of them spoke of a chambermaid who'd told them that six people had been shot dead in St Martin alone the night before, and there were demonstrations going on all over The Martinez Islands.

'My god, how terrible. I wonder how true that is though?' Kayte said.

'Apparently Prince Jaffa is definitely on his way back from Europe,' another said.

'Yeah, I think I saw something about that on the telly.'

'The chambermaid was in a right state, just hoping and praying he was going to restore peace as she was sure many more people would be dying out there today. Can you believe it?'

'No, I can't. It all feels so calm in here.'

'Anyway, we're fixed to leave tomorrow, and we're to be in reception at five am to head to the airport.'

'Oh, OK!' said Kayte. Reality was dawning. 'Well, we'd

better get ready to go out to Kidd's Beach then.' She spun around. 'Where's Chuck?'

'I guess he's up in his room.'

As everyone talked around her, Kayte's thoughts turned to Roger and where he was and what he might be doing now. She pictured him in a smart green uniform with medals, wearing a beret at a jaunty angle, sitting at a desk ordering his troops around, pointing at maps and barking orders into telephones. However, bizarrely, he was doing just the opposite. He was spending his time quietly at the main mosque in St Martin with Imam Bakri and leaders of the community, sitting cross legged on the carpeted floor, out of the rain. This was the only place where he knew peace could be restored.

He'd discovered it was the locals doing the killing. The very pillars of the community he was sitting with had ordered the murders as retribution for the brutality of the previous regime. Apparently old scores still hadn't been settled. Roger realised revenge was obviously a dish best served cold in The Martinez Islands. They'd waited all this time to do it. These were publicly sanctioned assassinations executed by the Home Guard he'd trained, now that they were strong enough. The elders had ordered the extermination of members of the old regime that Roger and Prince Jaffa had usurped 18 months ago. There were to be no court cases or punishments issued through any legal process, it was officially endorsed slaughter, hits, wet wipes, snuffs, whatever you want to call them. And, while Kayte was talking to her American friends in the restaurant, the Home Guard were going it alone, targeting and eliminating individuals who had demeaned and abused the population prior to Roger's arrival on the islands. His major issue now, and he knew it, was that both the local and international communities would choose to interpret the brutal killings as being yet another mercenary atrocity, whatever the truth was. Christ, he thought, another nail in my coffin. He sat back, leaning on a cold pillar, looking at robed holy men, listening to rain splatting onto marble, scrabbling to find a solution to this dilemma.

It was just gone twelve thirty when Kayte left the restaurant. Crossing back across the foyer, she saw the minibuses outside and bar closed. Relieved, she thought she'd find Steve up in the room. However, when she got there the room was empty.

'Where the hell is he?' she raged to herself, 'where the f-ck is he now?'

Before going down to reception to look for him, Kayte went back out onto the balcony for a breath of fresh air, to cool down and galvanise herself for the kitesurf of her life.

Although the rain had stopped and the storm was clearing, leaving just the faintest rumbles of thunder bubbling back from the far distance, the re-emerging blue sky was still heavily peppered with little black clouds moving rapidly overhead. The air was clean and smelt fresh and slightly perfumed.

She wiped her eyes and thought that all looked quiet across town thankfully. Between the far off rolls of thunder, all was peaceful. The only sound she could hear was of the heavy drops of water from the balcony above, rhythmically hitting the metal railing she was holding. She jolted back, shocked, as a commercial aircraft, an Airbus, suddenly came blasting overhead, flying low across the rooftops in front of her.

At that same moment, on hearing the plane, Roger slowly uncrossed his legs and stood up on the carpet. He said nothing and casually walked out of the mosque towards his waiting car, putting on his loafers, left in the usual place, as he went. His huge black Mercedes proceeded to waft through the empty, dripping and steaming town towards the airport to greet the Prince.

Before going down with some of her kit, Kayte flopped down on the bed, curled into the foetal position and lay staring at nothing. She rattled through a range of emotions, which ended in anger. *How could the bastard leave me alone when we're in such a dicey situation? How could he? We're supposed to be together! I just don't get it. I need to get out to Kidd's and get that prize money. I just have to.* Then, shaking her head in disbelief, she catapulted out of bed and dashed down to the foyer to find out where the hell he'd got to. Only to discover, from the receptionist, that him and Jim were last seen half an hour ago getting into a taxi. On hearing that, she really broke down, raging repeatedly to herself, *how could he? How could he? I can't believe it. I just can't believe it.* She stomped around the cavernous foyer. Not wanting to go up to the room alone, she paced around the whole circumference of ground floor, on the off-chance he may be lurking somewhere. Out on the terrace by the bar, she went into a fuming haze of absolute disbelief - not only had he left her on her own, but he'd blatantly ignored what the embassy had said. He obviously hadn't learnt anything from the day before. She ignored the admission of the fact that she hadn't told him about Alistair Fortesque's emphatic plea to not leave the hotel under any circumstances.

She went back to the receptionist. 'Are you sure you saw Steven Palmer get into a taxi? A tall man, blond.'

'Yes, yes, it was definitely him,' said the receptionist.

A few of the kitesurfing group were starting to muster, equipment was being piled up. Papa Jon was outside gesticulating wildly at the drivers to load up. She tried to ignore them all.

Kayte dived into the gift shop. She didn't know what to do, so she closely studied the assortment of odd objects displayed on the mostly empty shelves. She shook a snow globe paperweight. On the spherical glass dome the words 'Welcome to The Martinez Islands' were written. The scene was of an empty tropical island, in the snow! She wandered into the empty restaurant, went back out onto the deserted terrace by the bar and then turned back to reception. More of the group had gathered.

'Does anyone know where they may have gone please? Is the barman, Samoza, still in the building, he may know? Or do we know the phone number of the taxi company?' she pleaded, only to receive apologetic and negative responses. The barman had gone home and he doesn't have a phone, she was told. The taxis in The Martinez Islands were all one man band type outfits.

'Come on, Kayte,' someone called out.

'Hold on a minute,' she mumbled back.

She couldn't go up to her room on her own, haul all her kit down and leave without Steve. She was too uptight. She did pop up quickly to get Alistair Fortesque's business card and telephone number though. When she returned to the foyer, five minutes later, the atmosphere had changed dramatically.

It was suddenly buzzing with activity. Lights were on and Mr Toyful had appeared with a dozen staff. He was ordering them about furiously, scattering them in all directions.

'Will everyone please go up to your rooms now,' she could hear him say to the group who, obviously bemused, obediently grabbed their kit and filtered off as quickly as possible towards the lift. Papa Jon and the vans simply disappeared.

'Excuse me, Mr Toyful. I'm a bit worried because my boyfriend has gone off in a taxi and I was wondering …'

'I am sure there is nothing to worry about, my dear, he'll be back soon, I am sure,' the manager interrupted in his calm, reassuring manner, putting his hand gently on her shoulder. 'We have a very important person coming to stay, unexpectedly, and I really must get the hotel prepared for his arrival. Wait here, I'll be back in a minute and we'll see what we can do.'

He scooted off, waving and urging his team into action. She sat on a bench seat, a banquette arrangement right in the middle of the foyer, watching the action around her. More lights went on, the last of her kiting group went up in the lift, bouquets of flowers appeared and trolleys were being wheeled around, laden with all sorts of comforts, making the previously dull space brighten up and change in ambience for the better. Chuck rushed up to her from the lift.

'Oh babe, I guess that's it. I tried babe, I tried,' he said panting. 'Everyone was ready to bust the embargo and come with us.'

'I know Chuck, I know, thanks. If it wasn't for my idiot boyfriend we would have been on our way.'

He pth-pitt'ed Steve. 'He may well have cost us thirty thousand bucks.' And then he dashed for the waiting elevator.

Chapter Sixteen
All Change

After being momentarily lulled by the foyer's brightening ambience, Kayte suddenly recoiled. At the hotel doors, two motorcycles, with blue flashing lights, swept past and pulled up just past the entrance, letting a huge black Mercedes slip in behind. As the vehicle stopped, twenty heavily armed western soldiers rushed around it from the rear, burst into the lobby and pounded past Kayte, scattering to every corner. She was dumbfounded. They positioned themselves by the lifts, staircase, restaurant entrance and every other door.

One fully loaded soldier, a Robo cop type, rushed at Kayte.

'Who are you, Ma'am? What are doing here?' he roared in a deep American drawl, looming over her. Her jaw dropped.

'I'm Kayte King,' she said through chattering teeth. 'I'm with the k … k … kitesurfing party.'

'Stay right there, Miss King. I'll be back.'

He turned and charged straight for the reception desk, quick marching and, rattling like a one man band, he demanded gruffly, 'Where's the manager? I wanna see him right now.'

Kayte turned as the lift pinged behind her. Immediately the rude clicking of guns engaging echoed out through the foyer. A momentary silence followed as all eyes in the room swivelled; the lift doors sprung open. The soldiers poised.

'Hold it right there. Don't move,' a voice shouted out.

Mr Toyful slowly appeared from the lift's interior very sheepishly with his arms up saying, surprisingly calmly, 'Don't worry I am the manager, Heinrich Toyful. Is there a Sergeant Adams here?'

The bristling soldier at the desk strode across towards the lift. 'OK men, at ease. Let him through.'

Kayte collapsed back into her seat wanting to be invisible as the nervous Mr Toyful and the huge jack booted, confident Sergeant met, one looking up, the other down.

'I'm Sergeant Adams, US Marines, Delta Force. You must be Toyful, I recognise your accent from the telephone conversation.' He held out the biggest hand Kayte had ever seen, and she winced along with Mr Toyful as their hands clasped and shook. 'Is what I requested all organised?'

'Yah, it is, Sergeant, I have just checked and we have prepared a whole wing on 7th floor for you. It has 20 rooms in total.'

'Good man Toy-full, I'll take the master key now, much appreciated.'

He turned towards the entrance, beckoned twice with purpose and, flicking his massive index finger, gave his orders.

The front passenger door of the limousine outside was immediately opened by a soldier. It was Roger who stepped out and, in turn, opened the back door where a long robed, tall, dark-bearded man in his early 40s emerged serenely. Kayte recognised him from the telly. This must be Prince Jaffa. The two men then casually entered the hotel side-by- side, followed by a brief-cased, suited western man and more soldiers at a respectful distance. Mr Toyful stepped forward to greet the entourage. They made contact right by Kayte. Although she could tell Roger looked tired and despondent he still had a definite air of control about him.

As the three men greeted each other, Roger looked around, nonchalantly taking the scene in. His gaze halted when his eyes clocked Kayte, and, having turned back to brief Prince Jaffa, he beckoned her to join them. As she approached she was greeted by a warm, friendly perfect English accent, very erudite, 'How do you do Kayte? I am Prince Jaffa. Lovely to meet you.' He held out a ladylike, thin-fingered hand. She thought that maybe she was meant to kiss it or something but decided to just hold it for a second. He had a twinkle in his eye. 'How have you found the kitesurfing on our islands?'

She was dumbstruck. How could this man sound so calm in this atmosphere? And to be chitchatting with her! It was bonkers.

'Well, we've only been here for a couple of days, but it's been great on the whole, thank you,' she replied, amazing herself.

'Oh, that is super news. No doubt Papa Jon will fill me in later,' he said as if they were at a drinks party. 'But I must go now. I look forward to seeing you again. Very good to meet you, bye.'

He turned towards the lift and Kayte just managed to gently yank on Roger's loose, mint green shirt before he followed. She whispered, 'I'm sorry I need to ask a favour, my boyfriend has disappeared.'

He seemed to look at her blankly and all he said before joining the Prince was, 'Again!' He shook his head. 'OK, what room are you in?'

'502.'

'Wait for me there. I'll be with you as soon as I can.' And he was gone.

*

When Roger had reached the airport, an hour before they'd arrived at the hotel, he'd stepped out of his car and onto the tarmac at the bottom of the aircraft steps. He joined a gathering of other dignitaries, six military bandsmen and some local ladies in traditional dresses; beautiful flowing sari-esque robes, their heads garlanded with indigenous perfumed Ylang-ylang flowers. Ishaq, the Finance Minister was there too, shuffling around with a sinister grin. A threadbare red carpet was laid out and the same video crew, who had filmed Kayte and Chuck, were positioned and ready to roll.

They all waited on the old rug, the aeroplane doors opened, the band started to play but instead of Prince Jaffa stepping out to the mini fanfare, they were greeted by an unfamiliar, black suited white man who, as he came down the steps, pointed at Roger and beckoned him to come up to the aircraft. Roger strode up to the plane.

He followed the stranger up the stairs and, as the two men stepped inside, the cabin door swung shut behind them. Just as the door bolted the sound of some fifty weapons engaging greeted them, like a spontaneous burst of applause, intensified in the contained space. The fifty or so soldiers, who held the firearms, snapped up from behind seats, out of the galley, some were even lying on the gangway floor. Literally every conceivable space was filled with bulky, heavily armed men pointing their weapons at Roger. The view he had was a mass of over-muscled men jammed into a minuscule space like they were trying to break the world record for the most people that could be squeezed into a plane, making the scene before him look somewhat comical. It was all elbows, shoulders and square jaws.

Roger, typically, stood calmly and unmoved. He simply raised his arms up slowly so his fingertips were touching the cabin's ceiling. After a moment of deathly silence Prince Jaffa pushed forward, stepping over soldiers and rushed up to Roger, warmly clasping him. One of Roger's arms came down to pat the Prince on the back.

'My dear friend, my dear friend I am so sorry, so very sorry,' he gabbled, and quietly whispered into Roger's ear, 'My arm was held behind my back, my friend. There was nothing else I could do, believe me. Please just play the game and all will be fine, I assure you. I'll explain it all later. Just do as they say, please, my friend.'

The suited, brief-cased man immediately intercepted them from behind and said, 'I'm Colonel Mayhew, CIA. I'm in charge of this operation now. You are Roger MacGill, is that correct?'

'I am,' Roger replied coolly, ignoring the hand held out to him.

'Well mister, I'm afraid to tell you that the international community, a coalition led by us Americans, are giving you and your men 36 hours to vacate The Martinez Islands. Your time here is over. Do you understand?'

All Roger did was stare through him, without saying a word. He glanced across at Prince Jaffa, who nodded and shrugged feebly, and then looked back at Mayhew, waiting, forcing him to continue.

'We have a naval warship, *SS Nevada*, arriving into the port of St Martin anytime now with a further 500 marines on board and enough fire power to blow you sky high so you're gonna call your men up and let us do this peacefully. Is that clear enough for you?' Mayhew informed Roger. 'If you want a fight, we'll give it to you alright, and the one thing you can be sure of is this: you *will* loose. Do you hear me? Am I making myself perfectly clear?'

Roger knew that the less he said in these situations the better. To act hastily would only result in him repenting at his leisure. So all he said was, 'OK.' He wanted to add 'whatever' but didn't.

The American pulled out a neat little satellite phone and handed it to Roger.

'I wanna hear you make the calls. Get all your men to meet you at your barracks in two hours and order all your men here at the airport to put down their weapons and to stand out there on the tarmac so we can see them. Do it, make the calls.' He jabbed the mobile phone towards Roger.

'I'm so sorry, dear chap. I haven't got a clue what any of their phone numbers are,' Roger replied. Shrugging, he refused the phone. 'But please, stay calm,' he added. 'There's nothing to worry about. I assure you. I will deal with it.' Roger knew it was vital to calm the situation. He was well aware that, pumped on adrenalin soldiers, especially American ones, could be a highly unpredictable class of beast, even at the best of times.

Roger was ushered to one side as the gibbering Jaffa was urged towards the reopened door. The Prince hesitated before he went out, placed his delicate hand on Omar's shoulder and said earnestly, 'Dear friend, I will look after you. Do not worry. You have my word.'

He then turned, stood erect and, waving royally, descended the steps to greet his ministers and inform them of the new state of affairs. The tinny band made its effort.

Having called the control tower from the cockpit, Roger was led back to the shadows of the aeroplane's open door. He could see Jaffa on the tarmac below, holding Ishaq's hands tightly. The two men beamed at each other. He tried to read their lips.

'Sir, how wonderful to see you back. This is a great day, a great day,' he was sure Ishaq was saying.

'Indeed it is. Our money worries are over, my friend,' Jaffa agreed, smiling. 'I will tell you much more a little later but you must deal with receiving all the international aid I negotiated immediately. The Americans and British must pay us straight away. This is our priority. Come to me as soon as you can.'

Roger, interpreting their body language, suppressed all feelings of disgust. He knew that in the face of the overwhelming force he was faced with, the only rational course of action was to retreat. He certainly wasn't going to embark on a suicide mission. He closed his eyes and inhaled the fresh, post storm air deep into the recess's of his lungs, as deep as he could possibly take it. He held his breath until he could see white light flickering in his mind's eye. All he could do was play along, see what happened, buy some time, negotiate the best deal for himself and live to fight another day. He exhaled long and hard and, opening his eyes, was led down the stairs.

He was forced to sit in the front of his own car. That was a first. His old English driver had been replaced, left on the tarmac with a tear in his eye. The familiar route into town held no charm whatsoever for Roger. Vanished was the pride in his new road. He stared impassively, all he could see was the decrepitude of the place and felt, surprisingly, somewhat at peace.

The turn of events actually held no great surprise for

Roger, deep down he'd half expected it. And, if he admitted it, he welcomed it. It was a relief. His heart just wasn't in the place anymore. It had ground him out. He'd known the moment his money tap was turned off the writing was on the wall; his position on the islands would become untenable. The only two things of any importance were to get his men out safely and to retain favour with Prince Jaffa in order get some of his fortune back. It dawned on Roger, on that car journey, that the islands had drained him right out, not just financially but physically and mentally too. Even his kidneys hurt. Like an actual dripping drain, as opposed to an energy giving radiator. The Martinez Islands had steadily sucked the life out of him and left him devoid of any reserves. He'd literally given everything he had to these islands over the past two years. They'd shrivelled him up and left him empty; he was rinsed out. Nobody had given him anything back. He had given and given and everyone had taken and taken. He had nothing more to give. He breathed deeply; stop whinging and concentrate on conserving your already depleted energy levels, he said to himself. Just think straight and act calmly. It's over now.

He was fully aware that the next few days would demand the most delicate footsteps, manoeuvring, and clarity in choosing the most precise words to secure the optimum exit strategy - all the while maintaining some sort of position of authority on the islands. He just hoped nothing would go wrong. All he really wanted was his beach house, the hotel and his farm, to hell with the tens of millions he'd spent buying into the islands. Perhaps he could be of service down the line and call The Martinez Islands, maybe not his home, but his holiday home. Who knows?

Having stood down and disarmed his men at the airport, through the cockpit's two-way radio, Roger's private army were being escorted back to his barracks with orders to call in the whole mercenary regiment immediately, and peacefully. The Home Guard wasn't his problem anymore.

Roger, Prince Jaffa and Mayhew had got into the black

limousine, waved off by the small assemblage and headed back into town in complete silence. The wily old Finance Minister, unsurprisingly, was the most vociferous of wavers as they'd pulled away.

It was only when Prince Jaffa and Roger were alone in the hotel suite on 7th floor, with both men standing at the window overlooking St Martin shimmering below them in the pink and purple streaked afterglow of a crystal clear sunset, that Roger turned to Jaffa and said, 'My brother, you have my word there will be no more bloodshed here on my behalf, but I must have your word in return. You must swear to me now that my property shall remain mine. You will repay your debt to me, that is all I ask.' He took a step forward so that the two men were very close and forcefully, with an ice cold steely quietness whispered, 'Swear it to me.' He stared into the Prince's dark eyes. His words, 'swear it to me', hissed out like four bullets from a silenced pistol, on a trajectory firmly levelled at Jaffa's heart; aimed to lodge there and not plough on out the other side. Roger put his open hand forward.

'I do brother, I swear to you,' the Prince replied, reluctantly taking Roger's hand. He nervously shook it. His limp, sweaty palms made the act immediately unconvincing. Roger squeezed a little harder. At that moment, from that feeble handshake, Roger knew Jaffa had no intention of honouring any commitment whatsoever. As Roger gripped back, his blazing eyes said it all: *Let me down, you little piece of two timing squirming muck, and I will hunt you down, tear your liver out, and send your life into eternity*. Roger was sure the Prince comprehended every word of this unspoken threat. Jaffa began to tremble, his robe quivered like a dervish's around his ankles.

Conversely, Roger was beyond fear, he stood impassive. He knew that his lack of fear was what rattled the feeble man before him. Roger had learnt, a long time ago, that where there's fear, there's danger. And he was the opposite of all that. People and nature only pick off the weak first, it's easier. There was no way he'd ever be a willing victim. The last and only thing he could do now was put the fear of God into the man before him, willing him to do the right thing.

It was then, standing there, that Roger was reminded of his father's saying, 'son, never trust a man with small hands'. Why hadn't he listened to him earlier? Well, pretty well everyone he dealt with had flabby little hands though, he reasoned, and Jaffa's were no different.

'You have my word, Omar, my brother,' the Prince said.

'That *is* very good news, sir. An enormous relief to me. I thank you,' Roger said, before releasing his grip, turning and departing.

Chapter Seventeen
Ground Zero

Mayhew was waiting for Roger in the heavily guarded corridor when he came out. He'd been happy to let the two men talk privately, he even encouraged them, knowing their conversation was being recorded. They walked together across to the lift. When they got in, Roger pressed the fifth floor button.

'Hey, what are doing MacGill?'

Roger turned and glared at the American, yet spoke calmly. 'I'm going to see someone for a few moments on the fifth floor, OK.' He spelt it out. 'That girl I spoke to at reception is part of a kitesurfing group we've had here promoting tourism and she's asked me to sort something out for her. I won't be a moment.' He finished the sentence just as the lift doors parted and he stepped out before Mayhew could reply.

Roger knocked on the specified door opposite, which Kayte quickly opened. They could hear Mayhew behind them trying to sound authoritative saying, 'OK MacGill, five minutes max. I'll be waiting right here.'

Roger stepped nimbly into the room and flipped the door closed behind him. He stepped over Kayte's kiting gear and perched his buttocks on the dressing table, his legs outstretched. He gestured for Kayte to sit on the bed in front of him and said, 'So your boyfriend's gone walkabouts again has he?'

'Mmm, I'm afraid so,' Kayte replied, looking down. 'He

was last seen getting into a taxi three hours ago with that *Jim the journalist* and a couple of other guys,' she sighed. 'Apparently.'

'OK, but look Kayte, getting straight to the point, my guys found a camera up at the back of my beach house yesterday. The memory card was gone so we don't know what was on it but I assume this Jim, with Steve in tow, was snooping around taking photos. It doesn't look good, does it? Now tell me, what are they up to?'

'I haven't got a clue what Jim is up to. Really I haven't. I don't like or trust him but Steve's up to nothing, I swear it. On my life. He's just a cook in a pub back in Lee-on-Solent. I've known him for eight years. I swear he's doing nothing.'

'What's the pub called?' Roger interrupted.

'The Osborne View, why?'

'Oh, the old Osborne View eh! Carry on.'

'Well, Steve told me he'd waited at the pirate cemetery while Jim went off,' she continued, 'he told me Jim had insisted he stay back while he went on alone. They're just drinking buddies, that's all. They've never even met before. I swear it.'

Kayte talked to Roger whilst he sat impassively in front of her, wondering why on earth he was bothering with this trivia at such a pressing time. And whether Jim was spying or not was frankly inconsequential now, but he was inquisitive. It had crossed his mind on the journey into town that Kayte could somehow be involved with the British security services. That she may have had a small role to play in this coup to overthrow him. He couldn't deny he liked looking at this young lady before him, she had *something* he couldn't quite put his finger on. She felt very familiar and he sensed he knew her. Perhaps the associations of home were just what he needed then. Perhaps he was going under again. He recalled images of the pub she mentioned, perched on a rise above the sea with its wonderful view across to the Isle of Wight. He'd been there as a child with his parents many times to watch life on the water coming and going, eating chicken in a basket.

'Well, OK Kayte, I'll see what I can do,' he said dreamily as he emerged from his reverie. He didn't want to waste any more time on the subject. 'I'm sorry you didn't break your record here, you seemed so close. A huge shame. And …' he smiled, 'that you won't be able to send me a report on my house. Oh well.' He leant down and held out both hands, which she took. 'Look my dear, the solids have hit the fan for me here, the Yanks, and the Brits I guess, are taking over and I am being booted off the islands. All I can really do for you is speak to Alistair Fortesque, our British consul, and get him to put you on the next flight home.'

'Thank you, that's already been sorted out by him. I've been in touch today and he's due to call me,' Kayte said, somewhat galvanised.

'That's excellent, well done. I'll chase him up too. I understand the plane Prince Jaffa came in on is the one being held overnight and will leave first thing in the morning, be on it. I'll do all I can to find out what's happened to … Steve and I'll liaise through Fortesque. That's all I can realistically do, is that alright?'

'Yes, thank you. And please believe me, Steve is completely innocent.'

'OK, fine.'

Kayte's worried eyes looked up at Roger, seeking answers. They were still holding hands. The gentle human contact, the transfer of energy, helped them both feel slightly calmer, in more relaxed frames of mind. They both knew it wasn't the time to ask questions, every answer today would be depressing.

'You speak to Fortesque, Kayte,' he said gently, 'I'll do the same and we'll make sure you're on that flight tomorrow, that's the only important thing. To get home. Good luck, my dear.'

'Same to you, Roger. Same to you.'

'Thank you,' he said smiling. 'I think I'm going to need it.'

He released her, to her chagrin, stood up and walked purposely out of the door without looking back, leaving her alone again, in disbelief at the continuing dramatic opera she was living.

Roger and Mayhew brushed past the guard by the lift on Kayte's landing and went down to the foyer. Stepping out, they were greeted by Mr Toyful, Alistair Fortesque and his American counterpart with the flat-top haircut, Louis Bogdanovitch, who all came forward from the central seating area. The shop, bar and restaurant were all shut and the foyer had returned to a drab empty stillness, the silence only broken by occasional clinking of armed soldiers who still furtively clung to the recesses and extremities of the big space.

Roger introduced Mayhew to Fortesque, he didn't bother with Bogdanovitch as he assumed they knew each other. The four men began talking in muted but intense tones while Mr Toyful stood back respectfully. Roger clearly felt his dominance on the islands evaporate before him as the trio of agents, representing two of the most powerful nations on earth, stood discussing the unfolding of their plan without him. He could tell by the way they looked at him that he was now more of a criminal than a mere inconvenience. Someone they wanted out of the picture, locked up, neutered as quickly as possible. He was fast becoming utterly inconsequential to them. It's amazing what difference a few hours can make, he thought.

Fortesque, Mayhew and Bogdanovitch had been in secret communication over the past two months, but had never met. They were joined by Sergeant Adams.

'MacGill?' Mayhew demanded, 'you have 75 men in total on the islands, is that correct?'

'73 to be precise,' Roger replied, 'two are out of the country.'

'We must know their definite whereabouts, MacGill,' Sergeant Adams cut in. 'I have a map right here, point out precisely how many are stationed where.'

'Gents,' Roger said matter of factly. 'I'm really not sure. And we won't know until we get down to my barracks. With the problems we've had here over the past 24 hours, the boys have been shooting around everywhere.'

'Sergeant?' Mayhew asked.

'Yessir.'

'Take Mr MacGill over to that table over there,' he said, pointing, 'you both have a little chat. I need to have a private word with these two gentlemen.' When Roger and the huge Sergeant Adams were out of ear shot he continued, 'Ok, you two, obviously our number one priority is to contain MacGill and his men peacefully. Do you think we'll achieve this Alistair?'

'I do actually,' replied Fortesque, 'he seems calm enough. I can't imagine him thinking he's going to win any fight. And he's got soft here too don't forget. All he wants is an easy life. He'll bow out gracefully, I'm sure of that; I just hope his men do too.'

'I'm aiming to have them all contained within the next 18 hours. The target's midday tomorrow. Reasonable?'

'Sounds realistic. Eminently doable.'

'There's a transport aircraft on standby in Nairobi. I'm bringing it in to ship 'em out tomorrow.'

'And where will you take them?'

'Back to Nairobi, they can sort themselves out from there. Go to hell for all I care. OK, next item.' Mayhew was on a roll. 'We've got to inform the local inhabitants about the new setup. We must allay the people's fears about *SS Nevada's* force landing and what we are all about. "Temporary measures". "Not an occupying force". Those are the key words. Am I clear Louis?'

'Yessir, temporary measures, not occupying force,' Bogdanovitch echoed.

'OK Louis, you go up to Jaffa's suite now and nut out a speech with him, I'll approve it later. He's gonna make the speech in the morning. We're still pretty sure the local population don't have a clue what's going on, yet. The curfew will be kicking in soon. We must ensure the locals remain calm at all costs … until Jaffa makes this speech.' He looked at Bogdanovitch. 'We're here as a transitional necessity to ensure peace and stability for all, which will lead to greater prosperity. All that sort of lingo. That's the message. OK, off you go. I'll be back within two hours.'

'Yes, sir,' flat-top said, saluted and walked towards the elevator.

'What about the local dignitaries, Mayhew?' Alistair asked.

'Yeah, they're still contained at the airport. We don't want the bush telegraph exploding do we? I'm going to have them all brought back here. I've sent the Merc back to fetch them. I'd like you to stay here, to welcome them, make them feel comfortable. If that's OK?'

'Right, will do.'

'I must have absolute quiet on the streets until we can get MacGill's men contained, that is number one. Jaffa has already told the holy men to pull back the local police force. I've spoken to them too.'

'The Home Guard.'

'Yeah, that's them.'

'Are we sure that's been done. As they've been running amok the past 24 hours.'

'I know, that's all over, apparently,' Mayhew said with wavering assurance. 'I've spoken to Toyful. No staff leave the hotel or even make a phone call. Keep an eye on that for me.'

'Right, OK.'

'And keep an eye on the receptionists, only incoming calls. The men here are briefed to monitor that too.'

'Should be fine. Don't worry.'

Across the foyer, Roger was explaining to the Sergeant. 'It only takes a maximum of two hours to get anywhere on the islands. Rest easy, I'm sure we'll find the majority of my men at the barracks when we get there. I believe there may be twenty five on the two other islands, but don't quote me on that. They will have been contacted and helicopters dispatched to collect them.'

'OK, that's good. That's good. Two hours you say and they'll all be back?' demanded the Sergeant.

'That's what I said,' Roger confirmed. 'Have you notified all necessary air traffic control that two Augusta A119 Koala's will be in the air between Blanchette, La Boule and here in St Martin?'

'All in hand MacGill,' he drawled. 'All in hand buddy boy.'

Roger's eyes flickered. 'Please,' he said. 'Make sure, will you?'

'All in hand, buddy boy,' the Sergeant reiterated with all the airs of a superiority complex. 'All in hand. Wait right here.'

The Sergeant stood up and strutted the few paces over to Mayhew. 'OK sir, I'm ready to escort MacGill to his barracks. Twelve men are stationed at the airport. All that is secure. Eighteen are here and the rest'll come with me.'

'I'll feel a whole lot better when *SS Nevada* gets in. Have we had any news about when that'll be?'

'Yessir, she's just offshore now coordinating air traffic control. ETA in St Martin harbour is 0600 hours, sir. To dovetail with the broadcast to the people. We can get her in earlier if you want, sir?'

'That's good, that's good,' Mayhew said. 'That's good to know.'

'What about this friggin' Home Guard, who's coordinating them?' Sergeant Adams honked. Any army or military body, not from the USA, were pants in his mind.

'Don't worry Adams, I've been speaking to the head Imam here … Bakri he's called. He's the man in charge. They've all been called back to their barracks and are on standby if we need them.'

'Are we 100% sure they've pulled back on the smoke screen?'

'Yeah, yeah. Bakri said he's mopped it all up. We've got a clear slate now; there will be no insurgents. The curfew's still in place so there should be no opposition on the streets.' Mayhew turned. 'Go see what MacGill wants, he looks impatient.' The Sergeant was back in a moment.

'He's itching to get down to his men.'

Roger knew he had to allay any fears his men may be having immediately. Without him there with them he knew, only too well, that natural born soldiers, as all of his men were, always have a nose, a sixth sense, for changes in the air. The last thing anyone needed now was the mercenaries feeling any fear, getting tetchy or, worst of all, trigger happy.

'Come on gents, please, we've got to leave now,' Roger urged, approaching the troika of military attaches still in conversation.

Just as he said that the lift pinged open and - who should

come out? - but Kayte.

'Oh sh-t,' Roger said to himself, as she approached. He gestured to Mr Toyful who halted her progress and began to distract her.

'OK, one last thing, Sergeant,' Mayhew said.

'Yessir,'

'How we doin' on the containment and security of the American nationals on the islands?'

'Well, we've only got six national's, sir,' Sergeant Adams replied. 'All on a kitesurfing vacation and they're all right here in the hotel. They've been notified, sir, to stay in their rooms tonight and not budge one iota. They'll be on that flight out first light, sir.'

'Good man. That's great.' He pointed. 'And you, Fortesque? What about your lot, the British subjects.'

'They're all in hand,' the Brit continued, 'we've got three in the same party, the kitesurfers, and there are two contractors. I've organised them all getting to the airport at first light.'

'Hah hum!' Roger coughed, nodding his head back to Kayte.

'Well, actually that's not strictly true. Two of the kitesurfers, British, have gone AWOL. We're trying to locate them.'

'Wat! Whaddya mean AWOL?' Mayhew exclaimed.

Roger quickly interjected, 'Gents, please, we really have to go, now.'

'Deal with it Fortesque. We're outta here,' Mayhew barked, turning and heading for the exit, closely followed by the Sergeant.

'Alistair,' Roger managed to say, before dashing off himself. 'Please, ensure that Kayte here gets on that flight out in the morning and I'll do all I can to have these guys found, OK?' Roger held his hand out and they shook warmly.

'Yes, of course I will, Roger. Good luck,' Fortesque said. 'I told those guys emphatically to stay here in the hotel,' he continued, somewhat to himself, shaking his head.

Roger rushed to join Mayhew, who shouted as he left, 'Good

job guys, you all did well. Asta la vista babies.'

The three men sped off, escorted by outriders and followed by a truck load of GI's.

Chapter Eighteen
The Saga Continues

After the faint guffaws had died down from the American soldiers in the far corners of the room, there was silence. They'd all been tickled at their commander's reference to the Terminator film. Momentarily, Kayte, Mr Toyful and Alistair Fortesque stood looking around, slightly dazed, lost in the barren atrium waiting for the next phase of the operation to be executed – for the next burst of action to happen, but in the meantime all there was was tension.

The lift opened and Louis Bogdanovitch stepped out, breaking the silence.

'He wants to friggin' sleep,' he said, as he approached.

Alistair Fortesque turned to Mr Toyful and asked politely, 'Toyful old boy, fetch us a big jug of coffee would you? Kayte and I will be sitting just over there, there's a good man.' He pointed towards a sofa and table cluster off to one side of the foyer. 'Wait for me Kayte, I'll only be a moment.'

Mr Toyful and Kayte went their separate ways, leaving the two embassy officials alone.

'I don't friggin' believe it, man. I go up to his suite and the guy's lying in bed!'

'Oh well, let him have forty winks. Go back up in an hour.'

'Damn right, buddy. Like friggin' Hitler. Spending all his time in bed.'

'Louis?'

'Yip.'

'There's something I haven't told you.'

'Oh, you've been keepin' secrets from me Ally baby,' he joked, slapping the stiff Brit on the arm, hard.

'The journalist, James Singer,' Fortesque said, having recovered his balance, 'is actually one of us, he's a spook, working for British Intelligence, MI6 I think. I don't know exactly what his mission is. I wasn't fully briefed. I assume it's purely reconnaissance but he's gone off with her boyfriend ...' he nodded over his shoulder towards Kayte, '... for some bloody reason reason. I can only assume as sort of cover, a diversion.'

'Jeez, if they've been caught snoopin' around again by MacGill's boys, Gad knows what they'll have done to 'em,' he said chuckling.

'Louis, this is serious.'

'That's your problem ol' buddy,' Louis said smiling. 'There ain't anything much I can do. I've got my lot tucked up here, like sweetie pies, an' all booked on the flight to Nairobi in the morning. That's your problem buddy. Papa Jon and the vehicles will arrive for them at five am. I'll be here to make sure of that. And that'll be me done.' He clapped his hands together and pretended to wash them.

'Try and help, would you?' Alistair pleaded. 'Put some feelers out, at least.'

His counterpart became more serious. 'Sure, of course I will. I'll see what I can find out for you but you must get her on that flight, we can't have her hangin' and flappin' around, gettin' in the way now, can we?'

'No, no, quite, quite,' Fortesque agreed, and shuddered as he pictured himself dragging a screaming Kayte onto the aircraft, leaving her boyfriend stranded or dead in a strange land. He quickly shook himself out of this nightmarish scenario.

'Look, I see the coffee's arrived, give me five minutes with her. I'm going to make a quick call. I'll see you in a mo.'

Fortesque hurried towards the reception desk, his metal studded brogues *clickety-clacking* across the marble floor, crisply fracking the layers of tension within the hotel's lobby. He made his call and then approached Kayte, settled down and carefully poured himself a coffee before talking. 'OK, Kayte,' he said. 'I've just spoken to my man at the Home Guard and he did hear on the radio a couple of hours ago that two white guys were picked up in town. It wasn't by them mind, but it sounds as if it's Steven and James.' He sipped his coffee. 'That's better,' he said, and then continued. 'This chap is going to find out where they are and we'll go from there. Bogdanovitch over there, is going to see what he can do as well, but I'm afraid that's all I can do for now. Oh, and I'll try Roger later too.'

'Well, at least that's something. Thank God for that,' Kayte said. She sighed, relieved they'd been found. 'At least we've got some news. Was there anything else? Where they were or whatever?'

'No, I'm afraid not. Look, Kayte, the best thing you can do, my dear, is go up to your room and have some rest. Be down here in the morning at five sharp though. Papa Jon will get you all out to the airport, and we'll have Steve back here by then. I'm sure of that,' Alistair Fortesque concluded, trying to be as reassuring as possible. He sat back with the coffee cup, his little finger erect, standing to attention.

Ordinarily Kayte would have giggled at seeing that, but now she just stared at him glumly, continuing to reel from the unravelling events around her. She was on the verge of cracking under the strain of it all and the caffeine surging through her wasn't helping, she felt hot and prickly.

She was still utterly dumbfounded that Steve had abandoned her in this situation. If he'd only done what he was here on the island to do, they could have all slipped off to Kidd's Beach before all this military stuff happened and could have been back here at the hotel having broken her world record and been $15,000 richer. And they'd be happy. Instead he'd chosen to be the cause of such anguish. She felt betrayed, as if he'd done it on purpose, out of spite. To be so cruel and selfish was beyond belief. She was stupefied, glued to the sofa, unable to move.

As Alistair put his cup and saucer down, they were approached by the American consul. Alistair shot up and just managed to head him away from Kayte's earshot.

'All sounds jus' fine down at the barracks,' Bogdanovitch informed Fortesque. 'Our boys are disarming MacGill's guys without a hitch. Apparently there's only twenty five of 'em unaccounted for, but we know they've all been contacted and are being brought in as we speak.'

'Excellent news, we're getting there. Once that lot are all in, it should be plain sailing. Did Mayhew say when he'd be back here by any chance?' the Brit enquired, in a tone of optimism and relief.

'Yeah, he's gonna be here within the hour. He's released the ministers from the airport and they should be here any minute. We're to fix a general briefing with them and Jaffa, but he said we've got to wait for him to get back. I'll get Toyful to set up the restaurant up as a conference area.'

'Do that, I'll go up and inform the Prince - get him going and ready to meet and greet in an hour. Any news from that end on Kayte's boyfriend?' Alistair asked doing a reverse nod.

'Shite, I goddam forgot to ask.'

'Oh, don't worry, Louis. I spoke to that Colonel Richi at the Home Guard who thinks they may have been found. He's going to call me or come here soon anyway for a chat with the Prince, once Omar, I mean MacGill's, barracks are locked down, so I'll know more then. Help yourself to that coffee, its pokey stuff.' He turned back to Kayte and, holding out his hand, said, 'Come now Kayte, I'll take you up to your room.'

If he hadn't made that gesture Kayte wouldn't have been able to move. He could see she was wobbly and visibly shaken, so he put his arm around her shoulder and led her towards the lift. As they called for it, they heard the American soldier on duty getting on his walkie-talkie to say, 'Level 5, level 5, two personnel coming up, one male, one female, do you read? Over.'

Upon hearing, 'Roger, Rog. Affirmative. Over' from the other end they got into the elevator and went up into what was starting to feel more like a detention centre than a hotel. When they reached her door Alistair asked, 'Can I get you anything Kayte? Some food brought up, perhaps?'

'No, no thanks. I'm fine,' she replied and then changed her mind. 'Actually, I'd love a bottle of water.'

'Of course. Please now, just try and get some sleep my dear, and be down at reception at five o'clock sharp. I aim to be still be here. As soon as I get some news on Steve I'll let you know immediately.'

'Yes, OK and … thank you,' she mumbled as she closed the door.

Kayte lay in the foetal position on the bed once more. One moment she felt scared and alone, just wanting to go home. The next she had surges of determination, spurred by anger. Her fury at Steve for ruining the trip was unregulated. It was the only thing keeping her sane, focussed. Her emotions, tide tugged, had dumped her in the doldrums, floundering on a vast ocean of uncertainty. Her mood crested and troughed on waves of hope and despair, optimism and panic. Any affection for Steve had slipped its anchor and was now adrift on a sea of confusion. She was becalmed as her relationship headed for the rocks. This horrible nightmare scenario she was living through was a long way off being an experience to look back on and have a laugh at. It seemed, just then, the growing up Kayte had done over the previous 24 hours was rapidly unravelling as she cried herself to sleep, wanting her mother.

When she woke up she fumbled for her bedside clock - two am. The realisation of her current situation clicked into her consciousness rapidly: alone, *click*; Steve missing, *click*; Roger in danger, *click*; country rioting, *click*; coup, *click*; flight home, *click, click, click*; and finally, pack bags, reality check. The volume of insecurity shook her wide awake, she blasted off the bed and switched on the TV. I need information, she thought. Nothing. Just fuzz. Next, fresh air.

Out on the balcony Kayte was embraced by an oppressively sweltering tropical night. It had clouded over. After all the rain, the land now steamed in an unhealthy cauldron. All she could hear was the constant croaking of night creatures coming out of the darkness to close in around her. It was pitch black, no stars. Occasionally, attracted by her room's light, she'd jump back as large buzzing moths hit her face or got caught in her hair. Her spine tingled. There were no sounds coming from town at all, just this constant trembling racket from all these organisms vibrating under the weighty greenie grey sky, making Kayte shudder. As she turned to go inside two simultaneous flashes lit up the night sky: explosions, far out to sea. The pair of white fireballs burst and then, like dying fireworks, trails of phosphorescent light rippled downwards and fizzled into nothing. It was over in an instant. Kayte wasn't sure whether it had really happened or not. She rushed inside, slid the balcony door shut and closed the curtains tight.

She had the good sense to pluck out a Rickie Lee Jones CD and put it on her player. Although the sound quality was tinny, it did break the empty silence of the room and warm it up with something resembling the familiar. Having packed the bags with all the kiting equipment, to the sound of 'Skeletons' and 'A Lucky Guy', she peered out of her room door to see a bottle of water on the floor and the burley, fully kitted American GI, standing guard beside the lift.

'Excuse me, has anyone come to my door at all please?' she called out.

'No, ma'am, only the boy with the water,' replied the low toned, matter of fact voice, but there was a hint of friendliness in there somewhere.

'Have you any idea of the time at all?' she enquired, wanting confirmation her clock wasn't wrong.

'Two hundred and thirty hours precisely, ma'am.'

'OK thanks.'

Closing the door, alarm bells pulsed within her. She couldn't help herself. It had been hours since she'd heard anything. She had to go down and speak to Alistair or Mr Toyful, or anyone, and find out where on earth Steve was. She was having constant flashes of worst case scenarios as her imagination clamoured to overtake reason. For some reason she was even worried about Roger too. Going out on the balcony had definitely spooked her. She grabbed her key purposefully and went out of the room to be greeted at the lift by GI Joe.

'Just one moment ma'am, what are you doin'?' the guard said, his outstretched arm blocking access to the lift buttons.

'I want to go to reception please, my boyfriend is missing and I want to see someone,' she said, mustering conviction and trying to sound authoritative.

'Just hold it there ma'am.' He talked into his walkie-talkie before continuing, in no uncertain terms, 'No ma'am, no civilians are allowed in the foyer area at this time. I am sorry ma'am, please return to your room.'

'But I must go down, please, I must.'

'I have my orders ma'am, return to your room, now!'

Kayte realised the futility of arguing with this sort of individual, like nightclub bouncers, it was going to go nowhere and so she turned glumly and went back to her room.

After half an hour of repacking and with no news from Alistair, she resolved that she just had to go downstairs and try and do something to keep the search for Steve alive. She couldn't stay in this box a moment longer. Then a plan entered her mind.

She remembered seeing one of the guys on the beach larking around using a kiting rubber bungee strap as a catapult the day before, so switching off all the lights in her room she crouched on the floor by the door. She'd found one of her rounded shampoo bottle tops in the bathroom and gently edged open the door in the darkness. She positioned herself, poised to release the projectile down the corridor.

As soon as she was ready, she pulled the loaded bungee back as far as she could and then let go, sending the plastic orb ricocheting down the corridor. It flew perfectly, bouncing off two walls, making a hell of a racket before disappearing out of sight. She heard the *chick, chick* of a gun being engaged followed by the heavy thudding footsteps of her warden pounding down the carpeted corridor towards her. She closed the door to within a millimetre of it actually shutting, held by her fingernails biting into the wooden frame. She could just see his shadow flicker past the chink. She left it three seconds before she flung open the door and flashed across the corridor, scurrying into the stairwell opposite as fast as she could.

She didn't hear anything behind her, but she couldn't believe GI Joe hadn't seen her, or at least heard her door slam. She didn't look back and just fled, headlong down the stairs, adrenalin racing through her. She took three steps at a time, gripping the balustrade on the turns, her momentum swinging her around, on and down.

She burst into the foyer. The swing doors knocked a duty soldier off balance, which resulted in all the other soldiers, peppered around the foyer, cocking their semi's in unison. Kayte could hear a few voices barking out, 'Stop!' loudly. She stumbled and found herself crouched down, like a tiger, poised to attack. The position empowered her. Her eyes flashed around the room as all other eyes turned on her. She wasn't going to submit now and just hold her arms up feebly. She was passed all that, she'd found fearlessness. Spotting Alistair sitting at the same sofa cluster they'd sat at six hours ago, she sprung forward, sprinting towards him. Zigzagging and running as fast as she could, arriving at his side like a mini tornado an instant later. A gawping Alistair, having looked around from the intense conversation he was having with a local minister, jumped up like a seesaw to fend off the three soldiers who had arrived on her heels. They jabbed their weapons violently at the now cowering Kayte.

'Gentlemen, gentlemen, please, it is OK, this lady is with me,' Alistair pleaded, both arms out in front of him. 'It is OK, it's OK,' he repeated, trying to soothe them like one would crying children, 'it's all alright.'

When the three men stood down and shuffled off in deflated obedience, Alistair sat down and was again forced to put his arm around a shaking Kayte, who huddled closely by his side.

'That was bloody stupid of you Kayte King,' he rapped, his voice reprimanding, yet brotherly. 'You could have just gotten yourself killed.'

'What about Steve, what about Steve?' she blubbered.

'I haven't got anything to tell you Kayte, otherwise I would have come up. I'm sorry, I've got no further news.'

'But we must do something, anything. Where is he? You've got to do something Alistair, please, please.'

'I don't know, I just don't know,' he admitted. Guilt filled the silent moment that followed. 'Look, OK, just stay here,' he continued, 'I'll put another call in, OK? Hold on here. Excuse me minister,' he said and stood up. He was gaunt and looked as though he'd aged a decade overnight.

'It was six hours ago Alistair, please,' she pleaded. 'Find out what you can. Speak to Roger too, he promised me he'd do what he could.' Kayte was clearly in the last throes of an adrenalin buoyancy.

'Yes, yes, alright,' he said, slightly annoyed, as he headed up to the front desk. His gait had lost its purpose, his studs refused to clack.

Kayte trembled as the energy hormone wore off and the reality of having three guns pointed at her kicked in. The sweet looking local minister leant forward and said soothingly in broken English, 'Do not worry miss, it will all be fine, you will see.'

'Yes, yes. I'm sorry,' Kayte mumbled, trying to be strong and wishing what he'd said was the believable.

It wasn't long before Alistair reappeared and quickly informed her, 'OK, Kayte, I've left messages for both the head of the Home Guard and for Roger saying that I want Steve released right away if either of them has him in custody, and to inform me as to his whereabouts immediately. I'm positive the messages will get through very soon, they're both still up and about. And that is all I can do for now.'

Kayte looked up at him. 'Thank you,' she said.

Alistair Fortesque was utterly unprepared for this; in his book it was always a case of keeping calm at all times, especially under pressure. Certainly, letting one's emotions out, was a no-no written in stone. Indeed, Alistair Fortesque wasn't used to close female company at all, having been sent to an all boys boarding school from the age of seven. Then he went straight into the army at eighteen. He had one brother, five years younger, so simply wasn't used to women full stop; he'd spent so little time in their company. As a result he was being awkward, rather than patronising, and leant forward to help Kayte to her feet again.

'Come now Kayte. Let's go up to your room. It's going to be alright. It's all in hand, please don't upset yourself any more.'

As he helped her up to her room for the second time, Kayte felt more like a patient in a mental hospital having a nervous breakdown than the prisoner she'd felt like earlier. Feelings of being a minor celebrity guest in The Splendid Hotel had vanished entirely. She was a sad shadow of the image of vitality she'd been twenty-four hours ago. Her feet dragged as Alistair urged her in and settled her on the bed before leaving. Alone, she sat numbly staring around until she was roused from her stupor a few minutes later by a knock on the door. She rushed up, calling out, 'Steve, Steve, at last. Is that you Steve?'

'Miss King. I'm sorry. It's only me, Mr Toyful.'

She opened the door to see the tired looking, but still smiling, hotel manager holding out a tray with a steaming cup of hot chocolate. Kayte smelt the soothing aromas waft towards her.

'Come in,' she said, as if hypnotised.

He shuffled in and placed the tray on her bedside table. Pulling back her covers he told her to get in and puffed up her pillows. When she was sitting up, he passed her the comforting beverage and said, 'Sip this my dear, it will help you sleep.'

As she sipped obediently, spooning the froth, he pottered around, tidying up for a few minutes. Mr Toyful, an old hand at managing hotels in third world countries, enjoyed doing the small things his job entailed, it grounded him. Right now, tidying up was just what he needed. She put the cup down on its saucer and lay back. The last thing she remembered was Mr Toyful saying goodnight and switching off the lights as he left the room. Amazingly she fell asleep as easily as someone giving themselves up to the gentle motions of a spring tide and she surfed with surprising ease into morning.

Chapter Nineteen
Peace In
The Camp...

At the military barracks across town, fifty of Roger's mercenaries were being held in the confines of their Officer's Mess. Disarmed and heavily guarded by Americans outside, they languished on the floor of their mess room, the bar, the dining room, the entrance hall and even the corridors. Every conceivable inch of space was covered in burly bodies and kit. In the main Roger's men were fast asleep in their military sleeping bags, snoring heavily. The majority were absolutely exhausted from suppressing the fabricated unrest, which had gone on over the previous thirty six hours, but the ones that were awake sat glumly, fully aware that this mission, the longest and easiest of their careers, was at an end.

Many were settled into homes on the islands or living with local girlfriends. Some had even brought their wives and families over from their native countries, others were having children on the islands.

In a small shabby, ill lit side room, Roger was on the phone.

'Mayhew, where the hell are they?' he rasped into an old Bakelite hand set, 'they should have been back hours ago.'

The American at the other end of the line coughed. 'I'm afraid I have some bad news for you, MacGill.'

'What is it, Mayhew?' Roger sighed and shifted in his seat. 'Spit it out, man.'

'I'm sorry to inform you, but the flight movements didn't get through to the *SS Nevada*, she's shot your two helicopters down.'

'Jesus Christ, man, there were nearly thirty men on those two aircraft,' he exclaimed. His head dropped and he sighed again, louder this time, and quietly said: 'I trust you've launched a rescue?'

'Of course we did, it's under way now. Some bodies have been recovered already and, thank the lord, some are alive.'

'Dear God, that's something, and …?'

'I'm awaiting a full report from the Captain, I'll let you know when I have it. I'm real sorry MacGill, real sorry. It was an accident, a terrible accident.'

'You Yanks and your friendly fire, I don't know, I just don't know,' he said, shaking his head. He hung up.

Roger sat back and silently smoked a cigarette before he galvanised himself. He cracked the occasional smoke ring up at the suspended tin lampshade dangling on it's noose above him.

He'd already convincingly explained the futility of opposing such an overwhelming force to his men. It was going to be harder now. He mentally composed his words. They could have easily won the battle with the fifty soldiers currently on the island he'd said earlier, but five hundred more were arriving within a few hours. Then, if by a miracle they were able to overpower them, they could be sure that any amount of US soldiers would arrive within days, so where would they be then? Added to this, they would have to fight the Home Guard, who were obviously supporting Prince Jaffa. It was a war they just wouldn't win, he'd explained. The best they could hope for would be to get out in one piece with their families. That would be victory for them. And that was all Roger was aiming to achieve.

'If we kill one of them, we're all dead. So we'll do nothing and stand down. That's an order,' he'd told them.

He'd assured his men they'd all be paid up to the day they left. On hearing that, three cheers went up for their commander and he was patted on the back as he'd walked back to his office through his soldiers. He'd felt a huge sense of relief that none of these men were going to die for a lost cause. He'd closed the door behind him and was alone for the first time since he'd stepped out of his car at the airport twelve hours earlier. He'd collapsed onto the hard metal- framed chair behind his old desk and put his head in his hands.

He was completely used to the vagaries of fast moving, rapidly changing situations but, here and now, he was aghast that he didn't have one solid move to counter with. He had left himself a vulnerable pawn in a geopolitical game. He'd simply walked into the trap like a lemming with no cards left in his hand to play, virtually none at all. There was nothing of worth to bluff with either, well, only that weasel British agent, Jim Singer, and the squealing drunk, Steven Palmer, both bound and gagged in the two small offices next door to his. But what good were they?

He'd been completely side-lined out of the game. Roger could see that, in reality, he'd stumbled into a duplicitous political maelstrom the moment he'd become involved with the islands in the first place; with all their hidden twists and turns. It hit home that a soldier like him was completely ill-equipped for diplomacy. He was only mentally geared for straight lines and issuing orders. He had convinced himself that the international community was happy to play along with the political agenda for quite some time before anything remotely like this invasion happened. It was only a year after 9/11 and he simply hadn't appreciated how quickly the USA was moving in terms of the military establishing themselves in this region. The search for a suitable US naval base was widely known, somewhere that was a safe distance from, but within hitting distance of, the Middle East. But it was inconceivable that a decision would be made so quickly. That evening, Roger learnt that even lumbering nations could act quickly and decisively when mobilised.

He'd wondered whether his luck had really run out. Knowing that luck was a factor in any success, he'd puzzled whether, like an hourglass, his last grain of chance had emptied into the bulb.

Would it flip again, giving him a full barrel of sand or shatter? Only time would tell.

He stubbed his cigarette out, leaving it smoking in the ashtray, and summoned his men together again in the bar area. He stood for the second time that night on a rickety old chair towering over his men. He wasn't going to beat about the bush, he'd get straight to the point.

'I have some terrible news, my brothers,' he said, holding both arms up, palms outstretched. 'The two choppers coming across from the islands have been shot down, accidentally, by the Americans.'

The room immediately exploded into roars, shouts, threats and curses. Sleeping soldiers erupted out of sleeping bags like seismic earth movements. Ogres appeared.

'Quiet, please,' he said, with negligible effect. 'Quiet now, men,' he repeated, clapping his hands. 'I have heard there are survivors,' he ended up shouting above the cursing. 'As soon as I hear more I will let you know. But we must stay calm.'

Roger forced his way back to his office, being jeered at. One meaty old hand had even clutched his shoulder.

'Get me my f-ing gun, now, MacGill,' the voice's owner had said.

Roger lay back on the tiny campaign cot in the corner of his office. He listened to the uproar in the bar gradually subside as he stared up at the bundle of mosquito nets suspended above him, dangling like a swollen rain cloud. He cursed that wretched priest he'd confessed to after his parents had died. He was ashamed he'd done it, let alone even thought about confession. What the hell did he think he was up to? To Roger it was a critical moment of weakness. It was unmanly, and everything had changed after that. It had jinxed him, that act. These islands, this lifestyle he'd subsequently opted for had enfeebled him. He thought *civvy street* would be a walk in the park, his life would be plain sailing. Everything would be easy going. How wrong was he.

He lay awake. His men, as he knew they would, rumbled like

a seething mob, moved to venting their anger and frustration. It was as if Jim and Steve were here for that very purpose. He thought they may have been worth hanging onto as some sort of bargaining chip to negotiate with. But now, as he lay impassive listening to his men commence grilling the two helpless Brits next door, he lost all interest in them. He'd kept them locked up and safe for hours but now he had no will left to fend his men off; he'd allow them to release some steam. It was a form of therapy. It just had to be done. They'd lost twenty-three of their own men plus the four pilots. Revenge, retribution, call it what you like. He'd kept his men away from Steve and Jim earlier with ease, but now he just felt utterly drained, enfeebled; he'd let them just get on with it.

'It wasn't me I swear it,' he could hear Steve cry out. 'It was him.'

'What the f-k do you think you were doing, creeping around the bosses house and then going out during the curfew?' he heard Midge yelling at Steve, and then the slap, flesh-on-flesh.

'I don't know, I don't know. He dragged me along. I swear. I had nothing to do with anything.'

'Who dragged you along you f-ing pussy?'

'He did, he did.'

'Who did?' *Slap*. 'Give me a name?'

'Jim did.'

'Jim who?' Midge roared.

'Jim Singer.'

'Louder.' *Slap*.

'Jim Singer.' Steve squealed, a mouse's roar. Everyone heard, including the hapless Judas'd Jim in the adjoining cell.

Roger then heard doors slam and he knew they'd move to Jim's room now. His voice was as clear as Steve's through the flimsy partitioned walls.

'Did you hear that?' Midge hissed.

'I did,' Jim said.

'What did you hear exactly?' *Whack*.

'That it was me that dragged him out.'

'That's correct, and is it true?'

'Yes, it is,' Jim said.

'Right, what the f-k are you up to?' *Slap*.

It was four o'clock in the morning. There was a knock on his door, 'Enter,' Roger called out.

'Sir,' came a French accent from a dark-headed man peering around the door. 'Colonel Mayhew would like to see you outside if it is convenient for you?'

'Thank you Claude, let him know I'll be out shortly.'

'Oui, sir.' The head disappeared back around the closing door.

Roger stood up and had a quick squint at himself in the small, cheap, plastic framed mirror hanging askew on the wall. As he stroked his hair down flat with one hand, he could still hear the shouts and yelps coming from Jim's cell. He walked out into the corridor.

'Midge, here now,' he called out.

The giant South African came out of his interrogation chamber, red as a butcher.

'Yissir,' he said, to attention.

'Give it a break, my boy.' He pointed at Steve's door. 'Get this one a sleeping bag and some nosebag, and leave him alone. Am I clear? And the other one, just let him be for a minute too.'

'Yis, sir,' Midge replied, saluting.

'I'm going to talk to this Mayhew chap outside and find out more about what's happened to the lads. I'll be in shortly. Muster the men in the bar, I'll update you all there. And Midge … get the ruddy kettle on, there's a good man.'

He strode out into the heavily guarded yard where Mayhew was waiting, surrounded by a posse of his own soldiers. There were just the faint whispers of dawn's deep blue hues on the horizon behind, silhouetting Mayhew's team.

'Right, Mayhew, what's the update?' Roger asked coolly, taking the initiative as he approached the American military diplomat.

'I want to inform you that primary rescue has been completed,' Mayhew replied sharply.

'Well, it bloody better be. The sea's full of ruddy sharks, man.'

'We have rescued nine survivors from one copter, the shell hit the rotor and it gently dropped into the sea apparently, but we have no sign of the other. We assume all passengers have perished.'

'Jesus H Christ,' Roger said. 'Get me a list of the survivors names as soon as possible. Is the search continuing?'

'Yes, MacGill, it is. We have further search and rescue aircraft standing by to head right back out at first light. Nevada will be docking in the bay area any minute now, and the aircraft will head off immediately.'

'Right, and what else?' Roger enquired.

'Well, all's peaceful on the streets and Prince Jaffa is going to broadcast to his people at six am, so we'll take it from there,' Mayhew said, matter of factly.

'OK, when will I see you next?'

'I'll be back in 45 minutes.'

'I'll see you then. Anything else?'

'Yes there is MacGill. I need you to release the two Brits you have in there. The boys out here say they can hear you're givin' them a right roasting. I want them off this island.'

'We'll discuss this in 45 minutes,' Roger said, turning his back and strolling into the barrack hall.

Chapter Twenty
Paradise Lost

Kayte was woken up by exceptionally loud banging on her door. She stumbled up and opened it. A startled looking Alistair Fortesque stood in the corridor looking anxious, and had a clenched fist held up, poised to continue rapping.

'Crikey Kayte, are you alright? I've been knocking for an age,' he exclaimed. Kayte simply nodded and groaned a bleary eyed response. 'Come on, come on now,' he urged, 'the rest of your group are already gathering downstairs. Look, get yourself ready quickly; I'll take a load of your kit downstairs.'

'Ugh, OK, and what about Steve?' she mumbled, as she fumbled around.

'Good news, he's fine Kayte. I've just heard he's being released and is going to join us at the airport. The base he's being held at is out towards the airport, so don't worry. Come on,' he said. He'd heard nothing definite.

'Oh phew, well done, that's great.'

Kayte had dressed by the time he got back up again and they loaded a second lift with more baggage and boards, all overseen by the burly guard. Kayte joined Chuck and the crew in the foyer where the staff had laid out some coffee and old cakes on a trestle table. The only other sign of life on the ground floor was the clattering of tripods and the banging of metal boxes in the dining room as a news film crew setup for Prince Jaffa's imminent broadcast. Chuck rushed forward to help Kayte and the puffing, exhausted British diplomat, 'Hey babe, let me give you a hand.'

'Oh great, thanks, Chuck,' Kayte said, relieved to hear a familiar voice as much as anything else. They piled the rest of her luggage by the entrance.

'Any news on Steve, babe?' he enquired.

'Yes, I just heard he's fine,' she said, and then added sarcastically, 'thank God.' They looked at one another and smiled. 'Apparently,' she said continuing, 'they got arrested in town last night. I don't know what for, and they were held overnight. But I've just heard from Alistair here that he's being released and will meet up with us at the airport later.'

'Oh wow, that's cool, ace news. But what the heck did he think he was doing going off again, frikin' jackass?'

Kayte shook her head. 'Who knows, looking for a bar or something probably.' She bent forward to tighten a strap, her dark eyes flashed. 'That Jim's got a lot to answer for though. I've had a hell of a night.'

'Yeah, I'm sure you have, babe. You Brits and your booze. I dunno,' he said, chuckling.

'You don't know the half of it.'

They were interrupted by Papa Jon clapping hands in his customary appeal for attention. 'Good Morning everyone. Here please,' he called out. It still vaguely amused them to see the little man preen himself like a bird, thrusting his chest out and putting on an air of fake normality that deceived nobody. 'If you have all had coffee, please pack up the truck as usual and we will leave for the airport presently.'

As they loaded up in the pleasant chill of early morning, Kayte could see a deep blue sky dotted with cotton wool balls of rose tinted clouds, rapidly passing overhead. There was a deep calmness in the air after the storm and the prospects for a beautiful day in the tropics seemed guaranteed. The invigorating dawn wasn't giving the slightest clue as to man's upheavals going on around. Mr Toyful came out to say his goodbyes and apologise that they'd had a rotten stay at The Splendid, as if it was his fault.

'Kidd's Beach will be a marvellous hotel,' he gushed, 'you must all come again.'

Kayte looked up. She clocked that the hotel's fascia had completed its transformation. In the few days they'd been here the Splendid's exterior had gone from a dirty and mouldy old structure to a sparkling new creation. The complete opposite that happened internally for Kayte. From what had started as a fabulous opportunity for her, full of bright prospects, to a trip that had turned into a nightmare. The shabby hotel that had welcomed them now said farewell looking brand new. No one else seemed to notice.

The group was hushed, heads were down. Everyone was keen to get on board the vehicles quietly, not wanting to panic themselves or anyone else. Alistair Fortesque just managed to catch Kayte as she was about to get onto one of the minibuses.

'I'm taking my car to the airport, Kayte,' he said very quietly. 'I've got to pick up a couple of British nationals on the way, but I'll see you there in a jiffy, no probs.' He was trying to sound convincing. The dubious tone did register with Kayte, but before she could fully assimilate what the hesitation meant she was momentarily distracted and on her way, heading through the deserted town, still half asleep.

As the pocket convoy rumbled over uneven roads, Kayte could see a vague mist lingering in odd patches, like above buildings and only shrouding certain trees. The buses bumped along, splashing through puddles that hid potholes. The streets followed the shape of what were once sand dunes, wiggling in no great hurry to be anywhere. And then they were out on the new road, the tarmac steaming in the morning heat. They moved smoothly forward, towards the rising sun, glowing a strawberry colour on the horizon in front. The calm ocean flickered pink behind dark rows of palm trees on the coastline beside the carriageway. The only human life Kayte saw was a man towing a wooden wheelbarrow filled with three small children. They sped ahead in tense silence on the empty highway. Kayte felt dizzy, as if she had vertigo.

Before long, the vehicles pulled up in front of the old airport terminal to be met by more US troopers, who looked identical to the ones they'd left back at the hotel. They all wore the same army fatigues and carried the same weapons. They were even the same shape and size too, each with matching square chins. They obviously worked out on similar equipment as they had identically wide, chiselled shoulders and over-muscled arms. Kayte thought everything about them was square, even the way they talked; nothing rounded or pleasant.

When Papa Jon came back with two large trolleys, Kayte asked him earnestly, 'Did you see Steve inside, is he here?'

'Sadly I did not, Miss Kayte. But he is coming now for sure,' he replied in his ever optimistic tone.

'Oh sh-t,' she muttered to herself, feeling pangs of anxiety creeping in again.

Soon they were all saying fond farewells to Papa Jon who shook their hands warmly, nodding his head furiously.

'OK, folks, follow me,' said one of the GI's harshly.

He led them into the grubby old building where, to all their obvious relief, they could see the aircraft which would take them home out on the airstrip, waiting.

'OK, halt right here,' he snapped. 'Get in line and walk slowly past me with your passports out, one at a time, real orderly.'

He looked at the passport nearest to him, which was one of the journalist's, and waved her through the door and out onto the airfield. There were only four more soldiers in the building, no baggage handlers or airport staff. It was all empty apart from the dozen in the group shuffling in line through the ill-lit hall. When Kayte reached the GI, fumbling with her passport, she said feebly yet assertively, 'I'm going to wait here. My boyfriend is on his way. He's being brought out to the airport separately.'

'Everyone here is going to board the aircraft ma'am. There are more personnel arriving, and they'll join you on the aircraft.'

She was gently pushed forward, still in a daze.

'But, but …' Her words faded into hot air as she stumbled out onto the runway with the others. She kept looking back frantically as she was ushered out towards the Airbus by more American soldiers. When they reached the plane, they all had to pass their luggage from the trolleys manually to a crew member, who was crouched in the hold.

Kayte called out blindly, in a sudden panic, 'Chuck, Chuck, please help me, please. I can't leave here without Steve. I just can't get on board without him.'

Chuck, who was nearby, put an arm around her shoulder. She calmed. He could see her weighing up her chances if she ran for it. He then saw her eyes narrow and become feline. She'd become a cat woman. 'Don't worry babe, it's gonna be fine,' he said. 'Let's just get up on the plane and we'll speak to the Captain, see what he can do.'

He encouraged her up the stairs as fast as he could, towards the aircraft door. Kayte had heard those words far too much recently: it's all going to be fine. It plainly wasn't fine at all. But she agreed to be led forward slowly, one step at a time and reluctantly boarded. Kayte, obviously distressed, was helped to a seat near the entrance by their Australian stewardess.

'I can't leave without Steve,' she kept saying. 'Please, please, get hold of Alistair Fortesque, from the British consulate, he knows.'

'Hey ma'am, please speak to the Captain, would you?' Chuck interjected positively, 'and find out if he knows which passengers are still due to board.'

'Yes, of course I will, sir. I know more passengers are due shortly. What's the passenger's name?'

'Steven Thompson,' Kayte croaked.

'OK my dear, you get comfortable here and I'll be back in a moment.'

More passengers did arrive and two business men sat down

in the seats on the other side of the aisle from Kayte. She'd been purposefully seated to look away from the terminal and staircase, so whenever anyone stepped into the main cabin, Kayte had to crane around and peer up. One such arrival was Sonia from the beach bar, who could see Kayte was in an agitated state. She replaced Chuck and sat down next to her. She'd heard the full story from Kirk about Steve and Jim being caught snooping up at Roger's beach house when she'd got back from town two days ago, along with the violent scene that ensued. But when Kayte told her what had happened the previous evening, she just couldn't believe it; that they had not learnt from the experience, and had actually gone and done something similar again the following day, was unbelievable.

'Hey Kayte, I'm really sorry for you, but those two, I could tell were going to get in trouble. I told you , ya. All that drinking. You guys, I don't think, really understood the sort of place this is here. I tried to tell you and them. It's not a holiday place here yet,' she said, in her no nonsense manner. 'Africa is dangerous, full stop, ya. You can't muck about. Danger is around every corner and you have to be careful. Hey look I am sorry Kayte, I really am, but I don't have sympathy for them, they were warned.'

Kayte looked at Sonia with googly eyes. The German put her arm around her new friend. 'I know, Sonia,' Kayte admitted. 'But however furious I am with him, I can't leave without him. I can't keep worrying about him. If I leave him here, all I'll do is worry about him, and feel guilty myself. And I'm sick to death of worrying about him.'

Everyone on the plane, passengers and crew alike were displaying various degrees of anxiety, some better than others. They just wanted to get airborne, off the island, after all, they were, in effect, being evacuated from a war zone. Sonia carried on talking, partly to calm her own nerves and, although Kayte was glum, she was relieved to have a fellow girl to be with after being alone or in the strictly male company she'd had over the past twelve hours. She did manage to laugh at one point, saying with conviction and between tears, 'look the guy's an asshole. If he thinks he's having a hard time with them, he'd better just wait till I get my hands on him!'

She even managed to come out of herself and ask Sonia how Kidd's beach was after the storm, as the minutes dragged by.

'Well, after you guys left the other evening and I got back from town we could see a change in the weather coming in. Big black clouds appeared from nowhere, we saw them on the horizon, this is what it is like. So we rushed to pack up the bar as best we could and hoped and prayed and stayed in our lodge during the storm. It was a short one, sometimes they last three days, but it was savage, maybe even an anticyclone. And all that rain, my God, it was incredible. It just rushed off everywhere. Big rivers all over the place in a moment, coming down from the hotel above into the lagoon which came up about three feet and sunk a couple of small boats.'

'Oh, my God.'

'Luckily the bar itself was OK, but much of the hotel garden is a swamp, it's a real mess. Many trees are down and even some of the sand dunes have moved,' Sonia said, obviously having had a worrying 36 hours herself. Kayte pictured the wonderful paradise, that was Kidd's beach, ravaged and torn by the storm. She envisaged Roger's pleasure palace windswept and empty; only the French doors open and the long net curtains she remembered, frayed and swirling madly in the wind. All lit in the unhealthy green light she'd seen from her hotel room balcony.

'We didn't know about the riots at all until some of the workmen came in yesterday,' Sonia continued, 'and this takeover or whatever by the Americans, we didn't have a clue about until Roger himself called us late last night and told us about this flight. He said it was up to us.'

'How was he? How did he sound?' Kayte said, quickly turning to face Sonia.

'He was fine, ya, cool as ever.'

'Oh good, that's good. Go on.'

'Ya, well, Kirk and I talked and talked about what to do. In the end Kirk drove me here this morning. He will stay,' she said, 'all seems quiet out there.'

'Yes, it does. Very peaceful.'

'We hope, now that the Americans have arrived and Roger and his gang are leaving, the place will actually be much better, but we don't know who is going to finish the hotel and pay for everything. So we just have to take it day by day.'

They had decided that Kirk would stay and protect what they had at Kidd's beach. If things got really bad he would join her in Nairobi, where Sonia was going to stay with some friends until the situation settled in St Martin.

It was nearly six o'clock and, with the whining engine switched on and the crew getting ready for takeoff, Kayte's anxiety levels escalated to all new levels. She couldn't leave Steve here, however she felt about him. She just couldn't. They had come together and they would leave together. She'd never forgive herself if she left without him. The tension and violence she'd experienced over the past two days had rocketed her powers of imagination to dizzying heights, which didn't help. She pictured him being dragged through the streets like a trophy by savage locals. Or she envisaged him being interrogated by brutal soldiers as they beat and tortured him, tied to a chair in some sweaty dungeon. His screams and cries for help stifled by a gag. His clothes torn and blood running from whip marks. And then his head would slump forward as he passed out. *Stop it, Kayte!* she yelled to herself. Her dark eyes grew misty, a faraway light in them.

She stood up, stepped over Sonia and then dashed towards the flight deck crying out, 'Where's the Captain. Where's the Captain?'

When she reached the locked door separating the passenger aisle from the cockpit she banged on it with both fists distressingly. Everyone in the stuffy aircraft fidgeted in empathy. Panic's contagion filled the compartment.

Kayte turned around crying and pleading with the airhostess, who was pulling her back. 'You said you'd find out what was happening and you've done nothing,' she yelled. 'We were guests in this country. We can't leave without him, we can't … we can't.'

'Madam, please calm down, you must,' the stewardess implored. Sonia came up quickly to help. 'Hold her here please, madam, and I'll see what the Captain says.'

As she knocked on the Captain's dividing door Sonia ushered Kayte back up the aisle. When they passed the galley kitchen, Sonia stopped and poured Kayte a glass of water and ordered her to, 'Drink zis now.'

As Kayte gulped down the water obediently, the stewardess reappeared looking long-faced and said, 'Follow me.'

She led them further down the aisle, stopping at the main door where she pulled two levers down. The door hydraulically popped up and opened. After their eyes adjusted to the brightness, they saw a Land Rover appearing through a layer of mist or heat haze on the tarmac and approach the aircraft like something out of a mirage.

It pulled up below with a jolt and, from the front seat, out jumped Alistair Fortesque. He waved briefly up at Kayte as he rushed around to the passenger door, opened it and pulled out the dead weight that was Steve. The moment Kayte recognised his arm, leg and shorts she made a bid to run down, but the stewardess's arm shot out and she ordered in a maternally strict tone, 'Stay right here, dear, don't go down.'

Soon the two men were lumbering up the stairs arm-in-arm. Struggling, Alistair heaved Steve up with a lot more difficulty than Chuck had with Kayte. Steve's head was drooped down, one hand was on the rail and his other arm draped over Alistair's shoulder, as they slowly made their way onto the aircraft.

'Steve, Steve, it's me. Are you OK?' Kayte said, trying to wake him up as she took his free arm and helped him towards their seats. He glumly lifted his head and looked around. His eyes were bruised and swollen. He had a thick lip. There were various cuts and scratches on his face, hands and legs. He looked exactly like what she had visualised moments before.

'I'm OK, I'm fine, leave me alone. I'm just really tired,' he said, spluttering though blubbering lips.

'Is anything broken, Steve? Talk to me,'

He seemed to come round, momentarily, his head lolling, as if he'd done ten rounds in a boxing ring. He collapsed onto a seat and stared blankly up at her. 'No, I'm OK. I told you, I'm fine,' he blurted, defiantly.

'Are you sure Steve?'

And then cheers drowned her out.

'Hey, hey, Stevie boy. The hero returns,' Chuck shouted out. 'Yeh, haw!' Applause.

He flopped down awkwardly across three seats, the arm rests up. Kayte straightened, the relief was exhausting. Embarrassed, she looked across at Alistair Fortesque who was looking ashen himself. In fact most of the passengers had paled, every one impatient to get high up in the sky.

'Oh thank you Alistair, thank you,' Kayte said. She hugged him in the cramped gangway, repeating, 'thank you, I'm so very sorry.' Somebody had to apologise for Steve, he obviously wasn't going to.

The British consul managed to summon his last reserves of humour and smiled saying, 'It's all part of the service my dear, all part of the service,' in his best stiff upper lipness. He'd driven his old Land Rover as fast as it would go to Roger MacGill's barracks and stood on the edge of the parade ground, demanding Roger came out. He insisted on Steve's immediate release. Roger, to his credit, gave up willingly. Jim, he'd said, would be dealt with later.

At that, a few wolf whistles and further cheering came from the kiting group joyous to be witnessing the final scene of their eventful time on the Martinez Islands.

'Yes, sirree, that's our man!' Chuck yelled.

Alistair Fortesque backed down the aisle and reversed out

of the aircraft waving his hand and bowing in self depreciation. He went down the stairs thoroughly embarrassed, yet amused, hearing hoopla as he went.

'Three cheers for Fortesque! Hip, hip, hooray!'

No one seemed to be asking, or caring about Jim's whereabouts.

'Cabin crew, prepare for take off.' The Captain's voice buzzed through the intercom. 'Locker's down and seat belts fastened.'

The stewardess swept the aisle, clicking down the overhead lockers and making sure everyone was fastened up. She opted to ignore Steve who was out for the count, but did prop his head up with a couple of pillows and put two small blankets over him.

Kayte looked across at him, snoring as the plane taxied the runway. His swollen top lip vibrated as he exhaled. Any concern Kayte had displayed a few minutes before vanished, replaced with a combination of hatred and disgust. He looked so pathetic. She was thoroughly ashamed to be in any way associated with him. Her lumbering, arrogant caddy, lying oblivious to life opposite her had been a major contributor in ruining, not just her trip and her chances of beating her record and making a huge lump of money, but he'd mucked up the whole group's trip. He'd added to their worries. He'd made their trip worse. She couldn't believe that he'd got on the plane and not asked how she was or made any noises that he was pleased to see her. She thought people grew out of being selfish. Her grandmother had warned her of the destructive nature of hating another person, so she worked hard to steer away from entertaining that particular emotion, but she was close to it. The feeling of wanting to grab one of the pillows and suffocate him swept over her. She turned and looked out of the window. All respect, let alone affection, vaporised with the ferocious roar of engines as the plane charged up the runway, thrust skyward and became airborne.

Chapter Twenty-One
Paradise Found

As the plane's wheels started to grind into the hold, a loud cheer of relief went up, accompanied by some more, 'yee- haws', from the American contingent. The mood lifted. The delight of leaving such a stressful environment in one piece was palpable. The plane banked low around St Martin and Kayte could see evidence of the town coming to life for another day. Cars were moving on the roads and she could see a new seaborne town had arrived overnight. A big, grey warship was moored in the horseshoe shaped bay, and landing craft were heading towards the golden beach. She could see frantic activity on deck and twirling helicopter rotor blades flashed in the sunlight.

The aircraft soared upwards, away from paradise and towards the rising sun, as Prince Jaffa's broadcast was being aired to a jubilant nation below. She could see the protective frothing white rings around the islands disappear and merge into a vapour trail. Soon the mosaic of small islands, which had heralded her arrival to a tropical ideal just a few days before, came in and out of view as the plane banked and jigged on the thermals. The islands now clearly resembled scattered pieces of a jigsaw puzzle. Kayte wondered if she could just push them all together they may form some sort of a complete picture. All the little pieces in life, like the painter filling gaps on the Splendid, go into making a whole, a voice inside her said.

She then turned back in and, glancing across the aisle at Steve, thought of Roger left abandoned on the island.

The flight rapidly became humdrum, as if they were on an ordinary trip. Everyone settled, seatbelt signs pinged off and drinks were served from a trolley. The two suited business men in front of Kayte relaxed, their voices growing louder with every swig of the large pink gins they'd ordered for breakfast. Kayte listened in.

'There's no such thing as a good coup old boy, only bad or worse coups. Any military man who takes over a country, whatever their intentions are to begin with, ends up as a tyrant or at the very least a megalomaniac, it's doomed to failure,' said one of the men, laughing. 'Poor old Roger MacGill. He didn't have a chance in hell of succeeding back there. Every army officer thinks politics is easy; you just bark the correct orders and things happen. Which is a major mistake. Even ruddy Wellington failed miserably as a result of that approach. And changing his name to Omar, what a joke! What on earth did he think he was doing, God only knows.' More laughter.

'He's a bloody decent chap though, a true gent,' the other said. 'He's the sort of guy who wouldn't even look at his friend's wife.'

'Yes, yes, that aside, the truth is, successful governments succeed only if they allow decisions to be made by the people they affect, not through simply issuing orders willy-nilly,' his neighbour continued, 'that's what armies need but not populations. Strange affair. I think he thought he could just buy the islands. I bet he's spent thirty or forty million quid here in the past year or so.'

'At least. Any idea where all that dosh came from?'

'Well, I heard stories. I don't know how true they are but I do know boys like him do get incredibly well paid. He was the go to man if you had a security problem in Africa. He put or kept various tin pot dictators in power and no doubt got mining concessions thrown into the deal, that sort of thing. I heard he setup a couple of private armies for Arab sheikhs too. Anyway, poor bugger, I don't suppose he'll see a penny back - all down the old swanny. All I can say is, I'm just happy to be out of cloud coup, coup land!'

They both laughed. Kayte smiled. She instantly felt pleasantly relaxed and calm, lulled by the drone of the engines and English humour. She closed her eyes and drifted off into a half-sleep as the aeroplane sped through African skies.

She was in a guerrilla raiding party, crossing a desolate border with local tribesmen, Indians. She shot a few people and then crossed back over the boundary, but there was now a desperate hunt on to find her. She'd been seen taking photos of herself and the dead. The assailants chased her as she haired across the barren landscape. They pursued her so relentlessly that she eventually collapsed, worn out, run to exhaustion like an Oryx by Kalahari bushmen. She lay, prone, at peace, waiting for the coup de grâce; but it never came. Kayte stirred awake, feeling blissfully alive, to the reverse thrust of the aeroplane touching down and landing in Nairobi.

Steve was still fast asleep, even after the plane had come to a complete stop, so Kayte had to shake him vigorously to get any response at all.

'Hngh, where are we?' he eventually grunted. Sitting up, he looked around like a dopey camel lost in the desert. His swollen lip flapped comically.

Kayte just looked at him, appalled to be connected with him. No tenderness or sympathy had returned; that had gone for good. Even feelings of anger towards him had vanished too. She simply didn't care about him anymore. Apathy reigned supreme. The power nap had restored her faculties. And the realisation that she was back in control of herself again was such a relief that she calmly and coolly ordered him to just, 'Come on,' as she eased her way out of the plane, nodding a final goodbye to the sympathetic and smiling stewardess.

She didn't help Steve at all as he followed her lamely through the airport, trailing in her wake. He shuffled and limped through the motions as she strode out with purpose. She took control of getting trolleys, collecting their luggage and finding a porter to help them across to the international terminal. All the while, Steve tagged along, unable to offer any support or assistance whatsoever.

She said fond farewells to Chuck and the group, who were off to a local hotel to wait 12 hours for their flight back to the USA. Then said farewell to Sonia too.

'Wow, that was one hell of a ride, Kayte,' Chuck said, 'we could write a book about it.'

'The longest three days of my life, that's for sure!' she replied.

'So far, babe, so far.'

'Just a bloody shame we didn't break our records.'

'And get all that dough.' They both turned to Steve, their brow's clouding in unison.

'Exactly.'

'Oh, well it was a cool place to kite. We'll have a gas about this in no time.'

She hugged Sonia. 'It was great to meet you, I really hope the hotel works out and you're successful. It's a wicked place for kitesurfing, that's for sure.'

'Well, maybe you'll come and setup a kitesurf school, ya. When it all settles back down?'

'Yeah, right!' They both laughed.

When the departing group waved to Steve, lolling in the background, she could see them all desperately holding back laughter. Kayte was positive some of them even wanted to take a photograph of him. He stood, stooped over, all battered and bruised, his hair a mess, his eyes swollen and blackened, his t-shirt dirty and torn, the skin on his arms scratched, and dirt covered his shorts and shoes. He was a mess. Most of the passengers in the airport who saw him, including children, pointed. It was pitiful.

'Steve, get in the toilet and clean yourself up, you look like a tramp.'

She stood alone waiting for him to come out, staring glumly forward. If you looked closely, you'd notice her eyes definitely mist, like milky cataracts, as the iron curtain was finally drawn across their relationship. In the stuffy closeness of an African airport lounge, Kayte finally understood that she could have dealt with all the little faults in isolation, but concertinaed as they had, they'd all finally added up to one insurmountable problem. It was a straw that broke the camel's back moment. A darkness descended, their light went out. Extinguished. *Plink*. She knew there was no respect or sensitivity left for him. Here, in the humid morning, having had very little sleep, and importantly, able to be objective away from home, Kayte blinked and reached her quantum of solace, her rock bottom; she simply felt desperately alone with Steve.

When he eventually appeared, they silently followed the porter. Although it was only nine o'clock in the morning, the heat was already intense - a stagnant, stale heat which had condensed in the stifling, airless terminal. Their porter, dressed like a beacon in a bright orange suit, as if he'd come straight from Guantanamo Bay, led them nimbly through the crowds and around piles of luggage and bundles to their check-in desk. It was surprisingly quiet considering the number of people squeezed into every available floor space. So calm in fact, Kayte could even hear the rattle of ineffectual old fans rotating dangerously high above them.

Checked-in they went through to the departure lounge. Kayte left Steve with their baggage. Going off on her own she took her time to browse the Duty Free shop and had something to eat. She already felt the liberty she deserved. She bought some antiseptic cream for Steve and got a load of Kenyan shillings to phone her mother from a booth.

'Hi mum, it's me. Can you hear me?'
'Yes, darling. It's a bad line though.'
'We're on our way back. We're in Nairobi.'
'Already! Are you alright?'

'Yes, fine, I'll tell you all about it when I get back. Please call a taxi to meet us at Heathrow, the plane get's in at nine forty tonight. I'll give you the flight number. Have you got a pen handy?'

Call home done, she went back to Steve with a coffee. When she saw he'd revived slightly, she asked, 'So, Steve, what the hell happened?'

Lisping and blubbering through swollen lips, he started:

'Jim insisted we go for another drink when the hotel bar shut.'

'Insisted, did he?'

'Anyway, whatever Kayte,' he blithered, 'there were these two local guys with us who said they knew of a place that'd be open. So off we went, in a cab. It wasn't far. The minute we got there, the two guys left and Jim was constantly getting up and going outside, in and out of the loo. That's right. F-k knows what he was doing. Like he was on Charlie or something. Although I was pissed, I thought it odd, he just couldn't sit still.' As Steve talked he became more animated. 'Anyway, the next thing I know, a bunch of those mercenary guys burst in. One of them recognised us from the beach the day before, so they laid into us. They found a satellite phone on Jim that made them freak out so they started to batter us right there in the bar. Then they dragged us out and took us to some sort of army base I think, or police station, I'm not sure.' He paused and looked around shiftily. 'That was the last I saw or heard of Jim. They started asking me all these questions, interrogating me about what I was doing there, who I worked for and all that sort of crap; and they belted me. Anyway after a bit they just put me in a cell and left me there. I don't know what happened after that, I think they may have had another go at me.'

'And you didn't see Jim again?'

'No, no, I didn't,' he stammered. 'I don't know what happened to him.'

'And Roger, was he there?' Kayte enquired.

'Yes, he was actually,' he replied, brightening up. 'I don't know what time it was but he stopped them interrogating me. Then I was untied, given a sleeping bag and some food and I just crashed. The next thing I knew, I was being woken up and taken outside. It was just getting light and there was that Alistair chap, boy was I pleased to see him. We got in his landie and he drove like a bat out of hell to the airport, and that was it.'

'And you didn't see him again?'

'Who Jim?'

'No, Roger.'

'I did actually or I think I did.' Steve shuddered.

'Are you OK?'

'Yeah, yeah, I'm fine,' Steve continued, and suddenly lit up, 'I remember, yeah that's right, he was standing outside when they brought me out of my cell. He just stood there, that's right, and I thought *this is all about him.*'

'What do you mean?'

'I dunno, but the guy's deep, very deep.'

'What do you mean "deep", Steve?' She'd never heard any one use that word to describe anyone before.

'I don't know, I don't know what it is about him, he's just got one hell of an aura, that's all.'

'Oh, right, I see,' she said, a bit bemused. 'And Jim?'

Steve's eyes shifted and his head slunk down, he'd deflated.

She repeated. 'And what of Jim, Steve?'

'Ah, hum, hmm, I dunno.' He mumbled. 'As I said I didn't see him again after we were taken from the bar.'

Kayte didn't bother even mentioning the distress she'd been through on his behalf the night before, let alone disclose any strings she may have pulled or the efforts she'd made to help in his release. He didn't ask, or even make an attempt at an apology. Kayte didn't give a damn, she didn't want his thanks or any whiff of appreciation from him anyway or, more importantly, any sort of excuses as she'd be pressured to forgive him and that, most definitely, wasn't going to happen. In any case, she knew he'd be bragging and distorting the story in a day or two, bullshitting to his mates down at The Osborne View, so what was the point. All about Roger, she thought. No Steve, it's all about you, you muppet.

Their flight home took off on time. As the aircraft lifted above Nairobi, humanity's third world urban sprawl came rudely into view. From height, the major and minor roads all looked like a crisscrossing mess of twisted piping in one endless derelict industrial plant. The plane then flew over a vast expanse of featureless shanty towns. The brown coloured tin roofs below were either so rusty or completely covered in layers of dust that, from this overhead viewpoint, the shacks seemed to merge seamlessly with the sand coloured ground around them. It was only the etched paths and people walking, and the bright coloured headdresses surrounding them, that made the houses visible at all.

Kaye turned to see Steve wince, then open his tub of painkillers.

'Are you OK?'

'No, hon, I'm not,' he admitted. *Don't hon me*, she thought. 'Everything's killing me. My back, my foot, the lot. And these are my last two painkillers.'

'Here, take this,' she said, flinging him a sleeping pill she'd intended on taking herself. *Diddums.*

Chapter Twenty-Two
Homeward Bound

Kayte turned her back on Steve and stared out of the aeroplane's window. Carpeted below, hour after hour, lay the vast Sahara desert. It looked like a tan coloured ocean, frozen in time. The expanse of rolling sand dunes resembled perfectly shaped waves, cascading over a vast unmoving sea. She imagined that, in the future, a hover board could be invented to kitesurf the deserts. Instead of ramping off water waves people, in future, will be ramping the wavy sand dunes. Unseen by Kayte were tiny pin pricks on the desert floor below, nomadic caravans, ships of the desert, that were plying their slow and steady timeless trade across the inhospitable landscape, just as they had done for millennia and will do for millennia to come.

They then went over the Mediterranean Sea and into the bright, artificial lights of Europe as the sun set on Africa. France looked like a jewelled pattern, an enamelled mosaic, thought Kayte as she flew over it, but Britain seemed to have disappeared all together by the time they got there. Beyond Europe's coast, The Channel was nothing but an ocean of haze. She thought it odd that the flight's route, plotted on the rear of the seat in front of her, was missing the familiar shape of that very individual island she called home. Supposing that island had never existed: how different the history of the world would have been? Who else would have colonised India, America, Australia or Kenya? It was immaterial, she supposed.

They dropped into the ocean of cloud and found Britain again. It looked like a very muddy, ordinary place to have changed the history of the world. A steady drizzle soaked the land. Lights were on in all the buildings. Kayte stared at the twinkling human habitation below. The English villages and towns looked like burning volcanic deposits splattered onto the dark earth's crust, glowing orange in the neon-lit night. The busy cities however, from this height, looked like monstrous heaving lava flows on the move, and the traffic laden roads, glimmering rivers of ochre, pulsated like veins out in all directions.

The plane landed on time, the baggage arrived quickly and waiting with a cardboard sign was their taxi driver.

'We're going straight to hospital, Steve.'

Two hours later, they were sitting in the waiting room of the Accident and Emergency department at their local hospital, St Mary's, in Portsmouth, with all of Kayte's kiting equipment and their luggage piled around them. His foot had swollen up and had blackened badly.

Kayte phoned her mum. 'It's me again.'

'Oh, sweetie, hi,' Jill said all happy, and then lowered her voice. 'Two B&B'ers have just arrived. I'm settling them in.'

'It's a bit late, isn't it, mum?'

'Yes, I know. Work or something. Let's speak in the morning. All OK with you?'

'Yeah, fine. No probs. Sleep well, love you.'

Finally Steve was called into the doctor's surgery, having had x-rays as soon as they'd arrived. 'You've definitely torn some ligaments, and perhaps fractured your metatarsal, Mr Thompson,' he was informed. 'You're going to be out of action for a good few days, I'm afraid.'

'Doctor, can I have a word with you?' Kayte asked when Steve was wheeled off by a nurse.

'Of course.'

Kayte told the doctor what had happened to them, where

they'd arrived from and Steve's medical history, particularly about breaking his back.

'Please doctor, admit him overnight. I can't manage.'

'I understand. First, let me just find out if we've got a bed available.'

Steve kicked up a bit of a fuss, insisting he wanted to go home and that he was fine.

'Steve, don't be stupid. How are you going to get up to the flat? And you're going to have to come back in the morning anyway.'

Kayte, the doctor and the nurses persuaded him to just relax and spend the night there for observation.

'I'll come back tomorrow,' Kayte said. No farewell kiss.

She called a cab, eventually getting back to the apartment at 1am and, having heaved all her kit upstairs, crashed out immediately, fully clothed.

She woke early and although she was a little woozy with jet lag, she was elated to be back. Not in the scuzzy flat but in Lee-on-the-Solent, at home.

She didn't have a huge amount of belongings, but what she did have she began to pack up feverishly. When she went into the kitchen she stopped for a moment and looked out through the salt smeared window. There it was: the grey, grubby familiar Solent shrouded in it's dreary dimness. Today however, with contented eyes, it felt cosy and safe, non aggressive and peaceful. Little waves slapped and clapped the shore below with no great drama. Simply gentle motions, more like ripples, cascading onto the familiar shingle beach. Even the pebbles rasping sounded like applause today. She just wanted to hug it, wrap herself up in its snug folds and pull it up over her like a duvet.

'Morning, mum, it's moi,' said Kayte into her phone.

'Darling, you're up early. I thought you'd be having a lie-in.'

'Hey, look mum, sorry, but can I come and stay for a few days?'

'Of course, sweetie, what's happened?'

'I'll tell you all about it. I'll be there in an hour.'

'The kettle's on.'

She called yet another cab, and while she waited she did three runs back down with her kit and bags full of belongings. All she cared about was her kiting equipment. Slamming doors, she jumped in the taxi and left.

Jill was utterly gobsmacked to hear Kayte's story. She couldn't believe her daughter had been through such an ordeal unbeknown to her. She had pottered around normally, completely oblivious to what Kayte was going through. She'd pictured Kayte having a wonderful time, kiting in paradise, not wanting to come home.

'I just don't believe it, darling. I can't believe you've been through all that, I'm flabbergasted. Thank God you're OK,' she exclaimed.

'I know, mum, nor do I. I've only been gone five days, it seems like a lifetime.'

It took an hour and a half to tell and, three cups of tea later, after two crying sessions, Kayte got back to where she was. Back in her home kitchen, sitting around the big wooden table with pots and pans on the rack above, the Aga breathing warmth. It was cathartic therapy for Kayte to rewind and live through the ordeal in its entirety. She didn't miss a thing, right back to the bad vibes on arrival; the mercenaries at the airport and the poor dog getting run over the moment they'd arrived on the island. Jill kept insisting she go back and repeat things, to get it clear in her mind, so that the past few days fitted into some sort of order. They hugged a lot.

'Have you spoken to you're father?'

'No. I even forgot to tell him I was even going.'

'My God, if only I'd known,' Jill said, shaking her head.

'What, mum? What would you have done, come out waving your dish cloth?' They laughed.

'Actually, thank God, I didn't know,' she exclaimed, and threw the cloth at her daughter. 'So, what's going to happen with Steve?'

'I don't know, and I don't care. That's it, finito, it's over. I'm going to go to the hospital and tell him now. He's on his own. You wouldn't give me a lift would you? I've spent a fortune on cabs, and I'm exhausted; I can't cope with buses and ferries today.'

'Come on then, my little hero. Strike while the iron's hot.' Jill wasn't going to deter her daughter, no way.

Half an hour later they pulled up outside the hospital.

'You go in, I'll just pop in to Tesco's. Buzz me when you're done and I'll be straight back,' Jill said, leaning forward, 'Kiss?'

Kayte found the ward, walked up to Steve's bed and closed the curtain around them. He was sitting up in hospital pyjamas, with the top button done up, and was sipping tea through a straw.

'I'm leaving, Steve.'

He looked up casually. 'What d'you mean?'

'I'm splitting up with you.'

All he said was, 'Oh.' Then he turned his head away, and blankly looked out of the window. 'Don't tell anyone will you?'

'What *do you* mean?'

'Well, about what happened.'

She hesitated a moment while what he said sank in. 'Oh, I see, right,' she said. 'You mean will I talk about it in The Osborne?'

He turned back to her. They'd never got to the truth about what really happened and never would. Their eyes locked. It was a laser beam, clinical look; when two pairs of eyes meet, one pair holds and the other pair flees. Her stare out penetrated his, her eyes said it all: I'm through with you. And the moment he saw that, he knew any respect she may have had for him had spiralled into contempt. He turned away again, not physically but mentally. He could become nasty she thought. When the shabby truth is exposed, when someone's true colours are proved dim, and their moral fibre weak, even friendship becomes impossible.

In this case, Steve's shame, underpinned by his arrogance, was simply a blend of traits impossible to stand any longer. To Kayte, the foundations of his character had curdled.

'What am I going to do? I can't look after myself,' he whined.

She held her hand up towards his face, palm outstretched, said nothing, then turned and walked away. She pushed between the curtains and strode through the sterile ward.

'Kayte, Kayte, come back …'

She needed outside badly. The cold, fresh air. When she got to it, it gave her just enough strength to call her mum, who arrived immediately, as if on cue. She was pulsing on adrenalin.

'It's done, mum. I've done it,' she panted.

Kayte was asleep when they pulled up outside their home. Jill poured her a luxurious bath, unpacked some of Kayte's clothes and, while her daughter soaked, she got her old room ready. Kayte slept all that afternoon and curled up on the sofa that evening, still in her pyjamas, eating marshmallows and watching comfort telly. Purrfect.

The next morning she phoned Lisa, her best friend.

'Hey, Leese, it's me, I'm back.'

'Already?'

'You won't believe it, I've got so much to tell you. Come over to mum's.'

'You're at your mum's, why?'

'I'll tell you when I see you.'

'I'm in town, why don't you come for a coffee here?'

'Yes, sure, sorry hon. I forgot to ask, how are you?'

'I'm fine, meet me in Tiff's in an hour, OK?'

The two old friends sat by the window of their local café, tea room for an hour … in their seat; they'd been using Tiffin's for the past ten years.

'I don't believe you've done it, Kayte, I really don't. That's definitely the silver lining to the whole nightmare trip, he's the biggest w-ker I've ever met. Such an arrogant tosser. Sorry about my French, I just can't explain loud enough how the past few years, ever since you've been with him, have been awful. You lost your spark. To be honest, I'm as relieved as you must be. You're actually looking like your old self already Kayte, your eyes look different. The same as they used to when we were young. Since you've been with that guy, they've looked sad, as if you'd misted over. You've gone back to the old Kayte I know. You look great.'

'Oh, thanks sweetheart. I do feel young again, funnily enough. Maybe I was liberated. I know Steve ground me down. I was stuck. And yes, although the trip was such a rollercoaster in itself, so much happened, the whole experience gave me the strength and confidence to leave. If we hadn't gone, I couldn't have done it. I'm sure of that. I saw his true colours out there.'

'And they were dim, I'm sure. It's true. Well done. Anyway, looking to the future, what are you going to do now?'

'Well, I've still got money left from the attendance fee, about three grand.'

'Wow, fantastic. That's a good start, and?'

'Well, I don't know if I mentioned it, but I've been in touch with a group of kiters for about two months now, they are setting up a school in Corfu.'

'No.'

'Well, they've been hassling me for all sorts of free information about this and that, which was bugging me. And blow me, I got an email from them while I was away, which I opened yesterday, and now they've invited me over to help them. There's not much money in it but, hey, I thought it may be good for a few weeks or a month. What do you think?'

'Ab fab, go for it Kayte. Don't hesitate. Do it now.'

'Hungh, OK, I will then. Yes, boss,' Kayte said, saluting. 'I'll reply today and say I'm coming. May as well.'

'Sorted. Get on a plane as soon as poss. Go for it,' Lisa said, emphatically. 'And Kayte?'

'Yes.'

'What about this Roger chap? I detected a little twinkle in your eye whenever you mentioned him. I bet he's old though, isn't he?'

'I guess he is. Why do you say that? He must be in his forties.'

'Forties! Why the hell do you always go for older men?

They're getting older and older.'

'I dunno,' Kayte said, sheepishly. 'Well, guys our age seem so immature. Anyway I don't really fancy him. He's not right for me.'

'No, Kayte, you know exactly why: you've got a father- figure fixation, girl. Get over it.'

'What d'you mean?'

'Come on Kayte, you know you have. Let's not get into all that, we've been there before.'

'No, come on Lisa, what do you mean?'

'You know exactly what I mean, Kayte.'

'Because mum and dad split up.'

'Yes. Of course it is. Anyway forget it. Tell me about this Roger chap.'

'Well, he's actually called Roger Mc something or another. And can you believe it, he was brought up in Stokes Bay.'

'Stokes Bay! Bit bizarre. What's he like?'

'We're not suited Lisa. Just so you know. I know we're not suited.'

'What? Just an infatuation.'

'Yeah, probably,' Kayte said dreamily, 'it isn't just his good looks as such, or his beautiful voice or clothes or whatever … it's just it. He's got "It"', she exclaimed.

'Has what?' Lisa replied, slightly baffled. She'd never heard "It" as a description for someone.

'I dunno, he's just right on the pulse. He's sort of got a vibe a mile wide. You can … you know, feel him coming, oozing life. He's unforgettable. The sort of person who'd walk past you in the street once and you'd never forget him. Whereas most people, you can see them day in and day out but they pass right through. So many people pass you by, year after year. I mean look out the window.' A pavement of old folk, pushing shopping trolleys in drab clothing shuffled past. 'And it's only a few that make you stop. He's one of them. D'you know what I mean?'

'Mmm, yeah, I do. I guess. Larger than life?'

'Exactly. The sort of people that stick in your mind and fire your imagination.' Kayte turned and looked out at the stream of aged shoppers on the small town High Street outside. 'He even asked me if I'd have a look at his house on Marine Parade. Check it's alright.'

'Must be nice.'

'The guy's loaded.' She turned back to her friend.

'Sorry Lees, I haven't asked about you. So caught up in my own world. How've you been?'

'I'm OK, just really exhausted. The baby's kicking all the time, keeping me up. He's so large he's pressing up against my bladder now. I'm up and down all night, literally every 15 minutes, nightmare.'

Kayte bent down and touched Lisa's swollen stomach tenderly. 'Not long to go now. You'd better get used to it, girl! It's only the start of it. It'll be the screaming next,' Kayte said, looking up smiling, and then continued, a little concerned, 'I guess that's normal, is it?'

'Yes, it is. It's nature's way of making me want to get him out,' Lisa sighed, rubbing her tummy.

'I keep telling you I really don't know why you've been in such a rush to grow old. But, seriously, if I go out to Corfu I won't be here for when the baby is born, d'you mind?'

'No I do not. I'll be happier the further away from Steve you are. And Kayte … that's sweet, but I've got my mum and everyone else here, I'll be fine. Just go.'

Chapter Twenty-Three
Home Sweet Home

Two days later Kayte woke up frustrated. It hadn't been windy enough to kitesurf so she decided to walk up to Stokes Bay, a mile up the road. Pulling her hoodie tight, she turned towards the beach and took the coastal path, skipping past long rows of green beach huts, still shuttered up for winter.

The sea spray, combined with a drizzle so fine it was almost a mist, filmed her face and salty droplets clung to her eyelashes. She passed lines of vicious looking wooden groins tapering down into the sea; placed to help stop the beach being washed away. These sea defences were grotesque at the best of times but now, in the grey bleakness and through her blurred vision, they made the beach look more like a fenced prison camp, defended against invasion. The noise of the monotonous waves, breaking on the shingle and then rasping in retreat, created a horribly abrasive racket today.

Head up and striding out boldly, in spite of the conditions, and still buoyed on her joy of being home, she reached Marine Parade in no time. Who cares what the weather's like, she said to herself defiantly, it's only a matter of putting on the right clothes. A month ago this scene was the pits for Kayte, as depressing as it could get.

She stood for a moment looking at number 33, Roger's house. She could tell it was his before she got there. It was the tired looking one, exposed rudely against all the fine houses on the beautiful white stuccoed Regency crescent. The others were clean and fresh, his was peeling and grubby; bits of plaster had even crumbled away from the lintels, exposing the grey concrete beneath. Whatever it's cosmetic appearance, which could be easily remedied, the fabric of number 33 was a magnificent four-storey townhouse all the same. A tad tired, Kayte thought, weather beaten, but nothing that a bit of love, she meant money, couldn't put right. *Oh, my God, there are light's on*, she squealed internally. She mentally crouched, all embarrassed and scuttled straight home.

The following morning Kayte peeped out of her mum's kitchen window and began yelping with delight; it was an almost perfect morning for a kitesurf.

The weather today, was far from being gloomy, it was sunny and bright, bringing in a clear north easterly side shore wind that ran parallel to the beach. The conditions were ideal for kiting. The northerly was going to make it cold, but within a few minutes of working the kite hard, Kayte knew she wouldn't feel the chill one bit.

Kayte wheeled her converted trolley, loaded with her equipment, along the high path to *her* beach. Before descending, she could see that a small group of fellow kiting fanatics were already up and riding the surf; their kites resembling a small air-borne flotilla of multi-coloured sails, arcing and diving above the sea-shore in front of her, streaking shadows across the glassy veneer.

The joyous sight made Kayte rush to join them. The water twinkled and shimmered before her like a million diamonds refracting on the sea's surface and she could still smell the crisp saltiness of a fresh dawn, lingering in the air. For Kayte this view was happiness, the kiting omens were good; fun was a dead certainty. It was one of those rare late March days when the sun was hot and the wind was cold, when it was summer in the light and winter in the shade.

She got frantically pumping as fast as she could, furiously jacking up and down. The vigorous action warmed her up quickly and she exhaled big plumes of steam far out into the freezing morning.

As she sped to setup she could see one or two kiters out there, busting some lovely moves and probably getting heights of about four meters off the fin carved waves, about as good as it would ever get on this beach. 'Get in,' she enthused under her breath as she checked all was ready.

Wet suit on, kite up, Kayte rushed towards the milk white churning shallows, hitting the water running, getting straight up and out amongst the others with the minimum of fuss. She was off, breaking through the surf, bashing through the waves, her thighs aching under the strain, legs pumping frantically up and down like a pair of pneumatic drills on the ploughed swell beneath the board. Big smile, her eyes now darted from kite to front and sides, searching for a sweet spot, a flat area of water to pop and release her rail, always searching for a ramp-like wave to jump and fly off. The icy coldness in her face and the pace of the action, all combined to make Kayte's senses and limbs beat rapidly to a unified rhythm of pure adrenalin-fuelled joy. The blasting pinpricks of the freezing spray helped numb her perfectly on one cheek and rejuvenate her on the other. She pulled away from the shore, swinging and dipping her kite like a conductor orchestrating. She was jigging on water, she was that happy. It was a dance, a spiral dive, where she'd spin the kite down hard towards the water in a corkscrew and then pull out of the dive at the last moment, and then bash on.

As she described graceful arcs and swung out to sea, she didn't for one moment consider Steve, who was up at the pub preparing vegetables for the lunchtime shift. Whenever he hobbled out of the kitchen to the larders, he could glimpse the occasional flash of Kayte's neon kite dancing across the skyline.

'Are you OK, Steve?' his sous chef, Rich, asked, seeing his boss staring forlornly out to sea.

'Yeah, man, I'm fine,' he murmured, bailing out of his reverie. He pointed at Kayte's pink and black kite wiggling on the surf, 'I miss it like crazy though … it does my head in.'

'I'm sure, chef, but hey, we better be getting back to the veg, we've got loads of bookings in.'

'Yeah, right. The ol' veg eh, come on then, let's be having ya!' Steve joked keeping his chin up, and turned his back to the ocean and shuffled into his steaming kitchen.

Kayte, still a bit jetlagged, couldn't hack it for long. She'd spent her energy levels in short, vigorous bursts. She felt tired, so powered ashore. It was her arms. They'd noodled, big time.

She hadn't noticed the dark-haired man, sitting on a Hill Head bench looking down over the trees high above the beach to the still diamond-sparkling sea as she gathered up and deflated her kite. Packed up, she pushed her loaded trolley up the path towards level ground, head bowed under the strain.

'Here, let me give you a hand,' a vaguely familiar voice said, as she neared the top.

'My God, Roger!' she exclaimed, looking up.

As he took control of the trolley she collapsed forward, and with her hands on her knees, panted hard, gathering her breath.

'I thought I recognised your kite out there,' he said. 'I'll push.' As she followed, he turned. 'I don't suppose you expected to see me here.'

'Well, actually I did,' she replied, straightening up. 'Not right here exactly, but it did cross my mind that you may come back to Stokes Bay.'

'I had nowhere else to go,' he said smiling.

She looked at him. She didn't mention she'd been up to his house the day before and he didn't say he'd seen her scampering off. Here, in this light, minus the aura of power he held on the micro Indian Ocean Island, there was just a nice looking man in front of her. That was all. Fit, healthy and, yes tanned, but nothing that made her tremble. Just a pleasant looking, professional type bloke. A run of the mill small fish in Britain's big pond, not a biggie in the small one she'd met him in the week before. He was wearing boot cut jeans with brown suede ankle boots and a V-neck green cashmere jumper tied at the neck, no coat.

'It's such a lovely day, I thought I'd walk the coastal path and I was sure I recognised your kite out on the water. It looked as good as Kidd's out there.'

'Well, not quite that good,' she exclaimed, 'but not far off. Hill Head seems to catch the winds just right. It's a great spot. About as good as it gets for miles around.'

'I do love looking at it, I really must learn,' he said, smiling. 'Did you break your world record here?'

'No way, that was in Leucate in the South of France.'

'I'm so sorry you didn't better that record out on the island, Kayte. You got so close.'

'I know. Another couple of days and I may well have.' Then cheekily added, 'plus I missed out on that bonus which was an even bigger shame.' She heard Roger clear his throat.

'Anyway, Kayte, how about a nice cup of coffee? You look like you could do with warming up.'

'Yes, why not.'

They pushed the trolley across a car park on the ridge.

'I assume you got back in one piece,' he asked.

'Yes, it was fine.'

'That's good, and how's that boyfriend of yours getting on?'

'My ex boyfriend.'

'Oh. That's come to an end has it?'

'Yes, it has.'

'Is he OK though?'

'Yes, he's fine I think.' She looked across at Roger. 'Physically anyway, if that's what you mean?'

'Mmm, yes, I do.'

'And what of Jim, the journalist chap who was arrested with Steve breaking the curfew?'

'Oh him. He was OK. We released him when we left. I assume he's back here in UK.'

CHAPTER TWENTY-THREE

'That's good.'

They arrived at Tiffin's. 'Christ, I haven't been here for years, Kayte, decades actually,' Roger exclaimed. 'This place's been here for donkey's years; I used to come with my mother when I was a child.'

'I've been coming here since I was a kid too.'

Having ordered a cream slice, for old time's sake, and they'd settled at a table, Roger continued talking, 'So, what are you going to do now, Kayte, workwise I mean?'

'I'm not too sure about the long term, but some people I met are setting up a kiting school in Corfu. They've invited me out there to help get it going, so I'm thinking about joining them next week and giving a hand, but I'm not 100% sure. I haven't booked my ticket.'

'Sounds great, exciting. I don't suppose there's one here is there? I'm genuinely keen to learn. It'll do me good.'

'What a kite surfing school in Lee!' she yelled, as if he was joking.

'Yes.'

'No, there isn't.'

'Oh, that's odd.'

'What do you mean odd?' she asked. Then, after a moment admitted, 'Well, actually, I've thought about setting one up myself. I just don't have the money. There's a vacant shop I've had my eye on for a while, which would be perfect. I thought of pointing it out as we crossed the car park just now. It was an old hairdressing salon with big windows. And being right on the car park, it'd be ideal. Did you see it?'

'No, I didn't notice it, but I know where you mean, my mother used to get her hair done there. It's empty is it?' he asked, and sat back and looked at Kayte a little closer. 'Is that something you'd like to do, really?'

'Yeah, I'd love to,' she said, beaming. 'That'd be my dream come true.' He looked at her for a moment.

'What about your parents, Kayte? Are they local too?'

'My mum is, she's lived here all her life. Dad doesn't anymore though, he's moved to Australia.'

'I see,' Roger said, raising an eyebrow allowing his mouth to scrunch and drop. 'Is he in a position to help you financially, with the business at all?'

'Maybe, a bit. Anyway, what are you going to do now?'

'I don't know to be honest. The first thing I'm doing is getting the house in order. It's so dated. I had a meeting with a local builder yesterday. I'm getting straight onto it. Starting with clearing the place out then I'll put a new kitchen and bathrooms in, that sort of thing. Paint it inside and out.'

'Oh, that's good. I did walk past it the other day actually and saw it does need a bit of TLC.' She put her mug down and looked at him. 'And The Martinez Islands?'

'Mmm, work in progress, Kayte, work in progress,' he mused. 'Put it this way, I can't see myself going back there in a hurry. Anyway I'm sorry Kayte, I've got to get on but …' He unclipped a pen from his shirt pocket, scribbled on a napkin and handed it to her. '… I'd be very interested in helping with your business idea, as an investor only you understand? I won't get involved. Interfere. Draw up a business plan and let me see it. You've got my phone number there.'

'I will, definitely,' a surprised Kayte said, 'how long are you around for?'

'I'm going to be here for a while,' he replied, standing up. 'I'm actually pleasantly surprised to be back, to be home I mean. I don't plan on rushing off anytime soon.'

'That's good. Well, great to see you again. Small world eh!'

'I know, incredible. Quite incredible. Anyway, all the very best Kayte and do drop by soon.'

'I will. Maybe even in the next few days?'

'Great. I look forward to it.'

Chapter Twenty-Four
All Change

And four days later we find Kayte knocking on number 33's door. A young man, her age, in white overall's opened up.

'Oh, hello I'm looking for Mr Mac … Mac,' she said.

'McGill?'

'Yes, that's right. Is he in?'

'He is, he's upstairs. I'll give him a shout,' the painter and decorator replied in his soft Hampshire accent. 'Come in.'

'Hey, hey, hello Kayte,' Roger said moments later, bounding down the ornate staircase, 'how nice to see you. Come on through.'

She followed him out of the expansive hallway, negotiating ladders and dust sheets, towards the rear kitchen.

'You're getting on with it then?' she said, as they walked.

'Yup, striking while the iron's hot. I was up in the attic clearing out stuff. Apparently no one wants second hand furniture these days, or bric a brac. So I'm just being brutal; bagging and binning the lot. Sad really, but there we go. If you want anything, have a look around and just take it. I want to clear the place completely and start afresh. I'm not going to get all sentimental about things I've forgotten about. I don't want to live in the past. All that old baggage can really drag you down.'

'Oh great, thanks I'll ask my mum. I think she mentioned getting some new beds. She runs a B&B.'

'Great. There's half a dozen, singles and doubles. Tea or coffee?'

'Coffee please, white with one sugar.' She thought it amazing that here Roger was, less than two weeks later, happily doing up yet another house, having seemingly forgotten all about never moving into his nearly completed dreamlike project on Kidd's Beach. His resilience and adaptability were impressive to say the least. He had bounced back out of one very different world into another, quite seamlessly. She decided it was best not to mention The Martinez Islands at all today. It was as though the time they'd shared there was fast becoming a dream anyway. Somewhere from another time altogether. He exuded the futility in having regrets in life. She could see that there's obviously no benefit in crying over spilt milk when the forces of the universe are hell bent on spilling it. There's a silver lining to everything his actions seemed to be telling Kayte.

As Roger stirred, an image of Prince Jaffa wandering around the mansion on the bluff, sniggering whilst thanking Omar for spending all that money on building him a palace, flashed across her mind. 'I brought the business plan. I'd thought I'd better strike while the iron was hot too,' she said contrary to what she was thinking.

'Well done,' he said, smiling to himself, his back to her. 'I did wander down to the car park myself and, yes, I could picture a surf shop there, definitely. Any ideas on what you'll call it.'

'Yes, I thought about Extreme Academy. Having worked through the figures I think we're going to have to branch out a bit to make it pay though. You know, not just do kitesurfing but all water sports and mail order over the winter. Maybe even a funky coffee shop too.' She pointed at the table, to the document she'd brought. 'It's all in there.'

'Fantastic, great name. Sounds impressive.' *Smart*, he thought, she's thought this through.

Having carried an old 'Her's' mug on the grand tour around the house, sipping as she went, they arrived back at the front door.

'Come back the day after tomorrow, Kayte. I'll have had a look at the business plan by then and we'll go from there. Let me know if your mum wants any bits and pieces then too, otherwise I'll bin it. Thanks for coming by.'

*

'How did it go love?' Jill asked, as Kayte walked into the kitchen.

'He seemed very positive, still keen.'

'Wow wee, interesting,' Jill said, removing her hands from the sink. 'But Kayte, you haven't told me who exactly this Roger chap is?'

'Sorry mum, I'd forgotten his surname, but I just found out it's MacGill. Ring any bells? Sounds as if his family have been here for yonks.'

'Mmm, it does actually,' she replied, pondering. 'Yes, I remember, that's right, I knew a Roger MacGill years ago when I was a teenager. We did a sort of summer camp thing here when I was twelve or thirteen. It doesn't sound like the same guy though. That Roger was quiet. I can't imagine him growing up to be a mercenary.'

'He said his dad was in the navy.'

'Yes, this Roger's father was too, that's right, he was away all the time. The Roger I remember was a bit of a mummy's boy; she fussed about him all the time, I remember that. She wouldn't allow him to do this and that.' She hummed and tutted. 'I guess he was quite good at sport and was good looking, but he was quiet, and they seemed a bit … well, posh.'

'Anyway he's clearing out his house and wondered if we want anything. Beds or whatever, there's lots of nice stuff he's getting rid of.'

'Well, I do actually. Worth having a look around I suppose. I'd like to meet him too, this mysterious investor of yours.'

Kayte hadn't given her mum too much detail about Roger, certainly not as much as she'd told Lisa. She'd kept to the facts:

she'd met this guy on the beach, who coincidently came from the area; he was something to do with the regime on The Martinez Islands, she didn't know what; and that he was thrown out like them she presumed. She'd obviously mentioned the word mercenary, which she now regretted.

'Any news from Steve at all?' her mum went on.

Kayte had actually expected a barrage of calls and texts from him in the days following the split, but they never came.

'I heard he's OK, back at work. But no, no calls, nothing.'

'That's good, isn't it?'

'I guess so.'

'He's probably embarrassed,' Jill said, puffing up. 'His behaviour's been so damn shocking.' She scrunched her nose. 'You aren't missing him at all, are you?'

'I dunno mum. I don't know whether I miss him or whether I just feel a bit lonely.'

'Well, love, seriously think about the way he's treated you over the years. Reflect on that.'

'I know, he's taken me for granted,'

'Taken you for granted!' Jill repeated, exasperated. 'Is that what you call it? Abused you from the word go, more like,' Jill said, wiping her hands menacingly. She grabbed a bottle of white wine from the fridge. Kayte could see the act of extracting the stubborn cork from the bottle helped her mother release a burst of frustration. She poured and passed a full glass to Kayte, sploshing some on the table in the process and sat down opposite her. She calmed. The Aga throbbed and birds cheeped audibly through the open window. 'Look sweetie, I'm going to give you some home truth's about your father and my relationship.' She sighed. 'It's a similar story to yours, that's why. And I've had so long to come to grips with it. You may learn something.'

Crikey, Kayte thought, I wasn't expecting this. She took a sip of the chilled Chilean and sat back.

'I'm sure Steve's begun to reflect,' her mother said, 'and to look back too, not just on what's happened in Africa, but the way he's treated you over the years. All that will be coming back to him. He'll be realising he can't blame or be angry with you, that's the bottom line, Kayte. There's no guilt to lay at your feet; you've done nothing wrong. All he can do is whinge.' Jill looked closely into her daughter's wide eyes. 'I could see your lives diverging anyway,' she continued. 'And I'm sure he could too so he's obviously decided not to fight to get you back. He's just let you go. And I'm wondering if, subconsciously, he may have encouraged it, the split I mean, by being shitty.'

'Mmm, what d'you mean?'

'Shall I keep going, love? Do you want to hear more? Are you sure?'

'Well, yes … OK.'

'Try and look at it from his point of view. It was actually incredibly difficult for him from the very start of your relationship. I know this is going to be hard for you to hear but it was founded on your absolute love for him, you hero worshipped him. As if the sun shone out of his proverbial. You must realise that unconditional love, the sort of love you gave him, although hard to give is actually even harder to receive. Can you believe that?'

'Uhm, OK.'

'It's what I did with your father, and it actually drove him away in the end. I must take some blame for that. My unconditional love had enflamed him over the years. I know now that form of love ignited a particular viciousness in him, which was my fault. When you are loved by someone who can't see your faults as weaknesses, someone who airbrushes over them or even sees them as strengths, then you become smug at best, or downright beastly at worst. And if someone loves you so much that they cannot be hurt by you then, perversely, you try to hurt them all the more. This was the sad reality of what your father's and my relationship had turned in to. D'you see, darling?'

'Sort of mum, I do. Carry on.'

'Well, basically, I encouraged your father to be nasty to

me by over loving him. And OK, in the end it was me, like you did with Steve, who asked your father to go. He accepted it easily, like Steve has, and … as I just said … perhaps not only accepted it, but actually welcomed it. It's freed him up from horrible behaviour and, hopefully, will allow him to be a better person. Do you see?'

'Yes, I do actually.'

'Good. You've given so much and got so little back. I could tell, you were at the point where you were so drained by him you found the reserves, the inner strength, to move forward. To carry on. And, in the process you've given him the chance to grow too. You really have to move on with this one Kayte. Start fresh with someone else. Get off on the right footing. Otherwise we always seem to slip into old patterns of behaviour. Get it right Kayte. You've got your whole life ahead of you.'

'I know you're right mum. I will.'

'Good. And one last thing, the weird revelation about my relationship with your father now, which I think is why he's gone to the other side of the world, is that our relationship has turned full circle and he now holds me in higher regard than I do him, for the first time since we met. Steve is probably coming to terms with this too. His view of you has flipped. He respects you now, for the first time since you both met! He respects you for chucking him.'

'God, it's so complicated,' Kayte said, shaking her head. Jill topped their glasses up.

'It really is. Affairs of the heart are, they are impossibly hard to fathom. I was infatuated with your father just as you were googly eyed with Steve. Both you and I were literally something they could just stoop and pluck up. Lambs to the slaughter. Men like a fight and we gave them none of that; we didn't even give them a struggle, not even resistance. Not a whimper. So they didn't win anything; there was no reward for them; there was no sense of achievement in having won us. The important lesson here, darling, is that we gave them nothing to cherish. Getting us was a hollow victory. Therefore they just took us for granted, and why not?'

'I know.'

'We gave them a ticket to abuse us. You, just like me, were the giver and Steve the taker, plain and simple; you were the radiator and he was the drain. The more you gave the more he took.' Jill began to laugh about it all again. 'But now, perversely, the only one drained is him! He's a shell of the man you met.'

'Woe, woe, woe, mum, thanks. That's enough!'

*

Kayte phoned Roger to make the appointment, to verify he'd had time to read her proposal and to say that she'd be coming over with her mother, who was keen on some new beds. She didn't mention that they may have met and was eager to see their reaction when they saw each other. She rapped the big brass knocker, a clenched fist holding a ball. Roger opened.

'Come in, come in. Sorry about the mess,' he said warmly. Ladders, dust sheets and rollers were still propped up and strewn across the black and white marble hall floor.

'Roger, I'd like you to meet my mother, Jill.'

'How, do you do? Roger MacGill,' he said, holding out a hand. 'Come on through.' He led the way back to the dated kitchen.

'Wonderful houses these. It's the first time I've been inside one. I've always wanted to,' Jill said peering around.

'Regency, built in early 1800's,' he informed her. 'Surprisingly grand, aren't they? It's the only home my parents ever had; the only one I've ever known,' he said as he filled the kettle. 'Sit down, please, make yourselves at home.' The sheets of Kayte's business plan were laid out neatly on the table.

'Kayte told me you were born and brought up here, Jill?' he casually enquired.

'Yes, that's right. We have met actually, Roger, when we were teenagers.' He froze momentarily then spun around away from her with the wisp of a smile and instinctively put the kettle on without looking.

'Oh?' he enquired, still with his back to Jill and Kayte. He'd computed though.

'Yes, I'm sure it was you. We met at a few summer camps on Stokes Bay. We must have been twelve or thirteen, that sort of age.'

He turned to face Jill and looked, but he knew already. 'My God, I do, Gillian, yes, yes, Gillian Macready. Your name was a "Mac" too, that's why I remember it. And obviously Kayte King, the surname, threw me a bit.' He'd spoken fast. Suddenly, he craned his head back and let rip a peeling, high pitched peculiar laugh, just like a little boy's laugh. Then he went sheepish. Jill and Kayte looked at each other, slightly bemused. It was more a release than a laugh which had echoed around the room. 'God, that was thirty odd years ago. I can't believe it,' he continued, shaking his head. 'You look just the same.' He didn't notice Jill blush and Kayte's upper lip twitch. 'I thought there was something very familiar about Kayte. I just couldn't put my finger on it. And now I know, looking at you both together, so similar. You really are two peas from the same pod. It must have been because I vaguely recognised someone when I saw Kayte …' The kettle bubbled furiously then clicked itself off. 'Tea or coffee?' he enquired, changing the subject, and began chuckling and muttering loudly, more to himself, 'Ha, ha, how amusing, will wonders never cease.'

'No really, Roger, this is what coming from a small town is all about,' said Jill. 'Nothing out of the ordinary, surely?'

'Quite, of course, you're right,' he replied, coming back to reality, 'it was just so unexpected that's all. A delightful coincidence. It makes perfect sense now.' He placed their mugs on the table. 'Anyway, it's wonderful to see you again, Jill,' he continued, before sitting down.

After a few minutes of chit-chat he asked Jill if she'd like to wander around. 'Have a look on your own, make a note of anything you want, I'll have a discussion with Kayte about her proposal. Pop back here when you're ready. Sound like a plan?'

'Yes, OK, I'll do that,' Jill said, getting up. 'I'll have a good poke around … on my own,' she added cheekily.

Kayte, having felt sidelined was delighted to see her mother leave the room. Roger slipped a pair of thin tortoise-shell reading glasses on and immediately launched in to it: 'OK, Kayte, I'm going to go for it if you want me to. I think it's a great idea but it's going to need your determination, commitment and hard graft to make the business work. The first thing I want to do is register the company name: Extreme Academy. I think we agree on that. I think the name's perfect. We will each have 50% of the shares in the business. I will pay for everything except your salary.' He peered over his glasses at her. 'That's your commitment. The first profit will be wages though, definitely, but until then you'll have to beg, borrow or … . Are you with me on that?'

'Yes, absolutely.'

'Great, I'll pay for the lease on the shop, do the place up and pay for stock. I'm not expecting you to pay for anything. Now, look, I've been thinking and I do think it'd be good for you to go to Corfu, to learn exactly what they do and don't do. I've got a little bit of experience helping Sonia and Kirk setup the Kidd's surf shop. So, see what they do and the mistakes they make. It'll be a good exercise and there won't be much to do here anyway until I can pin the lease down. How does that sound?'

'I can't believe it. It's fantastic.'

'It's going to be hard work Kayte. Realistically it takes three years for a business to get up on its feet. You're aware of that. If you're not going to give it the commitment it needs, then it's not worth it.'

'Don't worry, I will,' Kayte replied quietly.

He liked that. The underlying positivity. The tone of Kayte's voice reassured Roger. It was something in the way she said *will*. He sat back and sipped his coffee. The steam briefly misted his glasses. He'd come to the conclusion that he needed something to do and, to hell with it, it would only cost him a hundred grand over a few years. If it floundered, well, it would be a bit of fun. His glasses cleared. He felt positive about Kayte though and instinctively knew the business would work. He liked the way her green, oval eyes never wavered. She gave off a cool confidence but not arrogance. Self assurance, combined with a giving nature would only succeed in the service industry. Roger looked at Kayte and assured himself that she'd be great in the shop. She in turn, believed in him. He was decisive. His faith in her was reciprocated. She just knew he had confidence in her abilities, which was the main thing. For a young person who doesn't really appreciate what qualities they've got; that meant the world. She knew he was a man of action and wasn't a screwy shark. The deal he was proposing couldn't be fairer. She was about to have a business, which she would own half of. That was all the incentive she needed to make it work. She read the look in his eye as saying … you can.

Chapter Twenty-Five
Love Rules

Within a week of their meeting to confirm the business was going ahead, Kayte boarded another plane and flew to Corfu. She'd arranged to go for three weeks, to advise the local crew on how to equip the centre, devise a programme for teaching beginners and train up the kite instructors. Roger had immediately got onto the lease and had arranged for his decorators to come straight into the shop after they'd finished his house. She'd made a start on ordering stock and would do more online whilst away. It was all systems go. Roger had registered the company as promised, that was easy, and they'd found a designer who was going to work on the layout of the shop, design a logo and corporate branding for her.

Time flew. Kayte loved the wild beach on the West side of the island, the people were friendly, committed and easy to work with. The tourist season hadn't quite started but they'd advertised well. As a result a few customers began to appear to register for courses and use the school. Westerners, Brits and Americans mainly, who Kayte was able to earn a few drachmas from, and have a bit fun with in the evening. They'd generally enrol for a week's instruction, or a five day beginners course so they'd stay in local guesthouses. It'd be the same back in UK. Kayte would use her mum's B&B for her clients. Although her stay on the island was only for a few weeks, it gave her the opportunity to teach the local instructors on the job and she got genuine fulfilment in getting people up and running on the water, sharing the buzz of kiting. To put something back into the sport she'd got so much out of was enormously rewarding. She was a minor celebrity too, she was a world champ, which gave the fledgling kite school added kudos.

After a couple of weeks of hard work, training the team and keeping busy, she was itching to get back to base again and crack on with her new venture. She'd had a great time, got a deep tan and the trip had enabled her to move on from the roller coaster Martinez experience. To have Steve at arms length made her feel truly liberated and now, more optimistic, she was ready to face whatever life threw at her.

It was a month since she'd got back from the Martinez Islands and that particular lunar cycle was a benchmark timeframe to mentally distance herself from the whole situation; to be truly objective about it. Those few weeks had given her mind the desired space to see her life in a clearer light. To be able to look back and assimilate quite what had gone on. To have not seen or heard from Steve allowed Kayte to get a firmer grip on her future and not waiver. Lisa was right in insisting she get away and Roger instinctively seemed to know it would be helpful. If she'd stayed, she may have had a moment of weakness and gone back to Steve. She'd be back where she started, locked into a bleak future. The break allowed her to feel emotionally strong enough to go home, head high.

And so Kayte slipped quietly back into England at the end of April.

'Come on Kayte, let's go for a drink at the Half Penny. I've got some news for you,' her mum said the following day.

'Come on then, let's go. Don't keep me in suspense.'

The Half Penny pub was incredibly busy; the cosy wood panelled bar they squeezed into was crammed full of laughter.

'Crikey, I've never known it to be so packed,' Jill exclaimed as they jostled up to the bar. They ordered their drinks and found a corner table. As soon as they'd sat down, Kayte asked excitedly, above the hubbub, 'So, mum, what's this news then?'

'Well, I wanted to tell you before you got anything second-hand or picked up rumours.' Jill bounced slightly on the banquette to turn and face her daughter. 'Roger and I are seeing each other.' She came straight out with it.

'What d'you mean?' Kayte replied, with a hesitant laugh, immediately taken aback. She looked at her mother with horror. Jill smiled and her daughter looked perplexed. 'Oh, I get it. You-are-seeing each other, like boyfriend and ...' she spelt out and twiddled her fingers, entwining them.

'Yes, we are.'

'Oh, I see.' Kayte looked at her mother with wide eyes. 'That was quick?'

'Well, it just happened, sweetheart. I hope you're happy for us.'

'Yes, of course I am, mum. As long as you are.'

They sat in silence for a moment, the ghost of smiles rippled across their faces.

'You seem to have really matured over the past month, my dear,' Kayte's mother said earnestly. 'It's incredible, I don't know if it was the horrible trip to those islands or splitting up with Steve but I can see you've really grown up a lot.'

Kayte recalled that memorable day.

'Yeah, you're right mum, it changed me entirely,' Kayte said, remembering seeing the letter with the enchanting stamps on the doormat two months ago. 'When all of this started.'

'What did?' Jill said. It was her turn to be confused.

'That kiting invitation, the letter, the paper missile that sent my life into a flutter.'

'Of course.'

'Just imagine if that day never happened, mum,' Kayte said. She was deadly serious, but her eyes were smiling. 'How different our lives would have been? Just think about it, mum. The long chain of events, which have unravelled because of that one link, has led us up to here. It feels unreal, like a dream. Do you know what I mean?'

'It is darling. It's amazing how one little thing in life sets off a motion.'

'More like a commotion!'

'Well, cheers. Here's to it.' They laughed and clinked glasses.

Kayte suddenly became agitated and kept looking around, trying to find something, or someone, she didn't know who or what. It was loud and it was hot. Everything felt as if it was closing in on her. She felt a presence on her back and didn't know how to interpret it. She was suddenly paranoid that Steve was going to appear. Something imminent was going to happen. Her mother hadn't noticed. 'Let's get another?' she said instinctively.

'Why not darling, let's celebrate.'

Jill looked across at Kayte.

'Are you OK sweetheart? You've suddenly gone awfully pale. Is something wrong?'

'No, I'm fine, mum. It's just very hot in here. I feel a bit dizzy, I'm going to the loo, freshen up a bit. I'll be back in a mo. I'll get the drinks.'

She moved off through the crowd, away from the heat to try and restore some sort of composure. Freshening up was an understatement. She was suddenly stoned, or high, sort of off balance and totally dazed, incredulous at life.

It all felt so normal though, that was the odd thing, as if it was meant to be. Roger with her mother. And, she'd introduced them. She didn't need a pee, she just needed to get some air. So having stood in the loo for a while, Kayte washed her face and, looking up into the mirror at herself, she smiled and thought, if this is life, well, it's not too damn shabby.

An image of Roger being normal at home with her mother was suddenly so beyond the realms of reality that she found herself laughing hysterically out loud in the toilets. So much so that she nearly wet herself. Fact, Kayte said to herself, is definitely stranger than fiction; I couldn't have written it.

The feelings she was experiencing were spiritual. She had witnessed, and lived through an explosion of coincidences. She was incredibly giddy for a long minute, trying to contain herself.

She fumbled for her phone and managed to text Lisa, asking her to call in ten minutes so she'd have an excuse to leave. Kayte was in an odd rhapsody, walking on air. Her appreciation of life had changed irrefutably. Her gratitude for it now felt so deep it was as though she was never going to come down.

As she approached her beaming mum, who hardly noticed her return, Kayte passed her a drink.

'Well, cheers mum,' she said. And they toasted, clinking their glasses. 'Here's to home.'

THE END.

Acknowledgements

I would like to publically bow down to Conrad, Dickens, Hemingway, Christie, Maugham, Tey and Childers amongst many others for their inspiration.

Enormous appreciation to all the work Hannah Sheppard at The Writer's Practice put in to the early drafts. Also to Dreya Wharry for her kitesurfing expertise. And latterly thanks for the skilled polishing of the manuscript to Gabriel at Spiffing Covers.

Gratitude to Gem Garrity, Annette Seth-Smith, Victoria Stroud and James Willis for their wonderful designs.

Many thanks to Rob Franks at Correct Score, to Mark and Becky at Luminata for the web work done on my web site: hwneild.com.

*

Love to my mother, Midge and sister, Frances for their support. Also Shari, Isabella's mother for her patience.

Thanks to Zoe Smith and Henry Bateson for the kind use of their homes for re-writes.

A big cheers to one and all,

Cocktails:

1. Captain Kidd's Rum Punch – 2 oz's gold rum, 1 oz muscovado sugar, ½ oz fresh lime juice, raw egg with a grate of nutmeg.
2. Martinez – London Gin, Vermouth, Maraschino Liqueur, Angostura Bitters, lemon twist.

NEXT TO COME FROM hwneild …

Vintage Roots. Due for release early in 2017. An intricately entwined blend of high adventure, soul searching and Nature. Vintage Roots takes a young man, coming to terms with the death of his father, on a ferocious journey to discover treasure, combat French mafia, and reconcile personal pain. Don't miss it. Sign-up at www.hwneild.com

Lightning Source UK Ltd.
Milton Keynes UK
UKHW040817290120
357813UK00002B/398

9 780993 531804